Paris Girls
Secret Society

Tom Brosnahan

Travel Info Exchange, Inc.

Concord MA USA

infoexchange.com

ISBN: 9767531-8-9
ISBN-13: 978-0-9767531-8-6
Version CS70505

www.ParisGirlsSecretSociety.com

Published by
Travel Info Exchange, Inc.

www.infoexchange.com

books@infoexchange.com

Comments welcome: tom@tombrosnahan.com

Contents

For Jane & Lydia
my Paris girls

Prologue

It was time. The sun had been warming them for awhile. It would be there to warm them when they emerged, shivering, when the sun was low in the sky.

He went down to the river, to the young ones. He had shown them what to do: find just these rocks, smash them and grind them. Mix them in this way with the sticky clay from the river and the black dust from the fire. Put the different colors of clay in the different skin bowls.

Bring knots from the trees. Light one from the fire so we can light others when we are inside.

As they climbed up the rocky cliff to the cave, the Magician remembered that day long ago when the Chief had led them out hunting. They had followed the great beast as the sun moved, and moved, and moved, a long day. Finally they had the beast surrounded. The Chief took his spear, hooked it in the spear-thrower and stood for a moment, arm back, still as the rocks. Then with great breath and a mighty grunt he swung his huge arm over his head and the spear flew faster than any bird—straight into the heart of the great beast.

The beast roared and kicked! It bellowed and thrashed! The earth shook when it fell!

With shouts they rushed to it, gathered around and stabbed, stabbed, stabbed!

The Chief's son ran forward with a rock and smashed the beast's skull.

The Chief pulled his bloody spear from the heart of the great beast. He held it above his head and roared like the beast. All of them roared like the beast!

The Magician smiled at the memory.

They would not be hungry, they would eat and eat and eat! After they had eaten, they would hack the rest of the great beast apart and lay the meat on hot rocks in the sun to dry so they would not be hungry when they walked over the cold mountains to the sea.

The Magician remembered, but that was long ago. They had not seen a great beast for many suns. The food was gone. The hunters wanted another beast, but they could not find one. The Chief and the hunters looked. They could not find one.

The females did not smile at the Chief now. ▬▬▬▬▬▬▬ *He knew what they were thinking. Find a beast! We want meat! So the Chief had told the Magician: you must make magic. Make a beast come!*

The Magician gathered the young ones and instructed them. They made the preparations as directed. Now they would perform the magic so a beast would appear.

The Magician and the young ones reached the cave entrance. A young one with a pine torch went first. When they had traveled deep into the cave, the Magician looked for the right place to perform the magic. The young ones gathered to watch.

With the young ones behind him in the cave, he dipped his fingers into one of the skin bowls and smeared the color on the cave wall. Another bowl, another color, another swipe on the wall. The Magician looked at what he had done. He touched here, he rubbed there. Then more colors on his fingers, more smearing and rubbing on the wall.

He worked and worked, making the magic.

As the young ones watched, the great beast, the auroch, appeared on the wall. It was the same as the great beast that had been killed! They could see it for themselves! Truly it was magic!

Truly, they thought, this magic must make the beast come to us. Then we will hunt, and we will have meat.

PART ONE

Secret Society

1

Café Aux Tours de Notre-Dame

Charity Cabot picked up her warm croissant, broke off a morsel, popped it in her mouth, lifted her cup of *café au lait* and took a sip as she listened to her two apartment mates reminisce about their soon-to-end college year abroad in Paris. They were sitting in the morning sun at a sidewalk table of the Café Aux Tours de Notre-Dame on a warm late April day in 1968.

Charity—shortish and slight, with regular features, a straight nose, thin lips, a sprinkling of light freckles, fine straight brown hair nearly down to her waist—was from Massachusetts, scion of an old Boston family whose young members, since the late 19th century, had always gone off on the Grand Tour of Europe as part of their education, then returned home, married into other Boston Brahmin families, and raised the next generation to go off on the Grand Tour. Her branch of the family was no longer Boston Brahmin-wealthy, but her father's job as majority owner of an electronics plant in North Adams made them wealthy by rural Massachusetts standards. Her mother raised her to be worthy of the status of the famous family name. In Massachusetts the name still opened doors.

"Well, if learning French is the yardstick to measure our year abroad, Charity gets the prize," Josie said.

"Oh c'mon, Josie. Your French is great! Besides, when you do your Josephine Baker impersonation, when you fix your hair and make-up her way, people think you're her daughter! You're beautiful! You just glide through French society."

Josephine—Josie for short—was the daughter of a federal judge and a prominent civil rights lawyer in Chicago. Her father, the judge, had urged her to take a college year abroad in France to experience a country and culture where racial prejudice was not endemic, where people were judged more on their character and cultural accomplishments than on the color of their skin.

"Charity, your French is perfect!" Josie said. "People think you're French, even here in Paris! You get the idioms right, you even know all that Parisian slang! You can pass for French, or American, whatever you want."

"Only until about five minutes into a conversation," Charity said matter-of-factly, wiping her buttery fingers on a napkin. "After about five minutes I guess I make some little mistake, or I don't get the idiom or the *argot* just right, and they look at me oddly and they say 'You're not Parisian, are you?'"

"And y'all think that means yore French is bad?" Amaleen exclaimed. "Good lord, when ah try to speak French they act like ah smacked 'em upside the head!"

"No surprise!" Josie said. "They never heard Hillbilly French before!"

They all laughed.

Amaleen was from Charleston, West Virginia, where her father's business success had taken the family to the top of the social pyramid—big fish in a small pond—but since his passing, Amaleen's mother had lost her inner compass. When her mother proposed that Amaleen go to Paris for her junior year of college "to get some travel experience and culture," Amaleen wasn't sure if her mother was thinking of her daughter or herself. With Amaleen in Paris, her mother could have all the affairs she wanted, and disappear on "nights out" without worrying her daughter would hear about it.

Amaleen wore her redneck country culture proudly. To treat her like a hillbilly was to pay her a compliment because in her mind West Virginians were God's People, authentic, no-nonsense, down-to-earth folks that no stilted status-seeker or city slicker could fool.

"So my French is pretty good," Charity said. "I'd rather be a little bit worse at French and a little bit better at what you're so good at, Amaleen."

"Which is…?"

Charity looked at Josie and they both smiled knowingly.

"Aw, c'mon you two! Ah jes' like to have some fun, that's all. We're in Paris, France, ain't we?"

"A little fun!" Josie exclaimed, her eyes wide. "The whole first term with Noireau and the second with Roussel! And both of them married!"

"Ici, c'est la France!" Charity said slyly. "Students sleeping with professors is *comme il faut.* "

"Ah swear ah dit'n do nuthin' to encourage 'em. They jes' wout'n let me be! So ah decided to have a little fun."

Amaleen got along well in Paris because she had a beautiful strong-featured face, long wavy light brown almost blonde hair, nearly six feet of an opulently feminine figure, a sassy walk, and a brash but knowing attitude that kept those around her wondering what she'd do next. She dressed as a hippy, but a well-heeled hippy—Hippy Couture, if you could call it that. The finest clothes embellished with hippy-like accents. It was a brash affectation, and Parisians loved it—particularly the men.

"A fling, yeah, maybe," Josie said, "and they like American girls—no commitment, we don't hang around. But you got those guys to take you everywhere! Weekends at châteaus in the Loire! Vacations on the Riviera! Dinners at *Le Train Bleu, Le Tour d'Argent, Fouquet!"*

Foucké indeed, Charity murmured to herself, making an obscene Franglish pun.

Charity thought Amaleen was a little too 'loose,' but actually, she didn't understand how a girl could do that. She herself had little experience of romance, and none during nearly a year in France. She was not good at putting herself forward, and was old fashioned when it came to sex, but secretly she envied Amaleen's man-killer ability…at least a little.

"When did those guys even have time to see their wives?"

"Not mah problem!" Amaleen said, and jammed half a

croissant in her mouth, blowing out her cheeks and bugging her big blue eyes at them.

Charity and Josie burst out laughing, making Amaleen laugh and spray croissant fragments across the table and onto the sidewalk.

"Remember orientation? And that first week together in the apartment? Amaleen, you haven't changed!"

Haven't changed? The three young women lapsed into silence, sipping their coffee and remembering how it had all begun, and how indeed they had changed.

2

Orientation

September 1967. Charity screwed up her courage and circulated through the big orientation hall asking girls if they had a place to live.

"I'm renting a big apartment on Rue Claude Bernard, less than a 15-minute walk from the Panthéon, and I'm looking for roommates."

The apartment was her mother's idea, located through Cabot family connections.

"It's big enough for two or even three girls," her mother told her. "Find some roommates to share the rent and you'll have more spending money to enjoy Paris. I'll feel better if you're with other girls—American girls. Nice girls your own age. You'll be safer and happier."

She knew her mother had urged her to take the apartment because of Charity's shyness. She thinks that if I have a room by myself I'll be a hermit and just study all the time and not socialize.

"Roomates aren't always friends," Charity said, looking directly at her mother.

Charity liked the idea of more spending money, but she liked even better the promise of freedom from family protection and social pressure, the opportunity to escape being a shy daughter and a Cabot. The family-name social status had followed her to

Radcliffe. Her name opened doors, but she carried it as a weight that only increased her shyness. In Paris she would be free to be herself—whoever that was. She needed to find out. Freedom from financial constraint might help.

As she circulated through the hall, Charity was worried. Nearly all of the girls already had arranged for apartments or dormitory rooms. If she lived in the apartment alone, her mother might be right: she'd come back from Paris fluent in French, with top grades, having done nothing but study by herself in her apartment. It was too easy, too natural for her to be alone.

Across the room she saw a big, buxom girl with light brown hair and a commanding presence. It was impossible not to notice her, but she was standing alone, looking lost.

"Hi, I'm Charity. I have a nice apartment not far from the Latin Quarter, and I'm looking for roommates. Do you have a place to stay yet?"

"Oh mah god, yore gonna save mah life! Mah name's Amaleen, and ah have no adea where ah'm gonna sleep in three days. Shore, ah'm interested!"

Damn, Charity thought. I did it again! *I don't think!* I peek out from my shell, try to be bold and daring, proud of my assertiveness, and it turns to mud. Now I've gone and asked a hillbilly to be my roommate. God! How do I get into these things, and how do I get out of this one?

But she had asked, and the big girl had accepted.

Charity thought quickly. If I can't stand her, I can always ask for a rent she can't afford.

Or is that just another way to assure that I end up alone, comfortable in my solitude because it doesn't threaten Shy Little Charity?

Look for other possibilities, she thought. Find alternatives. Get it right next time.

Charity kept circulating among the newly-arrived American students. Soon there were none left that she had not asked... except for one, a tall black girl standing by herself. Charity moved toward her.

"Yore not gonna aks that Negro, are yuh?" Amaleen asked, coming up behind her and grabbing her arm.

Like many of her Radcliffe classmates, Charity supported desegregation. She also empathized with a young woman who must have felt an outsider, the only colored girl in a room full of white people. Charity knew how it felt to be an outsider. She felt that way nearly all the time.

"I'm going to ask that young lady if she needs a place to live," Charity responded evenly, and pulled away. Maybe this colored girl will be okay. She's well dressed. If she drives the hillbilly away, maybe that's a good thing.

"Hi. Do you have a place to stay yet? I'm renting a big apartment on Rue Claude Bernard, not far from the Latin Quarter, and I'm looking for another roommate."

"Well…no, I don't have a place so far. I was set up for a dorm room, but there was some mix-up and now it's not available. Maybe…"

They looked at one another in silence for a moment.

"Try it, at least for now. If you find something you like better, I won't mind. But in three days you're going to need a place. I'm Charity. Your name is…?"

"Josephine. Josie for short."

Josie looked at Amaleen, standing a short distance behind Charity and glaring at her.

Charity turned and saw Amaleen.

"Amaleen, this is Josie. Josie, Amaleen. She's interested in sharing the apartment too."

They nodded warily to one another.

"After we've all finished with the orientation, let's go have coffee and talk things over."

The three rejects, Charity thought bitterly. Like the middle school dancing classes her mother insisted Charity attend, but which she hated. Dressed in her best, trying to act demure, she would wait expectantly to be asked by a boy to be his partner for the procession into the ballroom. She was always one of the last girls asked, by one of the shyest, least appealing boys. She and the boy had this in common: they knew they were the ultimate rejects.

He offered his arm, she placed her hand gently, diffidently upon it, and they paraded into the ballroom. He held his left hand up, she her right, his right hand on her waist, her left on his shoulder, and they pushed awkwardly through the motions commanded by the dance instructor. She looked into his eyes, hoping to see some sign of interest, but he mostly looked down at his feet as though trying to get the moves right, but in fact he was too shy even to look at her. At the end of the class, they glanced at one another with expressions of common suffering and mutual relief.

Charity complained so bitterly to her mother about the agony of the classes that her mother proposed a compromise: if Charity could show that she had learned all the dance steps, she could stop going to dance class. Charity stood up, pulled her mother up from her chair and waltzed her around the room. She knew it all. Learning the steps was not the problem.

Nor was coordination. Charity was already a winning player at tennis in high school despite her slight build, and she was an energetic competitor on the Radcliffe tennis team.

The three young women walked out of the orientation hall into a hot mid-September Paris day, the clouds thin, the September sun illuminating the city's monumental buildings, dark with age but brightened by the brash light. The Place Saint-Michel was crowded with Parisians shopping or waiting for buses, students and tourists gawking and photographing one another in front of the huge fountain.

As they strolled past the fountain, Charity considered what she was doing. She refused to judge a person by skin color, but that ethical commitment had been totally intellectual until now. She knew nothing about Negroes. She had no colored friends. There were none in North Adams. The few colored girls at Radcliffe tended to stick together in their own group.

By asking the colored girl to join them, they would be doing the right thing, but Charity still faced it with uncertainty.

Amaleen was thinking it over as well. For her, there was no question. Where she came from, the very idea of cohabiting with a Negro was unthinkable. Her mother must never find out. Most of the other Americans at orientation must have felt the same way.

What the hell, Amaleen thought. My mama ain't here, and this ain't the US of A. This here is France, a whole 'nuther country. The rules are different. Let's see what happens. Might be a hoot. Actually, I have no idea what Negroes are like.

The three young women sat at a café.

"Café au lait, s'il vous plaît, monsieur," Charity said to the waiter in a crisp, near-flawless Parisian accent.

"Hoowee, honey!" Amaleen exclaimed. "Why you botherin' to come to Paris when you already speak French?"

Charity smiled.

"Maybe that's all I know," she said with a wink.

"Uh-uh," Josie said. "You tossed it off too quickly. You know what you're doing."

"Well, I have studied French for awhile."

"Since when?"

"Seventh grade."

"I think you're beyond ordering coffee," Josie smiled.

Amaleen was silent, looking at Josie most of the time as though she were some sort of strange creature on display. She was pretty, Amaleen thought. No denying that. And well-spoken. Even classy maybe.

The waiter brought their coffees, big cups of creamy coffee-and-milk. When Josie lifted the cup to her lips, the color of the liquid was an exact match to her complexion.

"So," Josie said, "about the apartment…"

She asked a lot of questions. Where was the apartment, specifically? Was it a nice building? Did it get sun? Was it on a quiet street? How far from the Latin Quarter? Did it have a telephone? How many bedrooms? How many baths? Would she have her own room?

Sure is choosy for a Negro, Amaleen thought.

Charity was patient, but she too thought she was being a little particular for the last girl without a bed. But no, Charity thought, she's going to be paying money, she has a right to know what she's paying for.

Charity answered Josie's questions as best she could, but in fact she hadn't even seen the apartment yet. It would be available in three days, when their temporary lodgings at the university ran out and they had to move to more permanent quarters. All Charity knew about it was her mother's description of the apartment, second-hand from her friends.

They were all silent, looking at one another.

The thin girl is asking me out of pity, Josie thought. A white girl feeling sorry for the poor little colored girl. And the blonde redneck hates my guts because I'm not white. Damn!

"Look," Josie said. "I appreciate you're considering me, but I'm not asking any favors. If you don't think it's going to work out, I'd rather have you say so. I'm a big girl. I can take care of myself."

Charity looked at Amaleen, who avoided her eyes.

"Let's give it a try," Charity said. "We're all strangers, but if we all try, it should work out."

In their hearts, they were almost certain it wouldn't.

3

Parisian Brunch

Three days later, Charity came to the building on Rue Claude Bernard at 8 o'clock in the morning to get the keys to the apartment and instructions from the concierge. The other girls arrived at 9:30 with their luggage.

They put their suitcases down, greeted one another warily, and roamed around the apartment: a good-sized salon with two large French windows looking out onto Rue Claude Bernard which, though a wide street, had little traffic or noise; a dining table to seat four or, in a pinch, five; a sofa, two easy chairs, and lamps. The small kitchen—tiny by American standards—was rather primitive, but adequate. The bathroom had a sink, and a tub with a handheld shower attached to the wall. The toilet was in a separate tiny slot reached by another door from the hallway.

At the end of the hall on the left and right were two bedrooms with double beds, one looking out onto Rue Claude Bernard, the other to a small rear garden, not particularly well-kept, but green.

Also looking onto the garden was a very small room probably meant for an infant, but it now had a single bed in it.

"Who gets which room?" Josie asked Charity.

"I don't know."

They all stood in the hallway, glancing in the rooms, uneasy. It was obvious that one of them would have to take the small, cramped room.

Charity thought it over. Amaleen, almost six feet tall, would look like a giant in the small room. Would Josie sniff racial prejudice if she ended up with the small room?

"I'll take the small room," Charity said. "You two can decide about the others."

"You don't have to do that, Charity," Josie said. "It's *your* apartment!"

"What about flippin' a coin?" Amaleen asked.

"I'm the shortest girl," Charity said. And the best at self-effacement, she thought. I'm used to settling for less. Why change now?

"Are you shore?" Amaleen asked, looking hard at her. "Don't seem fair. Y'all invite us, an' you end up with the worst room."

"All I'm going to do is sleep there."

"Let's try the arrangement and see how it goes," Josie said. "We can always change it later."

She looked at Amaleen.

"Do you have a preference for one of the other rooms?"

"I dunno,…"

"Well, I'll take this one," Josie said decisively, going into the room with the view on the back. "We can always rearrange if somebody's dissatisfied."

They put their suitcases in the rooms and returned to the salon.

"Whatcha got in the poke?" Amaleen asked Josie.

"The what?"

"The poke, the li'l sack. What's in it?"

Josie held up the shopping bag in her hand.

"Ground coffee, milk and some pastries," Josie said. "I'll make some coffee and we can eat and talk things over."

Josie went to the kitchen, brewed coffee, took the croissants, *pains au chocolat*, *éclairs* and *réligieuses* out of their pastry-shop box, arranged them on a plate, and brought the brunch to the dining table.

"Introductions," Josie said. "My name's Josephine Duffin, Josie for short, like I said. I'm from Chicago—Oak Park, actually, Hemingway's home town. I'm going to the University of

Chicago in political science. I want to go to law school. My father is a federal judge. My mother is a civil rights lawyer."

Silence. Charity and Amaleen processed this surprising information.

"Charity?" Josie said, looking at her.

"Charity Cabot from North Adams, Massachusetts. That's about as far west as you can go from Boston and still be in Massachusetts, but it's beautiful there. Nice mountains. I'm going to Radcliffe and studying history and art. I want to be an archeologist."

"A what?" Amaleen asked.

"An archeologist."

"You mean diggin' around in the dirt 'n' such? Why'd you wanna do that?"

"Because I love it. I always have."

She smirked at the memory of when, during freshman year at Radcliffe, she had mentioned her goal to her parents.

"My family thinks archeology is a waste of time. 'Digging in dirt in desolate places in blazing hot climates populated—if they're populated at all!—with primitive, murderous natives,' they think."

As a little girl, she told them, she was fascinated by the archeological displays in the North Adams Public Library. John Henry Haynes, a wealthy 19th-century citizen of North Adams, had collected ancient Assyrian artifacts on his self-financed expeditions to the Middle East. Every time Charity went to the library to do her homework, she stopped to visit "the elf," a little clay statuette of a man with bushy eyebrows and abundant moustaches wearing a conical hat, seated with his hands on his knees. He looked just like a cartoon elf...but he was real, and thousands of years old! A sculptor way back then had fashioned something that a little girl, thousands of years later, could love.

She always said hi to the elf and surveyed the display cases to see the vases, spools and other artifacts from Haynes's excavations. She imagined ancient people using them and the objects came to life for her.

During a high school field trip to Cambridge she discovered Harvard's Peabody Museum of Archaeology and Ethnology, and fantasized about how the ancient Aztecs and Mayas must have lived. How can I understand myself, and other people, and our world, unless I understand where we all came from?

Charity knew her mother's attitude, expressed in little comments and warnings. How could her daughter participate in society and have all the good things in life if she was always running away to the other side of the world on digs, scraping dirt off old bones and broken pots with a toothbrush? What sort of life was that?

"My mother suggested I come to Paris and study art and fashion. She wants me to be a 'proper member of society,' meaning the society of her friends in Boston. I want to study art because it's important to archeology, but I have no interest in fashion."

"Sho' 'nuff for that," Amaleen said, casting a critical glance at Charity's simple monocolor blouse, pleated below-the-knee skirt, and two-tone loafers with white socks.

"What about you, Amaleen?" Josie asked.

"Amaleen Carlile. Charleston, West Virginia—that's *West Virginia*, not the Charleston in South Carolina. Mah daddy was in the coal an' salt minin' business. He died a few years ago. Mah mama lives in Charleston and she wants me to git some culture, so she sent me here. I figured it was worth it to git away from home."

They looked at one another in silence.

"Pastries!" Josie said. "We're in Paris! French pastries!"

They each picked up a pastry and took a dainty nibble, watching one another warily.

"Mah lord, these are *good!*" Amaleen exclaimed. She opened her eyes wide, dropped her jaw as far as it would go, crammed a whole *pain au chocolat* into her mouth and chomped down.

They all exploded in laughter. Pastry crumbs and chocolate sprayed across the table and onto the floor.

"Let's go out and see where we live," Josie suggested when the coffee and pastries were gone.

They went out to explore the neighborhood together, sauntering along Rue Claude Bernard to Rue Edouard Quenu and over to the Square Saint-Médard, with its little church of Saint-Médard de Paris, its cafés, and the southern end of Rue Mouffetard, the market street. Climbing the hill on Mouffetard they passed food shops, bakeries, pastry shops, cafés and restaurants. At the top of the hill they strolled into Place de la Contrescarpe.

"Hemingway wrote about Place de la Contrescarpe in that book that came out a few years ago, *A Moveable Feast.* I think he lived near here," Charity said.

She asked a waiter in one of the cafés. He pointed across the square.

"Soixante-quatorze Rue du Cardinal Lemoine," he said.

"What'd he say?" Amaleen asked.

"Seventy-four Cardinal Lemoine Street."

They walked across the square and along Rue du Cardinal Lemoine until they saw No. 74 on the left.

"From my home town to Paris," Josie said as they gazed at the nondescript building.

"So...Oak Park was Hemingway's home town?" Charity asked.

"Yeah. He grew up not far from where my house is."

"Uh...what sort of a place is it, this Oak Park?" Amaleen asked.

"Oak Park? Upscale suburb of Chicago. The houses are very nice. Ours has five bedrooms and a big back yard, two-car garage. Good schools. It's a great place."

"Josie, I hope I'm not being out of line, but is it...is it integrated?" Charity asked.

"It is because we live there," she said, "and we're not the only colored family there. Oak Park is more integrated than most towns. And I don't mind your asking. Let's get it all out front, girls. No need to tiptoe around."

They walked back to the Place de la Contrescarpe. On the west side of the square Amaleen noticed a large, obviously old picture illustration entitled *Au Nègre Joyeux* hanging on the side of the building at 14 Rue Mouffetard. In the picture, a Negro servant pours a cup of hot chocolate for a French *gentilhomme.* The setting is an 18th-century drawing room. She pointed it out to the others.

"Reminds me of the good old USA," Josie said. "I guess that shit is everywhere."

"I don't think it's right," Charity said. "I think it's awful."

"Try living it," Josie said. "But it isn't gonna last. I'm gonna make sure of that."

A week after moving into the apartment, the girls shared a simple dinner of food bought at a *traiteur* and fresh bread from a bakery on Rue Mouffetard.

"Anybody want some wine?" Josie asked. "I bought a bottle of white."

"Yeah, ah do," Amaleen said.

"I don't drink," Charity said. "Just water for me."

Josie poured two glasses.

"Amaleen, tell us about Charleston…the one in West Virginia," Josie said, winking at her.

"Well, it's the capital of West Virginia, an' the biggest city, about seventy-five thousand nice folks ah think. We got two rivers, the Elk and the Kanawha. We dig a lotta coal, we dig a lotta salt, an' we make a lotta babies. You got Hemingway in Oak Park? We got Daniel Boone in Charleston. Ah like it."

"Is that where your college is?"

"Yeah, ah go to Morris Harvey College right in Charleston, right across the river from the state capitol. Nice view. Actually, ah'm there for the music an' dance classes mostly. It's got a lotta those. Ah wanted to look at colleges in other places but mah mama nixed it, said ah had to go to college in Charleston, it was important for 'society,' meanin' her and her friends. Mah daddy had a lotta coal mines and salt mines, y'know? So she thinks this status thang is important."

They looked back and forth at one another for a moment.

"Well, here's how I see it," Josie said. "We're all from…what shall I say? '*Privileged* situations?' Amaleen is from the nobility of Charleston, West Virginia. Charity is a Boston Cabot. I'm a li'l colored girl from tony Oak Park, Illinois. We seem to get along okay. But if our folks ever got wind of our living together," she paused, "…the shit would hit the fan big time!"

They all laughed.

"Sho' 'nuff, Josie," Amaleen said. "That's sho' 'nuff."

"So I propose, ladies, that we call ourselves 'The Secret Society,' because we're all society girls in one way or another, but if our folks found out we were living together, there'd be hell to pay. So we keep it a secret."

"Your parents don't want you living with white girls?" Charity asked.

Josie looked at her, smiled wanly, and imitated her father's gruff voice, the judge handing down a verdict from the bench.

"'We don't need white folks' help to succeed! You stick with colored folk now, Josie. Our time has come!'"

Charity and Amaleen looked at Josie without expression.

"Well? What would *your* folks say, Charity?"

Charity thought for a moment.

"Um, well, they'd *say* 'everyone's the same, and if she's a nice girl, there's no problem,' but what they'd *think* would be different. They couldn't picture it."

"Amaleen?"

"Are you kiddin'? Mah mama would prob'ly die of a heart attack at the news, an' mah daddy, rest his soul, would want to send in the cavalry! 'An actual NEE-GRO?' I can hear him say it. 'An honest-to-god black-as-night NEE-GRO?'"

The girls looked at one another, paused, then burst out laughing.

"I'm *not* 'black as night,' as you can plainly see," Josie said smiling. She put her hands under her chin in a prim, jokey magazine cover-girl pose. "I'm *café-crème*, like Josephine Baker, my namesake."

Charity and Amaleen looked at one another, then at Josie.

"Who's Josephine Baker?" Charity asked.

"Josephine Baker? You don't know? Just one of the most famous singers and actors in France. She's American, but she got fed up with prejudice and segregation, moved to France years ago, and got rich and famous. She stood beside the Reverend Doctor Martin Luther King Junior at the March on Washington in 1963. She wore her Free French uniform and the Legion of Honor medal she was awarded personally by General Charles de

Gaulle for her military intelligence work for France during World
War II."

Josie lifted her wine glass and took a sip, lowered her eyes, then
looked at both of them directly.

"She told—she *showed!*—the world what a colored woman can
do in a society without segregation or prejudice. She lives in a
castle here in France now. Her own castle! She's friends with
Princess Grace and Prince Rainier of Monaco. She's over 60
years old and still performing. French people love her…and so do
I."

"*'Café-crème…* Ah like it! But it wout'n matter to mah mama,
honey. Ah could tell 'em you was beautiful, an' smart, an'
cultured, and…well, *rich,* an' it wout'n make a lump o' coal's
diff'rence. Y'all are *black,* an' for them that's the end of it. Mah
daddy would die,…if he wasn't already dead!"

They were silent, pondering Amaleen's loss of her father at an
early age. Then they all laughed again.

"Isn't it just *insane?*" Charity said.

"Ah'm gonna hafta make up some girls to tell mah mama I'm
livin' with 'em. She wout'n even like me to live with no girl from
snooty ol' Massachusetts. Too intellectual an' full o' themselves,
she'd say."

"What do you think my folks would say if I told them I was
rooming with…a *hillbilly?*" Charity said, looking at Amaleen in
mock horror.

More laughter.

"I like your idea of the Secret Society, Josie."

Charity put her hands, palms up, in the center of the table.

"The Secret Society. That's us."

The others put their hands in hers and gripped them tight.

Then eight months sped by…

4

Bells of Notre-Dame

Bonnnnng… Emmanuel, the biggest bell in Notre-Dame's south tower just across the street from the café, brought the girls back from their reveries of eight months ago. The giant 13-ton bell rang nine more times.

"Wow, ten already? I've got to go study," Josie said.

"Honey, why you botherin'?" Amaleen said. "The year's almost over. Pretty soon y'all will be back in Chicago an' you won't git to sit in the sun with us and sip coffee no more."

"It's not for grades, Amaleen," Charity said. "With Josie it's all about politics, you know? When she says 'study,' she means meeting with the student protesters and planning the revolution."

"What the heck y'all talkin' about anyway? Ah dit'n see no protests or no revolution."

Charity and Josie looked at one another knowingly. Amaleen was clueless about the demonstrations that had been roiling the University of Paris for over a month.

"C'mon, Amaleen, this is serious. Haven't you heard about the 'Movement of 22 March'?" Josie asked.

"It's jes' more o' them sit-ins and protests, ain't it? 'We want this, we want that…'"

"No, it's getting bigger every day—and it *has* to. You know how dysfunctional this university is. Too many students for the facilities, *huge* lectures, too few classrooms and labs, too few professors and no real interaction between students and professors, a lack of affordable places for the students to live and eat. It's okay for us, with our dollars, but for French students it's really tough. Their time at university determines the rest of their lives. They see how it's going and they hate what they see ahead."

"So how's marchin' around an' yellin' gonna help?" Amaleen asked.

"The university and the government aren't listening! They're doing nothing to improve the siuation! De Gaulle is a dictator! I hear the labor unions are planning big demonstrations, too. I'm going to show solidarity and support my fellow students."

"Ah know ezzackly what ah'm gonna do about it," Amaleen said. "Ah'm gonna have me another one o' them kaffay-oh-layz."

She signalled to the waiter for another coffee.

"Josie, we know you take this political stuff seriously, and we admire you for it," Charity said. "But we're Americans. French politics is not our thing. We'll be going home in a little while. We don't have that much more time in France. We want to get as much as we can out of our year abroad."

Josie looked at them with an ironic half-smile. How little they understood. They had not grown up colored in America. They had no idea of being denied entry to hotels, restaurants, toilets, the best seats in a movie theater, even water fountains just because of the color of their skin. No idea of having your car stopped because of a burnt-out tail light and being strip-searched. Of how it feels to see a photograph of colored people hanging from trees above a crowd of jubilant white murderers.

Josie had come to love her friends, but not their ignorance. This was the big challenge: getting intelligent, decent, caring, unbiased white people to understand prejudice personally, not just intellectually, not at a distance.

"Okay, ladies, I get it. You're not ready yet. If you're not gonna be part of it, then you better watch out and stay away from it. If you're not involved, if you don't understand what's going on, it can be dangerous. Don't go anywhere near the demonstrations. The cops are beating anyone they see. They don't care if you're white or black, girl or boy, protester or innocent bystander. They've vicious, just like in Chicago."

"But what about *you*, Josie honey? Don't get yore pretty li'l self hurt! Jes' political blabbin', no fightin', you hear?"

Josie sighed. Oh, Amaleen....

"I'll have another coffee with you, Amaleen," Charity said. "You're right, it's just too nice here to rush, and we're not gonna be in Paris much longer. But after the coffee I gotta go. I want to check out an artifacts shop I saw, maybe buy a souvenir of my time in Paris."

Josie kissed them on both cheeks, French-style, and went off to meet with the student protestors.

When the waiter brought Amaleen's coffee, Charity asked for another one as well.

"What's Noireau like?" Charity asked Amaleen.

"Professor Doctor Marcel Noireau? Yore askin' *me?* He's *yore* department. He's one o' them archeologists."

"I know, of course. Noireau is the most famous archeologist in France, and one of the most famous in the world. That means he's too famous for the likes of me, Amaleen. The great Professor Noireau does not teach undergraduates, especially not American year-abroad undergrads, especially not *girls!* He leaves that to the younger, un-famous instructors like Lagarde."

"Well, ah liked him because he's rich. We had lotsa fun. He took me to great places."

"I remember some of the presents he gave you. Pretty posh."

"That's the kind ah like, honey."

"But what's he like as a man—I mean, as a person?"

"Honey, he's nice, like a big ol' daddy, took sweet care o' me. But, y'know, these old guys are all the same. He wanted to lay me and show me off to the world that he still got the moxie. I'm used to that. Maybe these guys cain't stand the thought of growin' old. I'm not criticizin'. Ah shore don't know what it's like to grow old. Must be pretty awful. Anyway, he had his fun, I had mine. Even-steven."

"He's world famous, you know. If you're keeping track of your conquests, he's worth a lot of points."

Charity wondered if she had gone too far. She hoped Amaleen

wouldn't take offense.

"Oh honey, he's full of hisself about that archeology. 'I'm just back from Tokyo, I'm just back from Rio,' he'd tell me," Amaleen said, imitating the haughty professor's low voice. "'I travel all over the world to give my lectures and examine recently-found artifacts.' Tryin' to impress the naive young American girl. Honey, he's packed tight with a double load o' hisself. That's how he acted, that's how it looked to all o' his friends when he was showin' me off, but in bed he's really jes'… small an' kinda wimpy."

"Are you talking about the man or his…uh…male equipment?" Charity grinned slyly.

"The man. His ego. His attitude… *An'* his li'l dickie!"

Too much information, Charity thought, but it was worth a laugh, and I guess I asked for it.

"He wasn't that great in bed, ah can tell you that, but ah always acted like he was. That's what they always want."

"So?"

"So, he's insecure!"

"But he's rich!"

"He shore is. Plenty o' money."

"Inherited? Archeologists don't usually get rich."

"Ah dunno where he got it, honey, but he had it, an' he liked to show it off."

Amaleen sipped her coffee.

"We had fun."

They sat with their faces turned to the April sun, so welcome after the chilly, dreary, dark, wet northern European winter. Charity pondered Amaleen's description of the famous archeologist. It would look good on her resume to have studied with him, but she imagined that his few classes, always for graduate students, would be drearier than a Paris winter, all about him and not about archeology. What luck that she had studied with the passionate, lively assistant professors she had.

"So what about you, Charity? Ah dit'n see you playin' around none this year. You or Josie neither. Y'all jes' studied all the time, 'cept for Josie's political meetin's."

Charity was quiet for a moment. Studying archeology in Paris meant freedom from Massachusetts society: the cocktail parties and charity balls, the social-climbing class skirmishes. Here in Paris, an entire ocean away from Boston, she was free. Socially, intellectually, and personally free, although so far she had experienced only the social and intellectual freedom. She envied Amaleen her non-stop love affairs. She would have liked at least one. In that respect, Paris was no different from dancing class.

"For me, this time in Paris is not really for pleasure. I truly want to connect with all the people of the world from the beginning of time. Yeah, it sounds corny, but for me archeology is art, architecture, daily life, conflict and leisure, from the dawn of human existence. In America, archeology means the 'Indians' who were living there before the Europeans came. Here in Europe it means Greece, Rome, Byzantium.... In France, archeology goes back 17,000 years, like the paleolithic cave paintings of Lascaux. Amaleen, the cavemen scratched and daubed with their fingers. They didn't even have brushes! But the paintings are wonderful. It's *pure art*, expressions of dreams and visions straight from the human soul. No art-school training, no thought of artistic reputation, or sales, or posterity. All they wanted was to express themselves, and they did. It's wonderful!"

"Honey, that's too much to think about! Yore makin' mah head hurt!"

Amaleen took a sip of coffee.

"You dit'n at least have a fling with one boy here? Not even one?"

Charity shook her head slightly, self-consciously, and looked down at her coffee cup.

"It might have been nice," she whispered.

She thought of how she had studied hard, earned top grades, and won the respect of the other students and her teachers. She felt that the other students—the boys—were put off by her intelligence. She was 'too brainy.'

Or was she fooling herself? She knew she was plain-looking.

Charity remembered the time she had overheard her mother at a cocktail party telling friends that "Charity's profile is just like that painting in the Gardner Museum of the Duchess of

Urbino!"

Charity was mortified.

She looked up the painting in her art books. The small photo of the painting did look something like her, but it only depressed her. Then she read the history:

> *Battista Sforza, Duchess of Urbino, fluent in Greek and Latin, was "a maiden with every grace and virtue rare endowed." She was married at 14 to Federico da Montefeltro, Duke of Urbino, and though her husband was 24 years her senior, their marriage was an uncommonly happy one, described by one contemporary as "two souls in one body." When the duke was away from his domains, Battista acted worthily as his regent in all affairs, social, political and economic, that concerned his realm.*

When she was at Radcliffe, her mother's alma mater, Charity's art class went on a field trip to the Isabella Stuart Gardner Museum in Boston. She asked a guard about the painting. "Third Floor, Long Gallery," he said. She found it and saw that her mother was right: the profile resemblance was striking, but only because the duchess was no beauty herself. Not ugly, not pretty…just not remarkable either way.

Charity accepted the inevitability of her looks and her fate. She didn't care about fashion. She did like to be neat and clean, and she did her best with what she had. She couldn't imagine having the boldness and style—let alone the body—of someone like Amaleen.

Just one love affair? Yes, it would have been nice.

Charity brought herself back to reality, picked up her coffee cup and took a final sip.

She paid for her coffee, said goodbye to Amaleen, and wandered slowly across the Parvis de Notre-Dame, the plaza in front of the great church. By the time she was crossing the Seine on the Petit Pont, her mind had wandered off again to her favorite romantic fantasy.

5

The Old Curiosity Shop

Just one romance? Charity thought. Of course I fantasize about the most impossible one, the one I would have zero chance of experiencing.

Gaston Lagarde, her archeology instructor, was in his early 30s, handsome, suave and brilliantly intelligent. He spoke French, English, German, Spanish, Italian and even a little Arabic, Greek and Turkish from his work in the field. He drove an MG convertible on his trips out of Paris and was always dressed fashionably as befitted a highly eligible Parisian bachelor.

You could always recognize him by his broad-brimmed leather hat, a classy hippyesque affectation.

Besides his work in Europe and the Middle East he had researched the Pueblo peoples of the Four Corners region in the USA, and had spent time at the University of New Mexico. He understood American universities and was, unlike other French professors, more open and available to his students.

Every girl in his class had a crush on him. Charity was no exception.

But Lagarde took no special notice of any young woman in his class. Every time she or any other woman in the class spoke with him about their studies and perhaps sent him a subtle signal of interest, it elicited no response except gracious Parisian *politesse*.

There was that extracurricular field trip to Nîmes to see *La*

Maison Carrée, the perfect Roman white marble temple in the city center, and the intact Roman amphitheater nearby still in use for shows and spectacles after 2000 years. She maneuvered to be in front of him when boarding the train in Paris, dreaming he would notice her and sit next to her because she was one of the top students in the class, but he sat alone. During the walking tour in Nîmes, overcoming her shyness, she forced herself to stand right in front of him whenever he stopped to instruct the class in ancient architecture, history or society.

She took a seat across from him in the restaurant at lunchtime and sat demurely, listening politely to his conversation and smiling. The other girls at the table asked him lots of questions. Charity suspected they asked just to have him notice them. The one time Charity asked a question it was a complicated one about sequencing chronologies. She asked it not to get attention but because she didn't know the answer. He explained it at length, and technically. The other girls rolled their eyes and sneered at Charity behind her back.

She was proud of herself for at least overcoming her shyness that much. It was progress. But Monsieur Lagarde still treated all of his students with friendly politeness, and nothing more.

Nice fantasy, she thought as she walked along the Boulevard Saint-Germain—but just a fantasy. I bet every girl in the class has the same one.

She doubted that Amaleen ever had fantasies. Why would she? Her life was a fantasy-come-true: what she wanted in the way of romance always seemed to come to her.

Forget fantasies, Charity thought. She wanted a real, solid souvenir of her time in Paris, something archeological— something like the ancient little elf figurine she had loved in the North Adams Public Library.

She reached the Odéon Métro station and turned left onto Rue Dupuytren. Half way along the short street was an old-fashioned shop marked by a sign: *M Plouff, Antiquaire.*

She opened the rickety front door and entered a room characterized by utter disorganization. African tribal masks sat in piles with medieval suits of armor. Sculptures of Egyptian gods and goddesses lay prostrate on shelves beneath Roman oil lamps and Mayan textiles. Dusty piles of books crowded the corners. The windows hadn't been washed in a decade.

Seated at a battered desk in the center of the room was an old, bald man dressed in a threadbare, rumpled suit and wire-rimmed glasses. Beneath his salt-and-pepper moustache his teeth clamped the much-chewed stem of a squat, rough-carved briar pipe. The piles of antiquities and old junk hemmed him in like the walls of a tomb in Père Lachaise Cemetery. His nervous pipe-puffing filled the room with a noxious purple haze.

"Bonjour, monsieur!"

"Bonjour, mademoiselle! How may I help you?" he asked in French.

"I'm just looking for a small souvenir of Paris," Charity told him in the same language. "An old souvenir, antique. Would you have anything from Lutèce?"

"Ah! Roman Paris. Lutetia! You know the second-century town, the Roman town, was located where the Panthéon now stands, on the Montagne Sainte-Geneviève, which the Romans called Mons Lutetia."

"Yes. I live on Rue Claude Bernard, not far from the Arènes de Lutèce, the Roman theater. I'm studying to be an archeologist. I have been living right in what was once Roman Paris. That's why I want a souvenir from here."

He rose from his creaky swivel chair, shuffled to the back wall of the shop and rummaged in the drawer of a cabinet. She peered in the drawer with him: small clay pots and oil lamps, a few figurines, mostly nicked or broken. One, of a goddess figure, was in excellent condition. She pointed to it.

"What's that?"

"Ah, that is…ahem…a fine example of the earth-mother goddess. It is Neolithic, about eight thousand years old!"

"Where is it from? What is its provenance? What excavation?" she asked.

"Provenance? Well, uh,…it must be…you see, if it's Neolithic, it's probably…"

"You don't know," she interrupted. "You can't guarantee its provenance. It may be a fake, a modern replica."

The old man held the figurine up and smiled at it, admiringly.

Then his smile faded and he looked down at the floor.

"Well,…yes, it could be a fake, I suppose."

"You didn't find it yourself?"

"Oh, mademoiselle! How I would love to have gone on archeological expeditions! How I would love to have discovered these ancient works of art! So human! So full of meaning, even for us today!"

He held up the figurine between their faces again. They looked at it.

"Earth-mother! Symbol of life, fecundity, the miracle of birth and reproduction! These essential human traits worshipped in a goddess! A *fat* goddess!"

He smiled, and then was serious.

"For nearly all of human history, humankind's struggle has been to find enough to eat. The fat earth-mother symbolizes abundance, the health not only of herself but of her tribe, her people—hope and prayers for a happy future."

"But you don't know where it came from," she repeated.

"No, I did not acquire it first-hand. I have never had enough money to travel. Oh, in France, yes, to a few archeological sites, but never abroad, never even to Italy! Most of the artifacts in my shop come from the amateur collections of wealthy 19th-century travelers. They brought home these ancient works of art as curios, status symbols, to show their friends and to enhance their status. When they died, their heirs had little interest in them. The best, and those with provenance, would be bequeathed to museums. The rest, the less valuable, the ones without provenance, the…fakes—yes, there are fakes!—would be disposed of to *antiquaires* like me."

"Just out of curiosity, what would be the price of such an 'old' artifact?"

"Ah, well, for a piece in such good condition, I would have to charge…well, let me see,…"

He held the figurine close to his eyes, turned it back and forth, and pursed his lips.

"*Oui,*" he mused. "I would have to ask…a thousand francs."

"*A thousand?!* For an artifact without provenance?"

He held out the figurine to her, looked at it and frowned.

"You are right. Without provenance, I could not get fifty francs for it…even though it *may* be six thousand years old."

"Fifty?"

"Forty, then. Forty. Or thirty!"

"No, thank you. I'm looking for a Lutetia souvenir."

"Ah, yes, correct, a Roman souvenir. So we will look elsewhere."

He replaced the figurine in the drawer, closed it, and opened another. The drawer jingled as he drew it out.

"I am more confident in the provenance and authenticity of these Roman coins and medals," he told her. "There are so many of them, even here in France, let alone in Italy. So many that it would not be worthwhile to manufacture fakes."

He picked up several and arranged them on his hand for her to look at.

Charity pointed to one of the larger medals, about two inches in diameter, bearing the profile of a woman.

"Ah! Vesta, the Roman goddess of hearth and home!" Plouff said smiling. "Perhaps a fitting souvenir for a young lady returning to her home in…where are you from, young lady?"

"America."

"*Oh la la!* I would never have suspected it! Your French is so fluent I almost believed you to be a *Parisienne.*"

"Thank you, *monsieur.* What is the price of this Vesta medal?"

"Uh, I have already told you there are many Roman coins and medals, but in fact there are not so many portraying the goddess Vesta." He looked down at the medal in his hand. "Her most important symbol was not her human form but her sacred fire, the fire of the home hearth. I think it is worth…one hundred francs," he said without looking at her.

An ironic smile came to Charity's lips.

"I will give you forty," she said calmly.

He looked up from the medal into Charity's eyes. She returned his look, directly, without blinking.

"Or perhaps…but it is worth at least…well,…ah…—all right then! Forty! For a nice young *Américaine* who can speak like a *Parisienne.*"

He went to his cluttered desk and rummaged for something to

wrap it in. Picking up a used envelope, he dropped the medal in it, folded it once, and handed it to her.

She gave him forty francs.

"Perhaps when you retire you will be able to travel," Charity said to him in kindness.

"When I sell all the artifacts you see in this shop, then I may retire," the old man said, "and then I will be as old as that earth-mother figurine!"

They smiled at one another.

Charity thanked him and left the shop.

PART TWO

Early May

6

Amaleen Escapes

On May 2, 1968, after more than a month of demonstrations, student sit-ins, and minor violence at the university campus in Nanterre on the outskirts of Paris, the administration announced the imminent expulsion of several student protest leaders and declared the university closed. The next day, university students in the center of Paris protested these decisions, and on May 5th radical students occupied the university administration building in Nanterre. Police flooded into the campus and closed it down.

The next day students from all over Paris gathered in the Latin Quarter. As 20,000 students and faculty marched on the Sorbonne they were violently beaten back by police. The crowd built defensive barricades out of anything at hand and tore up stone paving blocks to hurl at police.

By the end of the day, 500 protesters had been arrested, and 350 police injured.

On May 6, the three roommates were sitting in the salon of their apartment on Rue Claude Bernard in the late afternoon.

"I hereby convene a meeting of the Secret Society for the purpose of determining what members of the Society will do given the current situation in the city," Josie proclaimed.

"But…why do we need a meetin'?"Amaleen asked.

"Because the Sorbonne has been invaded by police. Because there's fighting in the streets. Because students and faculty are protesting the unjust actions of the French government and the university administration, and we need to decide what to do. Shops are closing. Public transportation isn't running regularly. Trash is not being collected. Police are beating anyone not in uniform. The city is heading toward chaos!"

"We need a plan," Josie went on. "Do we stockpile food—if we can find any? Do we stockpile water? Do we buy candles and flashlights and batteries for when the lights go out?"

"Paris shore ain't no fun no more," Amaleen said. "It's gittin' downright dangerous!"

Charity thought wistfully of their carefree breakfast in the sun at the Café Aux Tours de Notre-Dame less than two weeks ago. A different world.

"Ah'm thinkin' o' gittin' outta this place. Ah got a friend's got a big place on the Loire. Maybe I can call him up 'n' see if ah can visit," Amaleen said. "Thanks for organizin' us, Josie, but you prolly won't hafta worry 'bout me."

"I don't want to leave yet," Charity said. "The trouble could settle down any day now."

"Fair enough," Josie said. "Good luck, Amaleen. I don't blame you wanting to leave. Charity, I'm staying too, and the apartment will be my refuge…sometimes. I won't be here most days. I may not be able to get back here every night. So let's get what supplies we can, replenish as we can, and keep in touch by notes left on the table here."

High school students, parents, union workers and others joined the Sorbonne protesters the next day, swelling the crowd to more than 50,000, marching and battling through the narrow streets of the Latin Quarter. When the police shot tear gas grenades at them, the protesters responded with molotov cocktails.

Amaleen went out hoping to find breakfast pastries and found all the shops closed, armies of protesters and police battling, and cries of "Long live the Paris Commune!"

That's it, she thought. I'm not putting up with any more of this. I've got my plan.

She returned to the apartment, telephoned her current lover,

Olivier, and said "Git me outta here!"

He came for her and her two enormous suitcases in his Renault and they drove to the Loire Valley.

"We goin' to the château?" she asked. She pronounced it SHAT-toe.

"Yes, my beauty. We will be safe, even if they come in suits of armor! We have our own suits of armor there!" he said laughing.

They arrived at the château on a hill with a commanding view of the River Loire. Olivier stopped the car at the castle gate, got out, and entered through a small door. After a few minutes the great main doors began to swing open slowly, one at a time, pushed by an old grey-haired man in coveralls. When they were open, Olivier drove into the courtyard.

An old woman emerged from the kitchen, wiping her hands on her apron.

"*Ah! Bonjour, monsieur le baron!*" she greeted him. "*Bonjour mademoiselle. Bienvenue!*"

"*Bonjour, Marie. Bonjour, Georges.* We will be staying here until there is peace in Paris," Olivier told them.

"Very good, sir," Georges, the old man, said. "We will prepare your room and a room for the young lady."

"Please bring us tea in the library," Olivier said to them.

They nodded. Georges went to take their suitcases out of the car.

Olivier led Amaleen to the library. After a few minutes Marie entered, walking carefully, carrying a silver tea tray.

"Is it gonna be boring here?" Amaleen asked.

"No! Of course not! We will take drives in the country. We will visit other châteaus. We will dine in restaurants. We will make love. I will invite my friends to come. We will have jolly parties. All of Paris is coming to the Loire because of the trouble."

After tea, she asked him, "D'you really have suits o' armor here?"

"Of course!"

He took her hand and led her out of the library and into the maze of servants' passages and stairways. They climbed to the third floor, beneath the roof. Dust coated the floor. Spider webs glistened in the dirty window panes. He opened a door to reveal a pile of armor pieces—helmets, bucklers, cuirasses, gauntlets—blanketed in cobwebs.

He picked up a helmet and blew on it. A cloud of dust billowed in the air.

"Want to try it on?"

"Git out!" she yelled, and grimaced at him.

He pantomimed putting it on his head. She was not amused. He threw it back on the pile, where it landed with a clatter.

Marie, the cook and housekeeper, made them a simple dinner. Georges—butler, gardener, groom, seneschal, handyman, whatever duties were left—now dressed in a baggy old black suit, served them in the vast baronial dining room.

"This place is beautiful with all the ol' furniture 'n' stuff, but it shore is drafty," Amaleen said. "And quiet! It's too quiet! We need some action!"

"Won't we have any action tonight?" Olivier asked with a knowing smirk.

"Tonight, darlin', ah'm gonna do sumpthin' to y'all that y'all never had done before, an' yore gonna remember it 'til the day you die. Gotta do *sumpthin'* to heat up this ol' place."

The next morning at breakfast, Olivier told Amaleen they were going to a party.

"My neighbor Benito is having a party at his château a few days from now," he said. "It is the grandest private château in the region."

"He a duke or sumpthin'? Aren't you, like, a duke or a prince or sumpthin'?"

"I am a *baron, le Baron d'Azé*. Benito is not of the nobility. He is proud of that. Every year, following May 1st, the laborers' holiday, he holds a 'counter-celebration' of wealth and privilege. He invites all of us, the traditional nobility of the region, to his château to celebrate status, wealth and excessive living—just the opposite of the workers' holiday."

"He invites y'all, but he don't have no title or nuthin'?"

"Yes, he invites all the nobility…to show off his higher status, which to him means greater wealth. He was born a poor

Corsican. Now he is among the richest men in the world. We nobles are all less rich than he is. Some of us are actually poor. We do not even have enough money to maintain the family château. He has much more than enough to make his own château the most splendid in the Loire. He has houses and villas in many other places, apartments in London and New York, Rome and Tokyo. By giving this party he is showing us, the nobility, that we are beneath him in status."

"He's a Corsican? What's that?"

"From the island of Corsica, in the Mediterranean. It was an Italian island, but two centuries ago it became a French island. Napoleon was from Corsica. Like Napoleon, Benito is short and has an inferiority complex—he fears that French people do not accept him as one hundred percent French, so he must show them that he is superior to all of them in every way."

"Sounds like a asshole," Amaleen said with a grimace.

"Oh no! He is quite charming. You will see. He is intelligent. He will enjoy meeting you because you, too, are proud of your... shall we say, country roots?"

"You bet ah am!"

"He does not gloat or act superior when we are together. That is done by the mere fact that he offers us his counter-celebration. He invites hundreds of people to his château, feeds them nebuchadnezzars of the best champagne, the rarest Médoc wines, kilos of the finest caviar, whole truffles on every plate, the rarest delicacies, all served by the handsomest men and most beautiful women available for service."

"Huh. Still sounds like a asshole."

"I will want to know what you think after you meet him," Olivier said with a little smile.

"I don't have nuthin' right to wear to no fancy shindig."

"Do not worry. If we can find a couturier that is working, we will have a fine dress made for you that accentuates your...ah... many *charms*. If none is working, we will find what you may like at one of the fashion houses, and have it modified."

"That's nuts! Some real expensive dress jes' fer one party? That'd cost too crazy much money!"

"Not at all," Olivier smirked. "I will have the bill sent to

Benito. It will be another symbol of my poverty and his superiority. He will appreciate the joke, especially when he meets you."

7

Aux Barricades!

Josie looked at herself in the mirror. She opened her purse and pulled out the publicity photo of the young Josephine Baker that she always carried. She held the photo up next to the mirror and compared the two. It really was quite amazing: the same long oval face topped by a large, smooth forehead above huge captivating eyes, a long elegant nose leading down to sensuous rosebud lips set above a slender girlish chin. Josie's café-crème skin color was somewhat darker than Baker's lighter tone, but a careful application of foundation and make-up could bring Josie's tone right to Baker's. With her eyebrows plucked the same way and wearing a long fall of sleek black hair, nine out of ten French people of Baker's generation, accustomed to seeing publicity photos of the entertainer, assumed Josie was Josephine Baker, or at least the daughter or grand-daughter of the famous American performer and movie star.

When Josie went to Josephine Baker's concert at the Olympia on April 5, she played down her resemblance to the star, not wanting to distract attention from her idol. Seeing and hearing the 61-year-old star on stage, Josie was in awe: her namesake, her icon, was still performing and bringing the house down! Baker had been out of the public eye in the USA, but her performance at the Olympia broke all attendance records for the theater.

Not all younger Parisians knew who Josephine Baker was. Not

everyone reacted when they saw Josie. Those who didn't know Baker well would pause for a moment in indecision, staring at Josie, thinking, "Who is this? The face is familiar. I know her. She's not a friend, she's someone famous...."

Her Bakerness gave Josie a priceless advantage. She would propose a course of action and the people looking at her would assent because their brains were busy trying to remember who she was, or busy being excited about meeting a celebrity.

It had worked on countless shopkeepers. She would shop for something, and if she wanted something special—a larger one, or gift wrapping, or a discount—shopkeepers would inevitably agree because their brains were occupied with her appearance. By the time her request fully penetrated, they had already agreed to it.

Would it work on police? She didn't know. Being a woman, and colored, and beautiful, and perhaps a celebrity, was the only armor she had. She would put it on.

Eight o'clock in the morning. Josie left the apartment and walked up Rue Claude Bernard toward the Latin Quarter. She heard noise on Rue Gay-Lussac and walked toward it. Up the street she saw a mass of students behind a long, two-meter-high mass of stone paving blocks extending across the street—a barricade. Several young people well behind the barricade were pulling up more paving blocks to strengthen their defenses, or handing them to the strongest men to throw at the police. Tenants in the apartments overlooking the street put transistor radios on their windowsills, broadcasting to those fighting below a running commentary of the demonstrations and battles all over Paris.

An older couple brought boxes of sandwiches and bottles of water from a nearby restaurant.

Off to one side, a slender young woman in hippy garb was sitting calmly on a wooden crate sketching the scene of the battle.

She's nuts! Josie thought. Stones and glass and tear gas cannisters are flying all around her and she seems oblivious. I bet she's American.

Josie approached her.

"Are you American?" she asked.

"Yeah, California. Isn't this exciting?" the woman said. "We had fights in the Haight, but this one's so much better! It's a real brawl!"

"Sister, you could get killed here! If the police break through, they'll beat you senseless. You'd better get out of here!"

"D'you really think so?" The woman looked puzzled.

Just then a tear gas cannister ricocheted off the wall only feet from the young woman's head. She stared at it as the cloud of gas spewed from it.

"Yeah, maybe you're right."

She scrawled *Flora* in the lower right corner of the sketch, closed her sketchpad, put the lid on her box of pastels, and wandered down the street away from the barricade, sniffling from the gas.

Josie watched her go, rolled her eyes, then returned her attention to the action at the barricade. She saw that several students, men and women, were the leaders of the group, shouting commands, directing the action, baiting the police. When one of the leaders left the barricade for a bottle of water, she approached him.

"I want to help! What should I do?" Josie asked in French.

The young man was drinking from the bottle, but when he saw her he stopped, held the bottle in his hand, and didn't move.

Ah, the pause-and-stare moment, Josie thought.

"Help the *medecins,*" the man said, continuing to look at her.

A group of white-coated students, well behind the barricade, had set up a first-aid station with medical supplies 'requisitioned' from a nearby pharmacy. Faculty of Medicine, Josie thought.

Josie went to the first-aid station. Four protesters lay on the street while the white-coated students performed first aid.

Without a word a young man in a white coat handed her a bottle of antiseptic and a roll of gauze, and pointed at another young woman lying next to them. Her head was turned to the side and her eyes were closed. Blood was running into her hair from a wound on her forehead.

"I...I don't know anything about medicine!" Josie said.

"You know almost as much as we do!" the medical student

barked at her. "All they teach us is science and theory! This is the first time any of us have treated real patients. Just put some antiseptic on the wound and bandage it. Then help us get her to the infirmary. You will do fine."

Josie knelt next to her, dabbed the wound with antiseptic, and gently holding the woman's head in her arms, wrapped gauze around her head and tied it in place.

"Help me take her into the café!" the man said to Josie.

Using a blanket as a stretcher, four of them carried the wounded woman farther away from the barricade and into a café that had been converted to an infirmary.

A dozen wounded lay on tables or the floor, or sat on chairs and benches tending their wounds as the medical students circulated with bandages, antiseptic, water and food. On a shelf, a radio blared a constant stream of news reports from around the city.

8

Charity Escapes

Friday, May 10, 1968, 22:00 (10:00 pm). Charity sat in the salon of the apartment in fear.

She was alone.

Amaleen had gone off with her lover to the Loire Valley.

Josie rarely came home since the troubles started, and when she did it was only to wash, sleep and leave again. Charity hadn't seen her since the Secret Society meeting on Monday.

Police and protesters were everywhere. Looking down from the salon window, she saw crowds of students and workers running along Rue Claude Bernard toward Monge. Some were bleeding or limping.

Charity knew she had to flee. She packed a small suitcase with a variety of clothing and tried to get some sleep.

Josie returned to the apartment around midnight, exhausted, having gone nonstop for two days.

The door to Charity's room was closed, meaning that she was probably asleep.

Josie collapsed into bed.

At 2:15 am, negotiations between students, workers and the government having failed, the police staged a massive attack. Charity woke in fear from the tumult and went to the window. In the distance she could see the reflection of flames off building walls.

Josie, deep asleep, heard nothing.

At 5:00 am Charity's alarm woke her. It was already light outside. She peeked into Josie's room and saw her asleep in her bed. Mustn't disturb her.

She left a note: "Josie, I'm leaving. Don't know where. I just have to get out of this city until things calm down. I'll keep in touch."

Charity was determined to go, but where? And how?

She thought first of the airport.

What if she ran into protesters, or the police? She remembered Josie's warning to steer clear of the demonstrations. What if the protesters forced her to join them? What if she came to a police roadblock? The police had been violent, and with so many cops injured by protesters, they would be brutal, taking out their anger on any student, even an American, even a woman.

She grabbed her suitcase, crept down the stairs to the front door and peered into the street.

Stepping out, she turned left and walked quickly. At the northern end of Rue Claude Bernard she looked up Rue Gay-Lussac. She saw trash, scattered paving stones, articles of clothing, overturned cars, spent tear gas cannisters. Broken glass everywhere. She heard shouts and cries and police whistles along the street in the distance, closer to the university. Not safe!

Would she even be able to get to the airport? Even if she got to the airport, would there be planes? Would there be seats available? Where would she fly to anyway?

No.

She would try to go to a train station. With few workers on the job, most trains had been cancelled, but she didn't know what else to do, except *not* to remain in the center of Paris.

The nearest train station was the Gare d'Austerlitz. The Metro wasn't running and there were no taxis. She would have to walk.

She retraced her steps down Rue Claude Bernard and made her way along Rue Censier and Rue Buffon, past the Grand Mosque and along the fence of the Jardin des Plantes. She listened for any noise as she crept carefully along. At intersections she peered around each corner to see what was happening farther along the street.

When she arrived at the Gare d'Austerlitz, it was chaos. Crowds and police filled the streets. An army of workers in traditional blue smocks surrounded the station chanting slogans. Just as she approached the station entrance, looking for a way in, a phalanx of police charged the workers, pushing their shields in front of them and flailing away with their truncheons. She was caught in the middle. The police pushed her into the mass of workmen, throwing her off-balance. The sky disappeared as she collapsed into a jostling prison of legs in rough, dark trousers, muddy worker boots and polished police boots. Elbows rammed her head and body. Knees jabbed her ribs. Feet in heavy boots kicked her as they tried to get free of her weight. Oh god I'm being trampled! Oh god oh god please don't let them crush me!

She shrieked in terror.

Her falling weight unbalanced the workers in front of her. They fell on the men behind them, collapsing like dominoes.

Her scream stopped the pushing crowd just enough for two workers to get their hands under her arms and lift her up and out. They cleared a way through the violent thrashing and pushed her into the station, tossing her suitcase down next to her before they disappeared back into the battle.

Inside were more crowds, workers, students and bystanders, pushing, shoving, fighting. Holding her suitcase up as a shield and pushing it before her, she made her way to a corner of the room. With walls on two sides, there was less danger of being toppled and crushed.

She took deep breaths, lowered her suitcase and looked across the room.

Then she saw it, the leather hat.

"Monsieur Lagarde!" she shouted, but he did not hear her over the tumult. He was pushing through the crowd to go deeper into the station.

She worked her way along the wall with her suitcase as a battering ram. Her blood was up. She *must* find him.

She made it to the train platforms, but she didn't see Lagarde in the throbbing crowd. She pushed her way to a flight of stairs, mounted the steps and caught sight of him again. He was heading for Platform 2. She elbowed her way down the stairs and through the crowd, pushing her way along the platform until finally she saw him again. She came up behind him and grabbed his shoulder. He turned, looked at her and gasped.

"Mademoiselle Cabot! Oh *mon dieu!* You are hurt!"

"Can you get me out of Paris?" she shouted.

"Come with me!" he said. Grabbing her suitcase and gripping her hand tightly, he pushed forcefully through the crowd and along the platform to a train carriage. He commanded others pushing onto the train to get out of the way for the wounded woman. They made space. In the carriage, he ordered a man to give up his seat.

She sat, closed her eyes and took deep breaths.

"Est-ce qu'il y a de l'eau?" Lagarde shouted. A woman nearby rummaged in a large bag on her lap and handed him a bottle of Perrier water. He knocked the cap off and handed it to Charity. The fizzing water stung her mouth and throat but was welcome and sustaining. She handed it back to him. He poured some on his handkerchief and gently wiped blood from her face, then from her arms. She watched in shock as his brilliant white handkerchief turned to a crimson rag.

Oh my god I must look a mess.

After a few minutes he handed her the handkerchief and said "You may want to clean your legs."

She looked down. Bruises, contusions, rivulets of dried blood. She touched the wounds on her legs gently. The bleeding had mostly stopped, but now she felt the pain.

Clutching the bloody handkerchief in both hands, Charity sat back, closed her eyes and began to weep.

When Josie awoke mid-morning, there was no one else in the apartment. A note from Charity said she was going to try to get out of Paris.

Josie showered, dressed, rifled the kitchen cupboards for something to eat, then returned to the barricade on Rue Gay-Lussac.

The café-infirmary was completely filled with wounded.

"Some of these people need to be in a hospital," she said to an exhausted medical student.

"Yes, but if we take them there the police will find them and beat them again, or arrest them."

Josie immediately went to work. When she had a moment, she watched the medical students and learned how to do more. The hours passed quickly. She felt the tiredness setting in.

Pace yourself, Josie thought. You're no good to anyone if you exhaust yourself and can't go on.

After five hours nonstop, she grabbed a bottle of water and sat down by two other women.

"What's the news?" Josie asked. The radio reports were in fast, impassioned French that Josie had difficulty understanding.

"We hear that high school students, the PCF and the CGT have joined us!"

"PCF? CGT?"

"The *Parti Communiste Français. Confédération Générale du Travail.* The big workers' unions. The fighting is all over Paris. We have even broken the police cordon on the Seine and we are now fighting on the Right Bank. The government proposed a peace, but we have refused. We want the government to resign! We want De Gaulle to go!"

"Wait!" one man shouted. "Listen!"

The radio announcer reported that the labor unions called for a nationwide general strike. All workers were to leave their jobs for 24 hours and to join the demonstrations.

"All of France is with us!"

The train started with a jolt. Charity opened her eyes. The carriage was packed with standees, but the pushing and shoving had stopped. The train was moving slowly. She looked up at Gaston, who was looking down at her with concern.

"You must have been terrified!" he said.

"Where are we going?"

"The train goes to Chartres, but I am getting out at Versailles. That is where I keep my car. Where are you going?"

"I don't know. All I know is I have to get out of Paris."

"You don't know where you are going?"

"No. Somewhere less dangerous than the Latin Quarter."

They looked at one another. A minute passed.

"You are right. Paris is dangerous now. I am driving to Sarlat," Gaston said. "You may drive with me if you like."

"Sarlat is in the south, isn't it?" she asked.

"Yes, the southwest. In Périgord, the Dordogne. I have a cottage near Sarlat. I will stay there until the danger passes and the university re-opens. It is a long drive. We will pass through many places. You may stop at any place you like."

"Thank you."

9

Périgord

Charity, in pain and fear, nearing despair, her eyes closed against the chaos, barely noticed that the short trip from the Gare d'Austerlitz to Versailles took almost an hour. The train stopped abruptly many times for no apparent reason.

Gaston tapped her gently on the shoulder.

"Here is where we get out," he said.

They pushed through the standing passengers to the door and stepped down from the train. The Versailles platform was crowded but not a battle zone as in Paris. They could breathe again.

"Do you think you can walk a kilometer?" Gaston asked.

"Yes, but please not too fast."

She was limping.

"Follow me," Gaston said, carrying her suitcase.

They walked through the town for 20 minutes to a walled compound. Gaston unlocked the heavy metal gate and led her through an untended garden to the front door of a large white mansion.

He unlocked the door and they entered. It was cold and dark inside, the windows shuttered, the furniture draped in white. He led her to the kitchen, switched on the lights and lit the gas oven.

"We'll have a bit of heat in a minute," he said. "It gets cold in the house when it's not occupied. I think we need some coffee.

Are you hungry?"

"A little."

She sat at the kitchen table. He went to prepare coffee.

"Whose house is this?"

"It was my uncle's. He is now deceased, so it is supposedly mine, but the lawyers are still…shall we say…*conversing* about it." He gave her a wry smile.

He brought the coffees to the table along with a bottle of water and a tin of biscuits.

They sipped the strong coffee. Ah! The bitter brew was delicious, the fragrant aroma and warm sips restorative. She felt the caffeine surge in her veins. She drank a glass of water and he poured her another.

"I will prepare the bathroom so that you may clean your wounds. The water from the tap is cold, but I will heat some water here and bring it to you. That will be quicker than turning on the water heating system."

After the coffee and washing, she felt much better, but she was sore all over, and her wounds and bruises were throbbing.

"May I rest for a little while?" she asked him. "I'd like to lie down."

"Yes, of course, but I'm afraid it will not be very comfortable. The beds are all so cold…"

He led her upstairs to a bedroom. Unlike the downstairs rooms, it looked normal, without sheets covering the furniture. He took blankets from a cupboard and spread one on the bed. She lay down. He spread two more on top of her.

"I will come in a little while," he said. "We should leave then."

When he gently touched her shoulder, it seemed like she had lain down only minutes before, although she knew it must be longer.

"You slept for a long time," he said quietly. "It is good! But now we must go."

They walked downstairs and through the servants' quarters in the rear of the house, locked the rear door behind them, took the MG from the carriage house and headed south.

The traffic was heavy and slow with frequent stops.

"How long did you say it takes to drive to Sarlat?"

"Normally about six hours, but today I do not know. This is slow. There could be trouble along the way. With the strikes and protests, who knows what will happen."

"Even outside Paris?"

"The strikes and the violence are all over France now. Nothing is working! We were fortunate to find the train. Someone said the only reason it was running was to go out of Paris and bring more factory workers to the center for *les manifestations.*"

"Do you know where you would like to go?" Gaston asked, turning to look at her. "You do not have to go all the way to Sarlat."

Charity stared straight ahead.

"I have no idea."

"Well, then, you may end up in Sarlat."

"I suppose it will do as well as anywhere," she said. "I've never been there. I've heard the Dordogne is beautiful."

They drove in silence. Charity closed her eyes and worked to regain her mental balance.

After an hour they were free of the city congestion and the driving was easier, with less traffic and no apparent obstacles, but it began to rain.

The MG is a sports car, built for racing speed and maneuverability, not for comfort on cross-country trips, driving hundreds of kilometers along national highways. The wind whistled through cracks between the soft cloth top and the flimsy doors and windows. Because of the car's tight suspension, every road bump shocked the riders through the thinly-padded seats.

To distract Charity from the frightening experiences she had suffered and from the dismal driving, Gaston talked as they drove.

"Périgord is famous for its cuisine. *Truffles, fois gras, cuisses de canard....*"

"I know truffles and fois gras, but...ducks' legs?"

"The legs are packed in duck fat to preserve them. The fat is delicious, of course, though high in calories. You must try them!"

"Perhaps you remember from our study of prehistoric archeology...the valley of the River Vézère near the village of Les Eyzies has several caves with Magdalenian artifacts and the most beautiful paintings," he said.

"Magdalenian? Please remind me."

"Upper Paleolithic, 17,000 to 12,000 years ago. The art in France's most famous cave, Lascaux, is of this period also."

"Yes, I remember now. I hope I can see them."

"You cannot see Lascaux, of course. It is now closed because of the damage caused by visits from thousands of people, but I can recommend other sites such as Font-de-Gaume and Les Combarelles, and yet others that are very little known. Some, in fact, that only I know. The valley is a treasury of wonderful archeology. Most of the other sites are not so impressive as Lascaux, but they have great archeological interest—besides the paintings, unusual tools and ornaments, things that the public finds dull, but which you and I find fascinating because they show us how people lived thousands of years ago."

She smiled at his saying "you and I."

"So, you have... a cottage?"

"Yes. In the hills between Sarlat and Les Eyzies. I enjoy exploring the Vézère valley for caves that may contain signs of Paleolithic life. My uncle was fascinated by archeology and wanted to encourage me. He was friends with Professor Noireau. Do you know Noireau?"

"I know *of* him, of course. He's so famous."

"Yes. He and my uncle were friends."

"Were?"

"My uncle—you may remember, I mentioned that he died and gave me the house in Versailles."

"Yes. I'm sorry."

"They both encouraged me to continue my explorations of the Vézère. Professor Noireau found the cottage for me, and my uncle provided the funds to renovate it. They both were extraordinarily generous!"

"How do you search for caves? What do you look for? How do you find them?"

"I rise early, pack a lunch, and drive along the valley looking at its cliffs. If I see a rock formation of interest, I climb up and explore. I've explored about two kilometers of the valley so far."

"Have you found anything?"

"Some of my finds may be worthy of a short article or monograph, but I have found nothing dramatic—nothing like Lascaux! I have discovered one or two caves with bones, charcoal, stone tools, marks on the walls. Though not of great importance, they do add to the overall picture of life in the Vézère valley 17,000 years ago."

"I think that's *thrilling!*" Charity said. "I'd love to be able to do that!"

They drove through the rainy night, uncomfortable and tense. The rain-slicked road was treacherously slippery and the reflected glare from the headlights of approaching traffic was beginning to give Gaston a headache.

"Lots of buses," Charity said.

"Workers going to Paris to join the demonstrations, I believe. Most of the trains are not operating."

The rain, the slick road, the bad visibility, the unsuitable car— at least it was better than tear gas, police truncheons, molotov cocktails and crushing crowds.

"At the next town we will stop for some food and fuel," Gaston said.

Few shops were open but they managed to find bread, cheese and fruit. They bought water.

At the fuel station, the attendant advised them not to follow the national highway. It was blockaded by striking truck drivers. He recommended a detour.

"But that will take hours!" Gaston said.

"If you want to go to Sarlat, you must go that way."

After several more hours, it was clear they would not reach Sarlat before midnight.

"I hope the chaos in Paris doesn't last too long. It'll be expensive, living in a hotel while I'm still paying rent for my apartment."

"If you wish, I will help you to find a *chambre à louer* in a private home. That may be less expensive," he said.

After a pause, "Mademoiselle Cabot,…"

She smiled.

"Under the circumstances, *monsieur,* don't you think *on peut se tutoyer*—you can call me Charity?"

Gaston stared straight ahead at the road.

"You are right. Then you must call me Gaston. Mademoiselle Cabot…uh, Charity, it will be past midnight when we reach Sarlat. It is a small town. We may be able to find someone awake at a hotel, but perhaps not."

He paused.

"I fear that I am about to make an improper suggestion. My cottage is small and, well, primitive, but it has a small room which I use as an office. It has a simple bed in it. You may stay there tonight if you wish. I think it will be adequate, and I assure you that I will be a proper host. You will not be disturbed. Tomorrow we can look for a more suitable lodging for you."

Charity was conflicted. Her classroom fantasy, so romantic when impossible, was anything but romantic when it became real: bruised and beaten, spending the night in a primitive cabin who knows where, with a strange man. For all her rich fantasies, she actually knew nothing about Lagarde as a person. In a fantasy this didn't matter, she could turn him into a romantic hero, but this was no longer a fantasy. He was real, and unknown. It would be the middle of the night, in a place she knew nothing about. None of her friends and family knew where she was.

Her parents would find his suggestion highly improper. The sexual freedoms achieved by women in 1968 were substantial, but they did not apply to Cabots in general, and to protected little Charity Cabot of North Adams, Massachusetts, in particular.

The anesthesia of shock that follows a wound had long ago worn off. Her skin, her bones, her muscles all throbbed with pain. She was dead tired. She knew what she had to do.

"*Monsieur*—Gaston—tonight I could sleep on a bed of nails and I would notice nothing. Your suggestion isn't improper, it's generous, and I thank you for helping me. I promise I will not be a burden."

Tomorrow can take care of itself, she thought, whenever I wake up. I could sleep for a week.

10

Refuge

It was just after midnight when they reached Sarlat. The old stone cottage was in the valley of the river called La Beune, a tributary of the Vézère, a 10-minute drive west of Sarlat on the way to Les Eyzies. Gaston turned off the valley road and up a hillside along a dirt track into the forest.

They felt the stiffness of the long ride as they got out of the car. They walked unsteadily to the door of the stone cottage, Gaston showing the way with a flashlight. He unlocked the door, entered, found two oil lamps and lit them. It was cold inside. He kindled a fire in the fireplace of the salon, went to the kitchenette in one corner, found a saucepan, lit the propane burner, then rummaged in the wine cabinet for ingredients for a drink to warm them. In a few minutes he returned to the couch with two *boules* of hot toddy and what was left of the food from the car.

"This is all we have, *malheureusement.*"

Charity took the bowl in both hands. Her slender fingers were stiff with cold, and the heat from the bowl felt marvelous. She lifted it to her lips, sniffed, the heated alcoholic vapors shot into her nostrils and she jerked her head back in shock.

"Red wine, cognac and some spices," Gaston said. "Perhaps it is still too hot to drink."

Oh. Alcohol. I can't drink it. But she was so tired, so tired. Alcohol was used in medicines. It could be medicine.

Charity took a tiny, tentative sip. She coughed and sprayed the red liquid toward the fireplace. It stung her mouth, her throat. It tasted awful.

The fire in the fireplace was burning now, but it would be awhile before it would blaze with heat she could feel.

Gaston looked at her, went to the bedroom and returned with a blanket.

"Here, this will help," he said, spreading it carefully over her, tucking it around her shoulders.

She held the toddy up to her lips, forcing herself to swallow small sips of the medicine. The spices were bracing. She felt the drink's raw warmth coursing slowly down her throat, through her chest and to her belly. Oh! That feels good!

Gaston sat down next to her and sipped from his bowl. They stared at the small fire in silence, waiting for warmth.

"At least here we are safe," he said.

After a quarter hour the fire was high and warm and Charity was surprised to find she had sipped half of her drink. Her head was dizzy, and her weariness about to overcome her. Fear, excitement and shock had kept her going for nearly 24 hours, but now that she was safe, her body demanded relief.

"I will prepare your bed in the office," he said.

"Can I just sleep here on the couch in front of the fire?" she asked, half asleep. "Any bed is going to be freezing."

"Of course! That is a good idea. If I wake in the night I will add more wood to the fire."

He went to find sheets, a pillow, more blankets, and a towel. When he returned she forced herself to stand up and help him make her bed on the couch. He handed her the flashlight and picked up one of the oil lamps.

"Goodnight," he said from the doorway of his bedroom, and closed the door.

The sun woke her, streaming through the windows, a flood of heat and light. By the sun's height she knew it must be late morning. She shifted her weight on the couch and swung her legs over the side.

"Ow!"

She was *so stiff!* Every muscle in her body felt sore, her bone bruises ached, but exhaustion had helped her to sleep soundly. Slowly she rose and, groggy, shuffled around the salon.

The cottage was a small old stone farmhouse with the spacious salon and kitchenette, a small bedroom, a small bathroom with sink and shower, a tiny closet with a toilet, and the tiny office. The big old roof beams looming over the salon looked ancient, but the kitchenette and bathroom were modern.

The bedroom door was open, and the room empty.

She walked out the front door. The stone terrace was flooded with sun which reflected off the rough limestone façade and made the cottage's red shutters blaze. The view from the terrace over the valley of La Beune and the Vézère was panoramic— spectacular.

The MG was gone.

She went back inside to the kitchenette and saw a note by the tea kettle.

I am shopping.

There was a box of loose tea by the kettle. She ran water into the kettle, put it on the burner and lit it, then went to the bathroom to wash. Oooh, the water was so cold!

When Gaston returned she was sitting in the sun at the table on the terrace wearing blue jeans and a heavy sweater. Her hands surrounded a large cup of tea.

"Good morning!" he said as he carried string bags of groceries and supplies to the cottage. "Or, perhaps, I should say, good afternoon! How are you feeling?"

"Pretty well I guess. I'm stiff, and still a little frightened. My head feels like a sponge."

"Of course, but here it is quiet, and beautiful, and you are out of Paris."

"Yes. The sun feels *so good!*"

"Warm!" he smiled. "The rain is finished."

She smiled in return.

He took the groceries inside. She rose and followed him.

"We are fortunate," he said. "It is market day in Sarlat. I bought just the things we need. *Saucisson, fromage,* some good

Bergerac wines, vegetables, fruit, bread, and for breakfast, croissants and pain au chocolat, and coffee and milk for café au lait."

"You will have to eat most of this yourself if I move to some other place today."

"Maybe not today. I asked at the market, but no one knew of any room available. Of course many of the market people are itinerant, they do not live in Sarlat. They go from town to town, market to market. But later I will ask in the cafés. That is where one learns everything about the town."

They sat outside in the sun for brunch: big bowls of café au lait, croissants, pain au chocolat and fruit.

While they were eating, a decrepit grey Citroen H panel van, streaked with rust and pockmarked with dents, came rattling up the hill to the cottage. The driver turned in a loop in front of the cottage and parked toward the road downhill. With a shudder, the engine died, the front door squealed loudly, and the driver emerged.

"Ah! Séraphin! Bonjour, mon ami!" Gaston exclaimed, rising from the table to greet the old man.

"Bonjour, monsieur le professeur! Comment ça va?" Séraphin replied.

"Oh, the troubles in Paris were unbearable! I had to get away. What more beautiful place of refuge than the Vézère? So we are here! We arrived late last night."

"Yes, I heard a car come up the road in the middle of the night. At first I was suspicious, but then I knew it was the motor of that small English car of yours. I know that sound."

"Yes, we arrived very late. It was a long drive."

Gaston introduced Séraphin to Charity as 'my friend and the faithful caretaker of my cottage.' "Séraphin's farm is at the bottom of the hill, near the junction of the main road and the road to the cottage. He is our guard and watchman!"

He explained to Séraphin how he had encountered Charity, wounded, trying to leave Paris, and that she had decided to stay in Sarlat temporarily.

"If you know of anyone in Les Eyzies or Sarlat who has a spare room to rent, please let us know," Gaston told him.

"I do not think there would be anything in Les Eyzies, it is only a village—and I know everything that goes on there!" he chuckled. "But Sarlat is bigger. I go to the Café de la Mairie in Sarlat sometimes. I can ask Rogier...."

Gaston and Séraphin talked for several minutes about practical matters: did the propane tanks contain enough fuel for their stay, was there a need for more lamp oil or firewood?

"I just want to make sure the water pipes from the spring up the hill are in proper condition," the old man said, and walked slowly around to the back of the cottage.

"*Tout est comme il faut!*" he exulted when he returned.

"The water is as cold as ever!" Gaston joked.

"*Ebe oui, professeur!*" the old man exclaimed. "It comes from deep in the earth! You will not complain when the summer comes and the sun is too hot. You will enjoy your cold water then!"

Bowing goodbye, Séraphin clambered into the Citroen, released the hand brake and coasted downhill.

"I rely on him," Gaston said. "He knows everything about the cottage. He keeps it in proper condition."

They finished their brunch.

"It is already afternoon," Gaston said. "The weather is beautiful. I think we need distraction. The prehistoric caves of Les Combarelles and Font-de-Gaume are only a short distance away, on the road to Les Eyzies. Would you like to visit them?"

"Oh, yes! Yes! That would be perfect!" Charity smiled at him, her eyes bright. She stood, cleared the table of the breakfast dishes and took them to the kitchen.

In a few minutes they were ready. They drove down the hill and turned right along the valley of La Beune toward Les Eyzies. After a short drive he parked the MG near Les Combarelles.

"Lascaux is closed, but at least we can visit Les Combarelles and Font-de-Gaume," he said. "They are almost as exciting as Lascaux."

They entered.

"This cave was formed by an underground river—it carved this tunnel through the rock," he told her. "What amazes me most," he said as they wandered, "is that in recent centuries people used this cave for storage and as a stable. They found Stone Age implements—tools, spear-points, axes, arrowheads— and they considered them mere curiosities, things to be used as paper weights or for decoration. It was not until about seventy years ago that archeologists came here and revealed to them the true significance of their cave and its artifacts."

As they passed by the hundreds of drawings in the cave, Charity was enchanted by the horses and the reindeer. Her mind wandered into fantasies of how these Cro-Magnon people had interacted with horses, and hunted reindeer, and how they had recorded these important animal inhabitants of their world on the walls of their cave shelter.

They left Les Combarelles reluctantly, but they wanted time to visit Font-de-Gaume before it closed for the day.

Charity was in awe as they explored Font-de-Gaume with its hundreds of polychrome paintings: bison, ibex, cave bears, aurochs, reindeer, horses, lions, woolly mammoths.

"What are these?" she asked him, pointing to some crude umbrella-like drawings.

"We cannot know for certain, but we believe they may be depictions of dwellings, shelters, perhaps a village—the Les Eyzies of 17,000 years ago!"

Staff in the cave announced its closing for the day. They left reluctantly and drove back toward the cottage.

"Tomorrow, if you like, I will show you one of the caves I have discovered. We must go early for the light. When the light shines in directly, as it does in the morning, it is easier to access."

"Please! That's just what I want!"

"Good! You will want to wear your blue jeans," he said, looking at them with approval, "and utilitarian shoes if you have them."

"I do. I'm an archeologist, remember?"

They smiled at one another.

11

Discovery

The next morning, Charity heard Gaston bustling about the cabin shortly after sunrise. The smell of coffee made its way into the tiny office.

She rose, washed and dressed, then joined him at the table on the terrace where he had set out breakfast.

They nodded to one another but said little, their faces turned to the welcome warmth of the sun, their thoughts on their tumultuous recent days, their hopes for the future.

"Time to go," he said after fifteen minutes, finishing his coffee.

Charity went to the kitchen to tidy up the breakfast things while Gaston took equipment to the car.

They drove from the cottage down the hill to the La Beune valley road and into Les Eyzies.

"This is a sweet little village!" Charity said.

"Yes, very pretty—and very old! Today you see a simple village of a thousand people, with neat stone houses built into a cliff. But people have probably lived here continuously for over 15,000 years."

He chuckled.

"After all that time, at least they have moved out of the caves and built their houses at the front of them."

They came to the Vézère, turned left onto the Avenue de Cingle and followed the flow of the river down the valley.

A few kilometers from Saint-Cirq, Gaston pulled off the road onto an unpaved track, drove a short distance and parked the car. They got out. He put some fishing equipment and fisherman's long boots on the front seat of the car.

"We're going fishing?"

"No, but anyone who sees the car here will think we are. We cannot let people think there is a valuable cave here. Too many cave robbers."

"The cave entrance is up there," he said, pointing up a steep rock cliff.

"I don't think I can do it," she said. "I still ache all over."

"If you walk and climb, it may help to exercise your muscles. But if you don't want to try…"

"I'll try. I'll see how far I can go."

He was right. As she moved, it got easier to move and the pain was less present.

The path uphill, a rough animal track, was difficult. They pushed aside bushes and low trees and clambered over rocks as they went. In some places they had to climb hand-over-hand.

Finally they came up beneath a high shelf-like ledge jutting out of the cliff wall. The top of the ledge was higher than Charity's head. She looked up at it and frowned.

"I can't do it. I can't get up there."

"What if I lift you?"

"Bon."

She faced the ledge. He put his hands on her waist and lifted her. He was strong! She got her arms and elbows onto the ledge and held herself there while he shifted his hands to her feet and boosted her farther up.

She crawled onto the ledge.

He leapt, gripped the ledge, and pulled himself up beside her.

The ledge was only a few meters wide, and about as deep. At the back was a narrow cleft in the cliff wall, invisible from below. The sunlight penetrated the cleft for several meters. She peered in.

It looked like a dead-end.

"Go in!" he said, and handed her a flashlight. "It continues, even though it does not appear to."

The cleft was narrow, but not a tight squeeze for her slender frame. She entered. It was a struggle for Gaston to squeeze through, but he exhaled deeply and wriggled in. Beyond the cleft, the passage was wider but low. Their bodies now blocked the sunlight so they switched on their flashlights.

"Proceed," Gaston said. "You will have the *impression* of discovery!"

Charity stooped and entered the low passage. At one point she had to squat and shuffle for several meters, foot by foot, being careful not to knock her head against the low, sharp rock ceiling.

After five minutes of slow shuffling, Charity stopped and said, "Are you sure?"

"Continue!" he said.

Finally she saw the end of the tunnel.

"At the end you can stand," Gaston said. "Do so, but do not step forward."

He crawled out of the cramped passage and stood beside her.

"Shine the light over there."

On the wall, crude figures of animals had been chipped into the rock. There were strange designs in paint and charcoal. Symbols?

He reached for her forearm and held it as they took several cautious steps forward.

"Step carefully," he said, "the rock is uneven."

As he said it she stumbled, but his hand on her arm steadied her. After a minute he stopped.

"There is a big drop ahead, too big for us to jump, but we can look. Hold my arm tightly so you don't fall."

He shone the flashlight down into a large cavern, the floor of which was five or six meters below. They were standing right at the edge.

"Are you afraid of heights?"

"No."

"Good. Look!"

He pointed the light beam into a corner and she saw a skull, a human skull—or was it Neanderthal? Around the skull were small dust-covered objects she could not make out.

"I have tentatively identified lamps, stone axes and knives, a spear and what may be a necklace of beads. I cannot be sure because I have not gone down there. I cannot disturb the site. It must be investigated properly, but there is yet no money for this work."

"But...this is amazing!" she exclaimed. Here was *real* archeology, a glimpse back tens of thousands of years.

"Do you think that you were the first to discover this place? That we are the only ones who have seen it?"

"We cannot know, but it is probable. Non-archeologists would have disturbed the site, but the site is obviously intact. The objects are arranged in some deliberate, perhaps ceremonial, distribution. I have made some photographs to document the site as I found it, but they are not the best. I do not have the proper equipment here."

"I feel like the archeologists who discovered King Tutankhamon's tomb!" Charity said. "The first humans to look upon this site for...for..."

"Perhaps fifteen thousand years,...twenty thousand...or more! We do not yet know," he said.

They shone the light around the deep hole for some minutes, then made their way out of the cave in silence.

Out in the sun, Charity sat on the ledge with her legs over the side.

"Not there, please," Gaston said. "Someone might see you. Please sit here near the cave entrance where they cannot see us from the valley road."

They sat in the sun and admired the view: the steep rock walls of the river gorge, the lush hills of Périgord well into their spring rebirth.

When the time came to leave, Gaston jumped down from the ledge and held his arms up to catch Charity. She jumped and her body slid along his as she came down, with their faces touching as she found her footing. For only a second they were motionless. Then Gaston released her, backed away, turned, and led the way down the steep slope to the car.

12

Château Weekend

'How do ah look?" Amaleen asked as she swirled around in her new dress, showing off for both Olivier and the full-length mirror in her room.

"Splendid!" he said. "A vision of loveliness. Or perhaps, more than loveliness, a vision of the power of feminine... ah... *influence.*"

"Y'all mean ah'm a knockout, right?"

Olivier grinned happily at her and put on an American accent.

"You said it, baby!"

They drove along the Loire. At this time of year, in May, nearing the solstice, it was still light despite the evening hour. At the top of the hill on the river's opposite bank, the hundred lights of a huge castle glittered in the dusk.

"There it is, Château Corsique," Olivier said.

"That's pretty darn good," Amaleen said. "If you wanna impress somebody, that'll do it, fer shore."

Olivier parked his little car at the base of the hill. Just as they got out of the car a Rolls-Royce pulled up and stopped beside them. A chauffeur emerged, opened the rear doors for them, and beckoned them into the car.

Sitting back in the soft leather seats as the chauffeur drove them up the winding drive to the castle entrance, Amaleen whispered to Olivier, "More points. This fella shore knows how to put on a show."

The Rolls approached the castle walls, drove across a drawbridge, through more walls into a spacious courtyard.

Drawing up before the high double doors of the mansion, Amaleen saw two liveried footmen in white gloves approach the car and open the doors. The footman who helped her out of the car was handsome as a movie star. When Olivier came around the car with the other footman, Amaleen looked closely and saw that the 'footman' was actually a beautiful young woman. Most of her hair was hidden under her livery cap, but there was no mistaking her beauty. She noticed a hint of scent.

This Benito does everything at 200%, she thought.

They strolled into the mansion glimmering with hundreds of soft lights on tables, on the walls, high in the ceiling. Long garlands of spring flowers swooped along the tops of the walls. Vases of large exotic floral arrangements were placed along the passage that led to the Great Hall, which had been filled with greenery and turned into an immense indoor garden. At each end of the hall was a fountain, loudly spashing on the east, quietly flowing on the west. Garden paths meandered past them and beneath young trees and flowering bushes, with stone benches here and there.

In the center of the hall, on a small grassy lawn as perfect as a putting green, stood a short, stout figure in a tuxedo. Even at a distance Amaleen could see his black diamond shirt studs sparkle. His patent leather shoes shone and, she noticed, had thick soles to make him appear taller. He had the physique of a peasant, short and thick, but powerful, and a head of dense black hair slicked and swept back.

Around him on the green were several dozen elegantly-dressed men and women chatting and sipping from champagne *flûtes*. Liveried footmen—and 'foot-women,' Amaleen thought—circulated through the crowd with trays of caviar and canapés.

As they approached Benito he saw them and smiled broadly.

"Ah, Olivier, my friend, welcome! And this must be the lovely Amaleen l'Americaine! Welcome to Corsique! My lady, you are a vision!"

His eyes swept over her, up and down, up and down again. He obviously liked what he saw.

"Supremely beautiful! What an elegant gown! But its beauty pales compared to that of the feminine vision it has the good fortune to surround!"

He looked at Olivier and winked.

"You have brought us a gift of great beauty this evening, *monsieur le baron!*"

So that is his little joke in response to my little joke of sending him the bill for the dress. Or does he mean "She's mine tonight?" Olivier thought it over. It was important to know his meaning. If misinterpreted, he could be dangerous. Olivier knew he would have to be careful.

"I hope you will enjoy our little Day in May celebration," Benito smiled.

A waiter offered them glasses of champagne. They toasted their host.

An elegant couple approached them.

"Excuse me, please. I must greet the Duke and Duchess," Benito smiled, and turned to welcome the new arrivals.

At the end of the evening the Rolls arrived at the door of the mansion to take them back to Olivier's car. On their seats in the rear of the limousine were elegantly-wrapped boxes, each topped with a small bouquet of spring wildflowers in a silver holder.

When they were back at Olivier's château and Amaleen was in her room preparing for bed, she opened her gift to find a designer nightgown of the softest, slinkiest silk, artfully cut to accentuate her feminine charms.

She tried it on.

"Fits perfect!" she murmured. "But o' *course* it fits, jes' like the dress. They measured me for that, so he knows mah size."

She looked in the mirror.

"Mah lord," she whispered. "In this ah could have any man in the world on his knees!"

Olivier opened his gift to find only a copy of the bill for the dress, with its astronomical price, marked PAYÉ.

13

Martine

Josie left the café-infirmary and jogged to the barricade in search of recently-wounded students. As she approached, she saw a young woman in red climb to the top of the barricade, waving her arms and taunting the police. The others at the barricade stared at her in astonishment, emboldened by her courage. Someone handed her a paving stone. She swung her arm and threw it as hard as she could at *les flics*, then set her fists on her hips in defiance.

She turned to acknowledge the cheers of the other students, and as she did so a tear gas cannister hit her in the back of the head. Stunned, she stood bewildered for a moment before collapsing. Students around her broke her fall and carried her back behind the barricade.

Josie ran to them.

"Bring her to the café!"

The young woman was slender, of medium height, and not heavy. As they carried her, Josie saw the blood show through her hair, the red patch growing rapidly.

"Oh my god!" Josie screamed. "She's *really* hurt!"

In the café-infirmary, the medical student in charge examined the wound, cutting away her hair with scissors.

"No, she cannot stay here. This is too serious a wound. She may die. She must be taken to hospital no matter what. We cannot save her."

The medics wrapped her head in gauze with a thick compress over the wound to stanch the bleeding. Two of the students put a blanket on a café chair and seated the wounded girl on it.

"Two on the legs, two on the chair back," someone said. Josie and three others picked up the chair with the patient, carried it out of the café and down the street away from the fighting.

The walk to the hospital was a journey through hell, past burning cars, people rushing along streets, piles of litter and mountains of uncollected garbage, but no one interfered with them.

When they reached the hospital entrance, a nurse looked at the woman they were carrying, looked out to the street for any police—there were none—then said "Follow me!"

Inside, they transferred her to a gurney, bumping her against it and almost dropping her, but she was unconscious and felt nothing.

An orderly pushed the gurney down the corridor and through a door.

Josie and the other carriers walked slowly out of the hospital and sat on the steps.

"Will she survive?" Josie asked.

"We do not know."

"She was so brave! I saw her climb up the barricade, stand openly on the top and shout at the cops, throwing big stones! They aimed right at her! It was a tear gas grenade, not a bullet, but they aimed at her head! I'm certain of it!" one of the other students said.

"Who is she?"

"Her name is Martine. Martine Lafoy. She is a sociology student. Sociology, but politics just as much. She is very political, very committed, very...vigorous. You saw her red clothes? It's because she is a Communist, but wearing red she also taunts the *flics*."

"Flics?"

"Police."

"Oh."

"She is saying 'Here I am! You can see my red! Go ahead and

shoot! You don't scare me!'"

Tears welled in Josie's eyes. She held her breath trying to stifle her emotions. One of the students put her arm around Josie and she burst out crying. The others surrounded her for comfort. A man put a bandage in her hand for a handkerchief.

They walked back toward the café-infirmary slowly. Before they reached it, Josie said, "I'm exhausted. I've got to get some rest," and left to make her way back to the apartment on Rue Claude Bernard.

The next morning Josie brewed a cup of tea and sipped it as she looked out the window to the street. When her cup was empty she left the apartment and walked briskly back to the hospital.

"You have a patient named Martine Lafoy. What is her condition?"

The nurse seated at the reception desk looked at Josie and said "We have no patient by that name."

"We brought her here yesterday! She must be here! Has she been moved? Has she…died?"

The nurse looked away, dropped her gaze to the desk.

"I saw her on the barricades. She was dressed all in red. She was incredibly fearless. We brought her here. I want to know how she is!"

The nurse looked up at her.

"You are not Parisian?"

"I'm not even French! I'm American! Martine is my friend!"

"All right. You are not government, then."

The nurse searched through papers on her desk, picked one up and read from it.

"Admitted yesterday at 16:32. Concussion caused by violent trauma to the back of the head. Comatose. Blood transfusion. No sign of infection."

"Comatose?"

The nurse nodded.

"May I visit her?"

"No."

Josie returned to the café-infirmary. The police controlled the street now. The barricade was being dismantled. The café was emptly except for café staff who were cleaning up after the riot, taking down posters, painting over grafitti, scrubbing away spills and blood stains.

As she left the café, a police sergeant approached her, lifted his nightstick and thumped it on her chest to stop her. He looked at her. She stared back. His expression softened as the Josephine Baker Effect took over.

"*Je suis chanteuse!*" Josie shouted at him. "*Je ne suis pas révolutionnaire!*"

It worked. The sergeant's face took on a puzzled look as he lowered his nightstick. Josie knew to grab the moment. She stepped forward and strode away.

The next morning Josie returned to the hospital.

"Mademoiselle Lafoy is no longer in a coma. You may visit her for a few moments. But please…only for a few moments."

An orderly led Josie to Martine's room. She entered and looked at Martine. Her head was wrapped almost completely in white gauze. Her eyes were swollen nearly shut. Her arms and legs were patched with bandages. Beside her bed, a pole held a glass bottle from which a plastic tube snaked to her arm and a needle dripped medicine into her veins.

"Martine, you don't know me. My name is Josie. I'm American. I saw you on the barricade. You were incredibly brave! The cops shot you with a tear gas shell. I helped bring you here."

Josie waited for a response. The patient blinked her eyes.

"I won't stay, but I will return tomorrow. If you need anything, I will do it."

Josie returned to the hospital every day at the same time. On the fourth day Martine was able to sit up. She could converse for a short time before tiredness overcame her. She asked Josie to contact her boyfriend, a medical student, and tell him where she was.

Josie spent the rest of the day asking everyone for Jean-Paul Plamondon. With every third person she asked, she got a little closer. In a café on the Place de la Contrescarpe she found him.

He was the medical student she had first encountered at the barricade on Rue Gay-Lussac.

"You are Jean-Paul Plamondon?"

"Yes."

"I have seen Martine. She is in the hospital and she…"

Jean-Paul grabbed her arm.

"You have seen her? Where is she?"

He leapt to his feet.

"I'll take you there."

They walked briskly from the Place de la Contrescarpe to the hospital and went to Martine's room. When she saw Jean-Paul she gasped and smiled. She raised her arm. He took her hand and squeezed it.

"Oh!"

"Sorry."

He released his grip.

Their eyes met and they gazed at one another without a word.

Josie quietly left the room. At the nurse's desk she wrote her address and telephone number on a piece of paper, gave it to the nurse on duty and said "If Martine needs anything—anything at all—please call me and I will help."

Josie came to see her every day. After a week Martine was able to leave her bed, walk, and sit at a table for meals.

"Thank you for coming," Martine told her. "It's boring here. I want to be out in the streets fighting! The struggle is not over!"

"Fight now to get well," Josie said, squeezing her hand. "Then you can fight in the streets."

The next morning Josie arrived at the hospital and went to Martine's room. Another patient was in Martine's bed. Josie went to the nurse's desk.

"She has been released. She will continue her recovery at home."

Josie stood dumbfounded. Tears welled in her eyes. Suddenly

she realized all Martine meant to her, what a powerful symbol she was.

The nurse opened a drawer in the desk, rummaged through papers, and found an envelope.

"You are Josie?"

"Yes."

"This is for you."

Josie tore open the envelope and read the note.

"Dear J, I do not have the words to express my thanks for all you have done. I'm sure you share my happiness at being able to leave the hospital. At this moment I cannot tell anyone where I am because the police are looking for me. The nurse gave me your note. I will contact you when I can. Stay well and continue the struggle! Love, M."

Several days later, Josie was surprised when she checked the apartment's mailbox and there was actually a letter in it. Mail delivery had been sporadic.

She didn't recognize the handwriting on the envelope. It bore no return address.

She slit it open with her fingernail and took out a small scrap of paper. On it, written in pencil, was a cryptic address in a suburb of Paris. Nothing else.

Still afraid of the police.

Josie dressed and did her hair and make-up to look like anyone but Josephine Baker. She put on her American sunglasses. She didn't want to be noticed, she wanted to disappear in the crowd.

She checked her face in the mirror by the apartment door, walked out and turned right to get to the Metro. One train. Transfer to another train. Then a bus, then a walk to the door of a small, modern, ugly apartment block in need of repair. She found the apartment door and rang the bell.

"Josie!" Jean-Paul exclaimed as he opened the door a crack and peered out. He opened the door wide and waved her in quickly. Martine came from the kitchen limping slightly as she walked, wiping her hands on a towel.

"Josie! How wonderful! You have come! How are you?"

"How are *you?*" Josie asked. "You're the one who almost got killed."

"I am fine!"

"She is not fine," Jean-Paul said, frowning. "She has terrible headaches. Terrible dreams. She forgets things, simple things. What the police did to her is a crime!"

"I'm fine because you are here," Martine said, wrapping Josie in her arms and kissing her. "That's what matters."

"Is it true, what Jean-Paul says?"

"Yes, it is true. But I will recover. I must recover because there is still so much to do. The revolution has not happened. The system has not changed. We must get rid of De Gaulle and the rest of them!"

"Until the revolution brings heaven on earth, we must eat," Jean-Paul said, coming from the kitchen with a string bag. "Today is market day. It is not safe for Martine to appear in the street. I must get some food."

Josie and Martine stared at one another, smiling, for a long time. Martine reached for Josie and hugged her tightly. When she loosened her grip, she looked into Josie's face and kissed her on the lips. She kissed her again.

Josie drew back, staring at Martine, confused. They stood in silence, staring.

Martine moved her head slowly closer to Josie's, slowly, not to frighten her. Smoothly her movement turned into a long, fervent kiss.

14

Sarlat

Back in the car driving through Les Eyzies after exploring the cave, Gaston suggested they go to a café in Sarlat and talk to local people about renting a room.

He drove among the low hills surrounding the town to the Place du Quatorze Juillet and parked the car in an open space shaded by long rows of large old pollarded plane trees.

"We will walk from here."

They strolled along the Rue de la République past 14th-century houses built completely of stone. Charity regarded them with wonder.

"Even the roofs are made of stone!" she said.

"It is a fitting town for archeologists, yes?" He smiled at her.

They came to the Place de la Liberté and went into the Café de la Mairie.

He ordered red wine, she a Coca-Cola.

"Archeology!" Gaston said, and raised his glass.

"Archeology!" she answered and touched her glass to his.

They drank.

"Does Professor Noireau know about that cave?" Charity asked, setting down her glass.

Gaston was silent. He glanced at her, looked away, and lowered his eyes.

"No."

"Shouldn't he?"

"No, I do not think so. Not yet."

"But, why not? He's the top archeologist in France! Couldn't he get the money to properly excavate the site?"

Gaston was silent for a minute. He swirled the red wine in his glass, held it up the the light, assessed its color.

"Miss Charity, our university course is over. I am no longer officially your instructor—although of course I value our, uh, acquaintance, and I am always available to answer your questions or help in any way I can. But...well, I will tell you the truth if you promise me you will not repeat what I say."

"I promise."

"Professor Noireau is a great archeologist. Of that there can be no doubt. He has discovered and excavated some of the most important sites in the world. He has been a great friend to me, his much younger colleague. He was also a good friend of my uncle's. Apparently my uncle had spoken with him about me and the Vézère valley because together they made the arrangements for the purchase and renovation of my cottage. Of course Professor Noireau has many contacts in this region because of its archeological importance. He used them to help find the cottage, and to buy it. I owe him a debt of gratitude."

Gaston took a long sip from his wine glass.

"Perhaps you are too young to know how things work in a university. The university is like the story of *Oedipus Rex:* the son kills his father and marries his mother. The father in the university is the most famous professor, and the mother is archeology. The great professors enjoy their prominence and do not want some younger colleague to threaten it. They put obstacles in the way of anyone whom they fear may try to 'dethrone' them and 'marry the mother' in their place."

"But what does that have to do with excavating the site you found?"

"If I were to reveal the site to him, he would come at once with a team, of which he would be the head and, because I am his *protégé*, he would declare the site to be at least partly his discovery. He would arrange everything having to do with the site after that. He would thank me for the 'hint' that allowed him to make the discovery, but he would probably exclude me from the excavation, the research, and particularly from *la gloire*...from the esteem, the fame if you will, related to the discovery. He and his august colleagues would take all the credit for everything. 'Young Lagarde had the hunch, but *we* made the true discovery and assessment,' they would say."

"I am conflicted about it," he concluded. "I want the site to be properly excavated and preserved, I admire Professor Noireau greatly but, however selfishly, I cannot bring myself to, ah, give it away to another, not even to my benefactor."

"I understand. I understand *completely!* I know just how that works. It's like the great sculptors in Paris—Rodin! His brilliant students, like Camille Claudel, would produce a great work of art and he would put his name on it! She was his model and his lover, and he still took the credit away from her!"

She looked at him.

"The Oedipus story is not just in archeology."

Gaston looked at her, looked deeply into her eyes.

Charity returned his gaze with the same intensity.

He looked away, but soon looked back at her.

They sipped in silence. Their eyes met, and met again.

Charity felt a need to change the mood.

"I enjoyed our little expedition today *so much!* It was a thrill to see an undisturbed, unknown site—my first! Merci, *monsieur!*"

She held up her glass to him and smiled. He touched his glass to hers, but his wine was almost gone. Gaston signalled to the waiter for two more drinks. The wine and Coca-Cola arrived. They raised their glasses and touched them again.

"This is a different sort of trip for me," he said, looking serious again. "When I come to my cottage, I explore the Vézère valley alone. That is what I prefer—or thought I preferred, but it was a nice change to have another archeologist with me."

He smiled. Her heart leapt at the mention of her as 'another archeologist.'

"If you don't mind a companion, I'd like to see more of the caves. It's thrilling!" Charity said.

They sipped in silence for a little while, recalling the day's exploration. Charity noticed that she had paid no attention to her aches and pains since the moment they had begun the climb up to the ledge in front of the cave.

His faced changed expression. He had made a decision. He took a sip of his wine, put the glass down gently and looked at her.

"Well, Miss Charity, we have got nowhere in finding you a room. I don't think we will succeed today, and perhaps not tomorrow. If you don't mind living with a strange bachelor for a little while, we can wait to see what to do."

Charity smiled wanly to herself. Living with this particular strange bachelor had been her most-often visualized fantasy in Paris. Now here it was, for real…and so…?

"When do you think we'll know what to do?"

"It is not at all clear. We cannot know how long the troubles in Paris will last, or when the university might re-open. Such a thing has never happened before. It could be a matter of days only, or weeks. I don't think it will be a month. We will read the newspapers—if we can find any. I have a transistor radio at the cottage, and if the radio stations are broadcasting we will listen for news. We must follow events."

They dined at one of the few restaurants open in Sarlat, a small traditional *bistrot* run by an old couple who did everything themselves, who had no need of hired staff, belonged to no union, didn't care what happened in Paris, and depended on the earnings from their restaurant to live.

"We will begin with *fois gras* with truffles, then *cuisses de canard*. Do you know how the fois gras is made? They force geese to eat corn. They push it into them. Their livers grow huge and fatty—and delicious! The *cuisses de canard* are served with local potatoes cooked in the duck fat. It is indescribably delicious, and the amount of calories is *astronomique!*"

They smiled at one another. Nothing like difficult times to convince a person to abandon boring dietary rules.

"I think the course you taught was excellent," Charity told him as they dined. "You were engaging, your knowledge of pre-historic sites is encyclopedic, and your English is excellent."

Uh-oh. Did I just go over the top? she thought. I am being too gushy.

"Thank you. You are very kind. I have been fortunate to visit many of the world's most interesting sites, and to work at some of them. Perhaps you did not know, I spent a year at the University of New Mexico and visited sites in Arizona, Colorado and Utah as well. I worked at the Anasazi sites. Simply fascinating! And some of the standing stone sites in the United Kingdom. We have standing stones in France, but theirs are better!"

He winked and smiled.

Charity decided to play it cool for the rest of the evening. They were mostly quiet after that, with only occasional comments on the food.

The dinner was delicious, they were tired, and they were both absorbed with thoughts of what the next week might have in store for them.

15

The Cousin

The next day Gaston and Charity rose earlier, but still not early, even though the sun flooded the house before 7:00 am. They drove to another part of the Vézère valley, clambered up to two more intriguing locations, but they found no new caves. They drove toward Sarlat in the late afternoon.

"We could go to the same café," Gaston said, "but...," he paused.

"But what?"

"If the people of the town see us together often, they may think.... You see, I don't want.... If they connect you with me, it may somehow be reported to others. In Paris? In Boston? I don't want your reputation to be compromised. It would certainly be the subject of gossip if people knew that a young woman—one of my students!—or at least former students—was staying in my cottage. But you can stay. The cottage itself is far enough away from the town that they might not know."

"We don't have to go to a café. We can have something to drink at the cottage," she said.

They returned to the cottage, washed and rested for a little while. Gaston heard her moving about.

"Wine is waiting on the terrace," he said.

She had changed from T-shirt and blue jeans into a comfortable summer dress. As she walked out the front door the late afternoon sun flooded the terrace. Two glasses of white wine glistened on the table, bejeweled by drops of condensation.

"This is cold white wine!" she said as she looked at him. "How do you have cold wine in a house without electricity?"

"The miracle of *gaz!*" he laughed.

"Gaz?"

"I have a *frigidaire* that is operated by propane gas."

"How? You burn gas and it's hot, like the propane burner in the kitchen, not cold!"

"To operate a frigidaire, all you need is a difference in temperatures. The heat from the propane flame expands the liquid in the pipes, it circulates through the pipes...oh, it's all physics and I don't really understand it myself. But the wine is cold!"

Oh. What to do. Well, I'll sip just a little, to be sociable, she thought. They laughed and clinked their glasses, Gaston took a hearty drink, Charity a tiny sip.

They looked out over the valley, impossibly green in its spring lushness: the fertile soil of the river flood plain just bringing up its first shoots of summer crops, the copses of trees in new leaf, white houses of a village, and in the distance a long limestone ridge showing gashes of white stone where the cliff was too steep for bushes or trees to grow.

The wine was slightly sweet and fruity. She took small sips. She was getting used to it, and it was beginning to have its effect.

"I'm not really a wine drinker, but this tastes good," she said.

"The wine is from Château Tirecul La Gravière near Bergerac," Gaston said. "The vineyards are of Semillon and Muscadelle grapes planted on north-facing limestone slopes. This one is mostly Semillon, but with some Muscadelle—a favorite grape in this region—to give it the little sweetness and scent of flowers. I chose it because...well, perhaps you are not so familiar with French wines. This one is, uh, *not challenging* to the palate. It is easy to drink."

"It's so beautiful here," Charity said.

"Yes, it is."

Gaston had arranged *l'apéritif*: olives, pâté, sliced sausage, cheeses and bread.

"This is *Rocamadour*, a *fromage de chèvre*—goat," Gaston said, pointing at the first of the cheeses. "This is *Chaumes*, from cow's milk, and this is *Échourgnac aux Noix*, also cow's milk, made in a monastery."

They sipped and nibbled.

"Do you really prefer being here alone?"

Gaston was silent.

"I enjoy my time alone, but I have not always been here alone."

She said nothing. He went on.

"I would come here with my cousin."

"So. Boys night out. It would be fun. Are you a hunter?"

"Ah. No. Not *mon cousin*, but *ma cousine*. I am—was—engaged to marry *ma cousine*."

She turned to him with a puzzled look.

"No!" he smiled, "she is not a close relation! She is the daughter of my uncle's wife by a previous marriage. The house we stopped at in Versailles, where I keep the car? That was my uncle's house. *Ma cousine* lived there with them when she was a girl. I would visit them when I was in *lycée*. We were friends for years, then we became lovers."

"So you're engaged now?"

"I am not sure. When my uncle died, his *testament*...what is the English word for when a person gives you some of his wealth after he dies?"

"Bequeathed. A bequest. Inheritance."

"Ah. Such a difficult word for a Frenchman to say! He... *bequeathed* me the house that you saw, and some more. He was a businessman and spent his life in an office. I think he was envious of my life, working outdoors, exploring the world. He was friends with Professor Noireau, as I have mentioned. They supported some of my archeological expeditions, and they really gave me this cottage. However, my uncle left an important part of his wealth..."

"His estate."

"Yes, his estate, to *ma cousine* Yveline, the one to whom I became engaged."

"So that should be perfect! The two of you are in love, you receive a generous bequest from your uncle, you marry and live together in a mansion, with a perfect little cottage in Périgord! What could be wrong with that?"

Gaston looked down at his glass. It was empty. He refilled it.

"If we talk about these serious topics, we may end up having only *l'apéritif,*" he smiled.

"Appetizers-as-dinner is perfect, if you ask me," she said. "I'm not hungry anymore."

She didn't want him to change the subject.

"But you were saying, about your *cousine...*"

"Ah, well, yes. Yveline and I did not agree on the division of my uncle's...estate, even though it was clearly written in his *testament...*"

"His will."

"Yes, his will. It was clearly written what he intended. But she did not agree, so she told her solicitor..."

"We say lawyer in America."

"...Her lawyer. She told her lawyer she wanted this, this and that. I was very surprised. We were engaged to be married! But she wanted everything in her name. I didn't want to have a disagreement with her, but she would not change her mind. Perhaps she believed that because she had lived in the house, it should be hers. I understand, but that is not what my uncle, her step-father, wanted."

"Our relationship suffered," he went on. "The lawyers are still discussing what to do. What is legal. The house is mine, but I don't want to live in it while we are in dispute. It gives me bad feelings. As for the engagement, it is not terminated, but I do not comprehend how we can be married. Our relationship has changed."

"I'm sorry to have brought up this unpleasant subject for you," Charity said.

"No, no, it is all right. I am glad I have told you. Now you understand."

He sighed.

"I had such plans for our marriage. As you said, it should be perfect! A girl I have known most of my life, a girl I fell in love with when I was young, a girl I thought I knew so well…. The generosity of my uncle…. He would have been *so happy* to have seen us married and living in his house! I am sad that his vision —that *my* vision!—has not come to pass."

It was late. The air was cooling. They moved in from the terrace to the main room of the cottage.

"I don't think I can stay awake much longer," Charity said. "I'm not used to wine. It's made me dizzy. I'm very tired. I'd like to go to bed and heal."

"Of course. Do you have everything you need?"

"Yes, thank you. I'll be very comfortable."

"Bonne nuit, mademoiselle Charité," he smiled.

"Bonne nuit, monsieur!"

She looked at him, hesitated, then gave him a quick kiss on the cheek, turned, went into the office and closed the door.

16

Monsieur M

Thierry Motte—Monsieur M—had a dream.

He would rise above the simple criminal jobs in which he was now involved and reach the heights of influence. He would specialize in doing special things for special people, and he would be the best at it. His clients would be the top, only the most extraordinarily wealthy—and he would finally be able to live as they did: the best of everything.

His dream began when his friend Lukas was asked to obtain a Fabergé egg, one of the fabulous bejewelled Christmas gifts fashioned for the Tsar of All the Russias. The world held a very limited number of authentic Tsarist Imperial Fabergé eggs—only 50 were ever made—but a Middle Eastern oil billionaire wanted one for his girlfriend—and could afford any price. Lukas had arranged the 'acquisition.'

"How did you get it?" Monsieur M asked his friend.

"None of your business! But in fact the method is simple: locate all the Fabergé eggs in the world, then decide which is the least protected, the easiest to 'acquire,' and…get it."

"Were you paid what was promised?"

Lukas smiled.

"More! The client was very satisfied with the neatness of the job. You cannot realize how much money some of these people have now. What to us is a fortune is to them mere pocket money!

Some of them have wealth equal to that of small countries! My client recommended me to others, and I now have three more clients and three new projects."

Monsieur M imagined how it would be: a client might want a Boeing 707 with advanced surveillance equipment and a "comfort crew" of exotic and fully available, movie-star beautiful women or men. Thierry would arrange it. The payoff would be *huge!* Or a client's eye fell on a stretch of prime beachfront property or a superb golf course in an exclusive community and he decided he wanted it. Thierry would arrange it.

A private island? Those would be easy.

He let his imagination go wild.

Raising the Titanic? Sorry, too much publicity. That was a job he would not accept if it were proposed to him. But just imagine the fee he could ask for that!

He trolled for clients, letting it be known among his circle of friends that there was a new 'fixer' in town. He called himself 'Monsieur M.' He thought it was more mysterious than Thierry Motte.

When a client finally contacted him with an exotic request, he was elated. This was the first rung on his climb up the ladder to great success!

It is true that he found the request just a little strange: find a cave containing prehistoric art, identify the most prominent piece of art in it, remove it, deliver it, and aid in finding a buyer. The client told him that the Vézère Valley in Périgord was the place to look. Numerous caves had been found there, some with spectacular cave paintings.

Who wanted such old stuff? It made no sense to him, but when he mentioned the project to Lukas—without details, of course—his friend said "Prehistoric art? I know just the person to buy it!"

"If you bring me a buyer, I will share the fee with you," Monsieur M told him.

"Of course you will!" Lukas replied with an arch look. "We are friends, but this is business. But," he cautioned, "this work of art must be authentic! No fakes! If you try to sell fakes to buyers, they always find out, and your reputation is ruined forever…and you may also be in danger. These people are powerful and not to be trifled with."

"That will not be a problem. I will be able to prove to the buyer that it is authentic."

"How?"

"That is my concern, not yours. I promise you, proving authenticity will not be a problem."

Monsieur M was not happy to take less than the full fee, but this was his first big job. He needed Lukas's help, so he must pay for it. He must also work carefully. He didn't want Lukas to know any more of the details than was absolutely necessary. He, Monsieur M, must be seen as the manager of the project. Its successful completion would propel him into the big league of fixers, those who could efficiently satisfy the requests of the wealthiest people. Once in the big league, clients and buyers would learn his name and come to him directly—no splitting fees.

The proposal for this project could not have come to Monsieur M at a better time. All the police and gendarmes in France were preoccupied with the troubles in Paris and Nantes and factories all over the country. Police presence in country places such as the Vézère Valley would be minimal, and mostly ineffective: all of the experienced officers had been sent to the cities to help put down the riots. In the small towns and villages, policing was being done by the youngest and least-experienced cadres.

He had his plan: take a few thugs into Périgord traveling through rock-walled valleys looking for caves. The caves were there, the client had assured him. Find one with paintings in it. Cut the most prominent painting out, spray it with a preservative lacquer, pack it carefully and deliver it. The client would provide authentication, the buyer would provide the money, and everyone would be happy. What was so difficult about that?

Monsieur M knew he would succeed. This was not nearly so difficult as stealing a well-protected Fabergé jewel. The caves and the art were there, open to the world. He knew he could get the thugs he needed cheap. He would use ignorant men who had no idea of the value of what they were stealing.

This had to be done discreetly, he thought. He would supervise the project personally. He and his men would be "government geologists doing a mineral survey." The cover was a good one because who knew what rocks they might have to take away, even from a rock cliff or a cave.

He made his plans, obtained equipment, recruited two men, and left Paris for the south.

Monsieur M sat with his two men in a café in Sarlat, growling instructions at them.

"Tomorrow morning—early! It will be light by 6:00—we will go by boat along the Vézère..."

"By boat? I thought we were looking for caves."

"Idiot! You can't see caves if you are on a road at the base of a cliff! You can see them from farther away. We will be in a boat in the middle of the river, able to see caves and rockslides in the cliffs on both sides. We will be government geologists conducting mineral surveys in the valley. Use your maps and cameras to document likely rockslides, clefts, the shadows you see along the cliff walls—anything that looks like it might have the entrance to a cave."

The next morning they went to the dock in Les Eyzies and haggled with a local for the hire of a motor boat.

PART THREE

Mid-May

17

The Hunt

Back at Olivier's château after the Day in May party, Amaleen wrote a thank-you note to Benito. She addressed it to "Mr Benito Vénière, Château Corsique, Loire Valley" and had no doubt that he would receive it.

Three days later, Georges brought her a box that had been delivered for her. She took the box and opened it: two dozen long-stemmed mauve-colored roses—symbol of 'love at first sight'—and a hand-written note inviting her to Château Corsique for the weekend.

"Let me know when you would like to come and I will send a car for you," the note read. It was signed "B."

She showed it to Olivier.

"Ah," he said with a wry smile. "I fear I will lose you to Benito's greater charm."

"Y'all won't lose me. Yore mah pal *and* mah playmate! But ah gotta see what this here's all about. It's too good to pass up!"

He smiled at her. He had imagined that this might happen. She was young and adventurous. He had caught a wild one. He must let her go.

Friday afternoon. Amaleen packed a large suitcase with her best clothes, not forgetting the fine silk nightgown that Benito had left in the Rolls-Royce for her after the Day in May party.

The hint implied by the gift of a nightgown was so unsubtle as to be entertaining, even seductive.

We'll see about that, Amaleen thought.

The chauffeur handed her into Benito's Rolls, they drove away from Olivier's small château, along the Loire and into the lush country to the north.

At Château Corsique she was helped from the car by a footman, welcomed by the butler and housemaid, and shown to a large sunny guest bedroom overlooking the castle park and the River Loire.

"Mr Vénière will return to the castle shortly. I will inform him that you have arrived," the butler told her. "He has taken the liberty of providing some apparel for this weekend's activities," he said, opening the walk-in closet. Hanging on the bars was clothing tailored exactly to her measurements: morning outfits, riding habit, lounging clothes, evening gowns, nightgowns, pyjamas.

"I hope you find them all to your satisfaction. Dinner will be at 8 o'clock. May I suggest that you might consider this for the occasion?"

He indicated an elegant but understated evening dress with a couture label.

"Tomorrow morning the hunt breakfast will be available starting at 6 am. Stirrup cup is at 8. You may wish to try on the hunt costume before dinner to assure that all is as you prefer. If it is not, please so inform the housekeeper and it will be modified to your requirements in time for the hunt."

He bowed and departed.

Amaleen changed out of her traveling slacks and top into the hunt costume: silk blouse and foulard, a black fitted jacket with gold-trimmed collar and cuffs, and a white vest trimmed in gold braid, tight white riding pants, long shiny black leather knee boots with gold spurs, black velvet helmet, and leather riding crop with a gold handle, all from Hermès.

The buttons on the vest bore the image of a black man's head in profile, tied with a white bandanna—a Moor's head, black and white, the symbol of Corsica.

It all fit perfectly. Of course it did. Benito knew her size.

Amaleen knew how to ride and hunt. It was part of the country tradition in Virginia and her mother did not want West Virginia to suffer by comparison. Hunting was a key to status. Amaleen had a hunt outfit at home. It was fine, but nothing so fine as all this. As for the hunt itself, her people rode much rougher than the sissy Virginians: fields, hills, forests, streams… she was used to it all. Nothing phased her in mountainous West Virginia, but the Loire was not West Virginia. She hoped she could ride well in unfamiliar country.

Dressed for dinner, Amaleen descended the stairs to the ground floor and a footman escorted her to a reception room where she saw a dozen other guests and Benito who was, as usual, at the center.

When he saw her he smiled broadly.

"Ah! Here comes our American princess!"

Amaleen lifted her hand to be kissed. She smiled at Benito.

"It was awful nice of y'all to invite me!"

Benito introduced her to the other guests: several couples from Paris, an elegant couple from Rome, two Spaniards, a Californian couple. The numbers worked out so that Amaleen and Benito were the final couple. In principle, she had no competition.

"Champagne, Mademoiselle Amaleen?"

"You bet!"

A glass was brought at once.

They chatted for a quarter hour. Amaleen, in her elegant dress, was the shining presence and the center of attention. She was by far the youngest and most beautiful person in the room. Was that Benito's plan?

"Dinner is served," the butler announced, and two footmen swung open the tall doors to the dining room.

Benito offered Amaleen his arm, escorted her in, and seated her to his right, the place of honor.

After dessert and coffee were finished, and the chef summoned from the kitchen for compliments, Benito stood.

"It is such a pleasure to have you all here! Normally we men would retire to the library for cognac and cigars, and the ladies to the parlor for tea and conversation, but as we must rise early for the hunt tomorrow, I suggest that we might prefer an extra hour or two in bed. Tomorrow, we have a good ride and, I hope, a good hunt waiting for us."

He offered his arm to Amaleen, and they strolled from the dining room to the center of the mansion where they said goodnight to the guests. After they had all climbed the stairs to their rooms, Benito escorted Amaleen up the stairs to her room.

"Goodnight, my beautiful princess!" He kissed her hand.

"Goodnight, Monsieur Benito."

She went in her room.

What now? She thought. How does this work?

I think I know.

She changed into the seductive silk nightgown he had given her after the Day in May party, got comfortable on the bed, and waited.

After half an hour, she dozed off.

She woke to a gentle knock on her door.

"Come in."

The housekeeper entered, bid her good morning, crossed the room and shot back the drapes on the windows. Sun flooded into the room.

"I hope you slept well, mademoiselle."

"Very well, thanks."

"I thought you might wish to wake because it is seven o'clock. Breakfast is being served, and only one hour remains before the beginning of the hunt."

"Thank you."

She dressed in the elegant riding habit and went down to breakfast.

All the other guests were already seated and eating. Several had finished. Benito was not there.

Amaleen sat and was served by the footmen. As she was sipping her coffee, Benito entered. His hunting dress was identical to Amaleen's: Château Corsique. Smiling broadly, he greeted all of his guests with a few pleasantries. He took his seat next to Amaleen.

"I trust that you slept well, Miss Amaleen."

"Very well, thanks."

"Good, good!" He smiled at her, a knowing smile. Other guests glanced their way then looked down, hiding their smiles.

"Our Château Corsique hunting dress has never looked more beautiful than it does on you," he said.

Breakfast finished, Benito rose.

"Several of you have hunted at Château Corsique before, but some have not, so I will explain. French hunting is quite different from English hunting. Today we will engage in *la grande vénerie*— the most noble, the Great Hunt: we will hunt *un cerf*—a stag. We may ride briefly across fields and meadows, but most of our riding will be in deep forests on the estate of the château—the habitat of the stag. We may encounter streams and ponds. We may be riding for most of the day. It depends on the prey!"

"I realize that our friends who are hunting with us for the first time will not recognize the many particular horn soundings that guide the hunt," Benito continued, "so I have assigned a hunt guide to each of you who are first-time hunters here. The horns are the music of the hunt, but also its bugle calls, notifying us all of what is happening and calling us to the action. There are said to be 4000 horn calls! We use only a few dozen, such as the calls for the sighting of the stag, for when the stag attempts to throw the dogs off his scent by doubling back or entering water, a special call for when the stag is at bay, and of course the *hallali* announcing the death of the noble prey. Your guide will interpret the calls for you so you can follow the progress of the hunt wherever you are in the forest, and ride to where the action is happening."

"I am very proud of my *meute*, my pack of hounds," Benito smiled. "They will bring down the stag, and then our Huntmaster, Monsieur Clive Harrows, will deliver the *coup-de-grâce* in the traditional manner using his hunting dagger. Then," he said, glancing at Amaleen and smiling, "the stag will be dismembered—butchered—at the site."

He smiled at everyone, then grew serious.

"I must warn you about *la curée*, the end of the hunt. It involves much blood. After the stag has been butchered, the horns will sound the appropriate call for the age and size of the *cerf*, then the *hallali*, then *le mort*, the call of the Death. After these calls comes the one for *la curée*, and upon hearing this call, the Master of Hounds lowers his whip. That is the signal for the dogs to attack and feast upon the stag's entrails. It is…a ferocious moment."

He smiled and his eyes shone as he pictured the bloody scene in his mind.

His expression changed to one of seriousness.

"Please, do not take excessive risks! No one will think less of you if you do not clear an obstacle or gallop in the dense forest. Injuries such as broken bones are possible, so we have a medical crew following the hunt. If you tire—or are bored! (laughter)—our hunt crew will escort you back to the château so you can rest or engage in a more amusing activity."

They trooped out of the mansion to the stable courtyard where their mounts were waiting, saddled and ready.

Amaleen noticed Benito talking with the Huntmaster just inside the stable door. Though low-key, it was clear they were disagreeing about something. Both of their faces were grim. Benito was insisting. There was silence, then the Huntmaster turned away and mounted his horse.

Benito approached Amaleen and smiled.

"Mr Clive Harrows, the Huntmaster, will be your guide, my lady," he said, pointing to Harrows. "He speaks perfect English— being English himself! He will interpret the horn calls for you and keep you safe."

When they were all mounted, footmen circulated with trays of silver stirrup cups.

"Au cerf!" Benito shouted, held up his cup and drained it in a single gulp.

"Au cerf! The stag!"

As they started off, Clive Harrows did not wait for her. He rode off at the head of the hunt, as was his prerogative.

Amaleen trotted up past the others to his side.

"Thanks for bein' mah guide," she said.

Harrows looked straight ahead, said nothing, spurred his mount and rode on.

18

Hallali

Benito's hunting party rode for a half hour across fields, into the forest, and along paths beaten long before by hunters and their prey. Along the way the hunters dispersed into small groups on different paths, following the groups of hounds, keeping in touch by horn calls. Amaleen was in a group of six with Clive Harrows.

Amaleen knew Harrows was unhappy—bitter!—at having been told to "take care of the young American girl." It was far below his stature as Huntmaster. They were arguing over me back there, she thought. Benito won because he's the boss, but now this jerk hates me.

Suddenly the baying of the dogs changed to a higher note.

"Ah!" Harrows shouted, "there is our prey!"

They looked ahead along the path into the forest and saw a huge stag leap across a stream with the dogs not far behind. They spurred their mounts and followed the pack.

The stag was huge, a 12-pointer, noble and swift. It raced through the forest and used every tactic to throw the superb hounds off its trail: doubling back, circling around, leaping over streams and swimming through ponds. The hounds kept up their music and were occasionally thrown off the scent, but not for long.

Amaleen and Clive Harrows rode in pursuit of the dogs and the stag for an hour and a half. The other riders in Amaleen's group fell behind, tired, but Amaleen kept up with Harrows, never more than a hundred meters behind him. Sometimes he was out of sight in the dense forest, but the baying of the hounds never failed to lead her back to the track.

The note of the hounds' music changed again to a medium-low barking—they had the stag at bay!

The barking became frantic—the stag was down!

Amaleen came around a bend in the path and saw Harrows standing beside the fallen stag, both of them surrounded by the snarling dogs. With his huge hunting dagger raised in his right hand, the Huntmaster knelt to give the stag the *coup-de-grace*, but just then the stag, attempting to rise, dashed its head to the side. The huge antlers swept around, catching Harrows in his chest and belly. His face frozen in a mask of surprise, fear and pain. His muscles in spasms from the shock, Harrows dropped his dagger and fell back as the stag's head thrashed again in a last futile attempt at defense against death.

Seated on the ground, a dazed look on his face, Harrows gripped his bleeding torso with both arms. Bloodstains spread on his shirt, soaked through his white vest and flowed in a crimson current down the white cloth of his riding pants.

The dogs, perfectly trained in the ceremonies of the hunt, were confused. This was not what should happen next! The stag's throat should be slit cleanly, the Huntmaster should rise and they, the ferocious dogs, against their nature, should stand back and wait for the stag's head to be severed and for the body to be slaughtered, after which they would hear the *hallali* call from the horns, then the call for the *curée*. Their eyes would move to the Master of Hounds. When he lowered his whip, they would lunge forward and gorge themselves on the warm, bloody entrails.

In an instant Amaleen saw the danger: both the stag and Harrows were soaked in blood, but the Master of Hounds was nowhere to be seen. The confused dogs might ignore their years of training and attack both living, flesh-and-blood beings, the stag and the Huntmaster! She leapt from the saddle, pushed her way through the ravenous dogs to Harrows, picked up his dagger in her right hand, grabbed the stag's huge rack with her left, thrust the head back to expose the neck, plunged the dagger into the left side of the neck and drew it cleanly across the throat to the right.

Blood spurted from the dying stag's mortal wound. Its mouth gaped, its eyes flashed wildly, its great head sagged and was still.

Amaleen, gasping for breath, released the antlers, dropped the dagger, and stood transfixed at the bloody sight.

The dogs understood now. That is what is supposed to happen. They fell back and waited, panting and moaning.

Harrows gritted his teeth and grunted as the pain of his wounds overcame his strength. He could no longer sit up. He fell back on the ground.

"Help!" Amaleen shouted. "Help!"

The dogs bayed, increasing the chaos. She stood over Harrows, the dogs retreated, and as she shouted again other riders came into view. One of the guides jumped from his horse, raced to Harrows and began first aid. Another rode off to bring the medical team.

Benito arrived, surveyed the scene quickly, dismounted, and rushed to Amaleen.

"Are you all right?"

"Yeah, shore."

The others in the hunt rushed up, dismounted, and conversed quietly, glancing at Harrows as stretcher bearers arrived to carry him away.

Benito bent over, picked up the Huntmaster's bloody hunting dagger, and gave it to a guide.

"See that this is returned to him," he murmured.

He turned to his guests.

"Now we must give the dogs their reward," Benito announced. "It is already confusing for them."

The Master of Hounds came forward with two hunters who severed the stag's head from its body and slaughtered the carcass, leaving the entrails.

"Sound the *hallali.* "

Six French horns sounded the *hallali*, the Death, and *la curée.* The dogs' eyes were fixed on the Master of Hounds and their panting and growling was reaching fever pitch as he lowered his whip. The dogs surged forward onto the mass of warm guts, gnashing and tearing in a frenzy of hunger, blood lust, and animal savagery.

One of the men who had butchered the stag handed something to Benito.

Holding it high, Benito said "The right front foot of the stag, the prize of honor!" The skin of the leg had been peeled back, divided into three strips, and braided above the hoof.

Smiling, Benito approached Amaleen and handed her the bloody trophy. She took it and stared at it in confusion.

"Thanks…I think."

She stared at it in silence.

"Never had one o' *these* before," she mused.

She stared at it some more.

"It'll make a good…"

She cocked her head to one side, staring at it.

"…or maybe a…?"

She frowned.

"Wonder what mah mama will think…"

On the ride back to the château, Benito rode with Amaleen.

"What happened?" he asked her. "I did not expect a Master of the Hunt to be so badly injured by a stag."

"That stag was a brute!" Amaleen said. "Ah never seen anythin' like it. He looked like he was down, but he wasn't. He attacked the man just as he was makin' the kill."

"You mean the master made the kill as the stag attacked him? He made the kill even though he was wounded?"

Amaleen hesitated. She took a deep breath.

"Yep, that's what happened. He was just about to slit the stag's throat an' the stag stabbed him with that big rack."

Benito stared at her, then looked away.

"I have never heard of such a thing. He is a hero!"

Amaleen looked down.

"Yep, he's a hero all right."

At dinner that evening, the Count of Cercedilla rose to

propose a toast.

"To our host Benito and his brave Master of the Hunt!"

They all raised their champagne glasses and drank.

"Thank you, *monsieur le comte*, but I must make a slight amendment," Benito said, smiling. "Mademoiselle Amaleen was the one in at the kill. I arrived just afterwards. She is an amazing rider! If that is how they teach ladies to ride in West Virginia, I must go there to learn…so that I may ride as well as she does!"

"Mademoiselle Amaleen!" They raised their glasses and drank.

Amaleen blushed.

"They don't teach us ridin', Benito, we grow up ridin'! Ah got on a horse when ah was three an' ah been ridin' pretty much ever' day since then, 'cept in Paris."

Becoming serious, she added "Ah shore hope the hunt master's gonna be all right."

"I have heard from the hospital," Benito said. "Master Harrows' wounds were dramatic but not too deep. He has been treated successfully and will make a complete recovery—except, perhaps, of his pride! He was, ah, shall we say, *insulted* by the stag. But I must add that Mademoiselle Amaleen tells me that the stag was a 'real brute.' For a man to kill a stag after the brute has thrust him so terribly is certainly a heroic act!"

Amaleen raised her glass in a toast to the Master of the Hunt.

That evening, Amaleen put on the sultry silk nightgown again and lay in bed wondering what might happen, and again she dozed off.

The housekeeper woke her the next morning at 9 o'clock.

"Let me show you the château," Benito said to his guests after they had finished their Sunday breakfast.

With footmen preceding and following to open and close doors, Benito led them through the reception rooms, the library, and the great hall, then up into one of the towers.

Cobwebs festooned the corners of the narrow, low-ceilinged, dust-covered walkways. The ancient blown-glass windows were grimy and dark.

"I leave the towers as they were when I became the owner of the château," he said. "For all I know, the towers have not changed in centuries."

They came to a small door that gave access to a narrow platform outside, high above the stone-paved courtyard. The footman opened the door, but Benito blocked the way.

"We will not go out here. It is too dangerous. You may look through the door but please do not step out. I wanted to show you this because legend has it the lord of the château in the 1400s struggled with his rebellious son on this narrow platform. Both lost their balance and fell to their deaths on the stones below—a tragic moment in the history of my fine home."

Benito led the group down dusty stairs into the lower rooms of the tower. A footman opened an armored door and they entered a spacious circular room illuminated by small spotlights aimed at sculptures and other objects as well as paintings, mosaics and icons on the walls.

"This is my museum," Benito said. "I am an avid collector of historical works of art. Please feel free to examine them as you wish. You may even touch them!" he smiled, happy to contravene the usual museum prohibition against handling art objects.

Amaleen wandered through the huge, high-ceilinged room past full-size statues of Grecian marble, medieval sculptures, a large triptych from a church, exquisite oil paintings by—could it be?—the Old Masters. This was a treasure-house!

The room was well laid out, but one small portion of it was different: uncrowded and rather plain. She sauntered over to it and looked into a glass case containing small, obviously primitive objects: stone axes and knives, arrowheads, beaded jewelry and figurines.

"My antiquities," Benito said, approaching her. "My museum includes art from every period of human history—and pre-history, as you see here. From every age of human endeavor. The objects in this display are from the Stone Age, many thousands of years old."

Benito walked to the door of the room.

"I'm glad that you find my little collection interesting! Please spend as much time here as you like. When you are finished with art, please join me in the library. We will decide on activities for the rest of the day."

The chauffeur handed Amaleen out of the Rolls at the front door of Olivier's château. He welcomed her at the door.

"Thanks fer lettin' me stay here. I couldn't go back to Paris with all that trouble."

"Of course, *chérie*. How was your weekend?"

She told him everything…or almost everything.

19

University

It was drizzling, so Gaston and Charity breakfasted at the dining table in the cottage. As they sipped their coffee, they talked about the university and when it might re-open.

"I hope there will be some changes," Gaston said. "The university system is broken!"

"Broken how?"

"Too many students for too few facilities. We are overwhelmed! Not enough faculty or administrative staff to make it function properly. Students are not required to think creatively. The teaching programs are too rigid and designed only to help students pass the *license* examinations—but even so, most fail! Even if they pass, the only job they are qualified for is teaching... and there are already too many teachers!"

"The students are right to demand change, but they do not know what they want," he said.

"What should they want?"

"I have spent time at universities in America. There is more discussion and intellectual freedom. Teachers guide the students, but allow them to experiment with new ideas. Your professors realize that the world is always changing, and they must adapt their views and their teaching as changes occur. TStudents help the professors adapt by exposing them to the new developments and ideas."

"But…you are a French *maître de conférences*, like an assistant professor in the States, and you encourage student participation in your teaching."

"Yes, because I learned to do so in America! My teaching methods are not entirely appreciated by others in our faculty." Gaston laughed. "After learning how to participate in my classes, my students ask similar questions and make similar comments in other classes, and it irritates some of my fellow faculty members. They want to give their lecture and then walk away and do something more amusing."

"So the student protests are valid?"

"The protesters are correct when they say the university must change, but they are not capable of presenting a plan for effective change. They have chaotic, pointless discussions where factions collide and never come to a resolution. They call this 'people's democracy' and 'the new university,' but it is neither."

"The new university must have a plan that all interested elements agree upon at least in general," he said. "Interested elements include more than students and faculty, they include the Ministry of National Education and the professional groups the students will join: teachers, doctors, scientists, administrators."

"Every group—students, faculty, government—will believe that it has the best plan, but the optimal plan will be the one developed through the creative conflict of facts and ideas. It will satisfy none of these groups completely, but it will meet the needs of all to the greatest degree possible. The university must fulfill its function for all."

"Now you are the idealist" she said. "It sounds like utopia."

20

Auroch

This was the third morning that they had set out from the cottage to search the Vézère valley for caves. They had gotten into the habit of starting early, right after breakfast on the terrace —in the sun, they hoped. If they began early there was less chance to be observed, but today, with the rain, they started late.

"We'll start where we ended yesterday," Gaston said. "Because we have not found any new caves of interest in two days, it must happen today! We must find a place to get out of the rain. The probability is good!"

She smiled at him.

"I hope we find a cave," Charity said, "but even if we don't, it will be a good day. The river and the valley are so beautiful, even in the rain. It's spring!"

And I'm with Gaston all day, she thought. It won't last, we'll be back to our normal lives in Paris soon, so I have to enjoy every minute here...with him.

He drove down from the cottage to the valley road and along the river to the point where the previous day's explorations had stopped. As they drove, the drizzle slowed and finally stopped. The sun peeked through the clouds.

"Any geological disturbance," he said. "A rockslide, a cleft, anything that is not solid rock wall."

He drove slowly, stopping frequently at the side of the road so they could get out of the car and scan the cliffs with binoculars. If another car passed, they turned and looked at the river and Gaston lifted his camera. Just two tourists enjoying the beauty of spring.

By noon they had found little that looked promising. One rockslide had drawn them through the bushes and up the steep cliff, but they found nothing. The cascade of rock looked as though it had fallen from far above against the hard cliff wall of rock.

"I will try a little test," he said.

He reached in his pocket and pulled out a cigarette lighter. Thumbing the wheel, he ignited the flame and held it close to the broken rock cascade. The flame rose steady, unmoving.

"Sometimes, if there is a cave, air will pass through the pile of rocks into or out of the cave, moving the flame. There is no movement here."

He replaced the lighter in his pocket.

"It is not a scientific test!" he laughed. "Not every cave has air moving through it, but the limestone in this region has many fractures and holes that may allow air movement through the interior spaces. Sometimes this simple little test is useful."

He smiled at her.

"We would not want to remove these tons of rock just to find a solid stone wall."

Back in the car, driving along, Gaston saw a good place to pull off the road by a grassy plot on the riverbank.

"Perfect for our picnic!" he said.

Charity spread a blanket on the grass and arranged the bread, cheese, pickled vegetables, pâté, fruit, water and wine.

They ate mostly in silence, gazing at the river, the trees, the wildflowers. Birds flitted above them. The river, powered by the spring flood, made a quiet rushing and rippling sound.

Gaston stretched out on the blanket looking in the direction of the cliffs and closed his eyes. Charity stretched out beside him. I love this, she thought. I just love this. I am happy, happier than I can ever remember being.

They dozed.

A car passed and honked its horn at them.

"*Con!*" Gaston cursed. "Sorry, mademoiselle. I apologize for my language."

"*Il est vraiment un con,*" Charity joked—'he sure is a jerk'— and they both burst out laughing.

Gaston looked up at the cliff and was still.

"Please give me the binoculars," he said.

Charity reached for them and handed them to him.

"Maybe… We should look at it. Yes, we should go there."

He pointed to a dark spot on the cliff and handed the binoculars to Charity. She looked through them and saw that the dark spot was…ambiguous. Maybe something, maybe not.

"We go," he said, standing.

They gathered the picnic provisions, put them in the car, crossed the road and began to clamber up the steep cliff. It took some time because they had to move laterally, edging far to the right because the direct course to the spot was too steep.

When they got to the dark spot, they saw it was just an extraordinary growth of dark plants. No gap or opening in the rock.

"Bad luck," Gaston said.

They started back down as a boat motored slowly along the river.

As they began the climb down from the dark spot, Charity gripped a rock to steady herself as she climbed over other rocks, but the rock was loose and her hand pulled it enough to topple it.

"Watch out!" she called to Gaston.

The rock tumbled down the steep slope toward him, but Gaston leapt aside and it passed harmlessly.

"Gaston. Come up here."

He climbed back up to where she was. She pointed to the gap where the rock had been: emptiness. He lifted his flashlight and shined it into the darkness. No obstacle. He lit his lighter, held it to the hole, and the wind being sucked into the opening extinguished the flame.

"Well! Good for you!"

They pulled the broken rocks down and soon made an opening big enough to enter. The passage into the rock was fairly large and going deeper was not difficult.

Twenty meters into the cave they saw drawings on the rock walls.

"*Mon dieu!* We have found it!"

Their flashlights revealed drawings of animals—bison, deer, bear—scratched into the rock using some sort of tool. The scratches were primitive, the drawings crude—but that they were pre-historic drawings they had no doubt. Some were colored with charcoal or crude paints.

The walking was not difficult. They penetrated farther into the cave with their flashlights illuminating the walls. A few meters farther in they stopped and stared: large, beautiful polychrome drawings of dozens of animals!

"Look at the cow!" Charity said, shining her light on it.

"Auroch," Gaston said, "a prehistoric bull. Now extinct. *Merveilleux!*"

They looked at one another. Charity saw the passionate excitement in his face. She threw her arms around him and hugged. He hugged her back.

"We must be careful," he said. "We are responsible for the first examination. We must protect the site!"

Handing his flashlight to her, he took out his camera, rolled the film back, took out the roll and replaced it with one of fast 400 ASA Ektachrome.

"Hold the lights for photos." She held them steady, moving from left to right on the wall as he snapped pictures.

"There is so much here!" he said. "We must go farther into the cave, but it may be that we cannot see it all today. There is no way to know how deep it goes without exploring it all."

Shining their lights ahead, they penetrated further.

"Be careful of holes!" he said. "Do not always look at the walls and ceiling. Watch your footing. Do not dislodge any rock. Do not step on any artifacts or other evidence of activity!"

Charity was in the lead. They found nothing for another twenty meters. She stopped.

"I can't see the walls ahead. My light's not hitting anything."

"Careful!" he said.

Where the walls ended they found a huge room fifteen meters wide and seven to ten meters high. The floor was uneven, but they saw a way—a track? A path?—on the left going to the wall, and on the wall, more paintings.

"Mon dieu!" he said in a low voice.

A frieze of art extended all along the wall intermittently for at least six meters.

"Step carefully!" he said. "There may be artifacts under foot. Try to step only on stone you can see."

They worked their way along the wall taking photographs.

"I only brought three rolls of film," he said. "I never imagined we would need more than one hundred frames! We will return tomorrow with more."

She held the flashlight as he wrote in a pocket notebook, looking up now and then to survey the room.

"As we walk back, I will pace the distances," he said.

She followed, casting the light for him and not interrupting his concentration. Every few meters he stopped and took notes.

When they emerged from the cave, the sun blinded them.

"Sit for a moment," he said.

They sat on the rocks without speaking.

"We must cover the entrance well."

They pushed, pulled and lifted the heavy chunks of rocks until the entrance was disguised. They were sweating in the warm late afternoon air.

Gaston tore a dead bush up by the roots and placed it in front of the rocks, then stood back and looked at their work. Charity wiped the perspiration from her face and looked at him. He returned her gaze. Their arms went out and they embraced, holding one another tightly.

They clambered down the slope to the river road. As they emerged from the bushes, Gaston saw a boat tied up near their picnic place and three men resting on the shore.

"Merde! Écoute, Charité, we are lovers."

He grabbed her hand and smiled at her. She smiled in return. They put their arms around each others' waists as they crossed the road. When they reached the car, Gaston embraced and kissed her.

Charity knew what he was doing, but she was not prepared for how it felt. She kissed him in return, but it was too real! It was her dream come true…but this was so different from her fantasy! She was dizzy with confusion. Her emotions surged inside of her as she felt the excitement of their discovery, the passion of her romantic fantasy, but the absurdity of play-acting it out, fake passion, to deceive the men from the boat. She felt unsteady. Gaston supported her as her legs wobbled.

Clutching him, she chose to live her fantasy. She let herself go. She embraced him as in her dream, fervently, their lips hot together, her hands moving over his back and pressing him to her, her legs pressing against his.

With a little laugh, he let her go. He looked over at the men from the boat.

"*Pardon!*" he said. "*Nouveaux mariés!*"

Newlyweds.

Charity felt a rush of emotion.

Gaston and Charity climbed into the MG and drove away.

"I think we fooled them," Gaston said. "I *hope* we did."

Back at the boat, Monsieur M stood up.

"Go look up there," he said, and pointed up the slope toward the dark spot.

The other two men climbed up the steep hillside following, more or less, the route Gaston and Charity had taken.

When they returned to the boat, they stepped in, they cast off, and they motored slowly along the river.

"Anything up there?" Monsieur M asked the two men. "Openings or caves or…"

"Just solid rock and rockslides," they said.

"Are you sure? Nothing? That couple, the '*nouveaux mariés*', there's something odd…."

Monsieur M frowned and was silent.

That evening, in the cottage, Charity and Gaston talked little, lost in thought. Only the necessary, short conversations: something to eat, preparations for tomorrow. They said good night and went to their rooms.

Charity woke when Gaston called quietly to her from the office door. When she emerged for breakfast, all was ready, including his full photography kit, measuring equipment, special battery lamps, and a picnic. They breakfasted quickly. Gaston packed all of the equipment into two knapsacks and they set out.

"We will be carefree hikers today," he said. "I will park the car some distance from the cave, out of sight from the road. We will hike along the river, enjoying the spring weather and scenery. When we see no one around, we will go up to the cave."

They reached the cave without incident and uncovered the entrance. Once inside, Gaston pulled rocks and the dead bush as close as he could to disguise the entrance.

They got to work: first a photograph, then measurements, then a careful description of the size, style, colors and composition of the pictures. They moved methodically along the cave wall.

Hours passed.

When they reached the large room, Gaston said *"Déjeuner pique-nique!"*

They sat on the dusty stone floor and ate in silence, occasionally casting their flashlight beams on the walls in wonder.

"After we finish our survey, we will not return," he said. "It would not be advisable. We take a chance at discovery, our breath and sweat may cause damage.... We will not see this again until a proper examination can be mounted."

21

The Dagger

This time it was two dozen pink roses: 'true, pure, gentle love.'

Amaleen telephoned to Château Corsique and arranged a travel time for Friday afternoon.

The Rolls delivered Amaleen to the front door of Château Corsique where she was again greeted by the butler and the chief housekeeper, who escorted her to her usual guest room. The closet and dresser were already filled with the clothes, cosmetics, toiletries and flowers Benito had ordered for her.

It could seem like I belong here, Amaleen thought, but I don't feel that way. There's something too slick about this place and about Benito, but I can't put my finger on it. It's not his wealth—I'm fine with that—and it's not that he's *nouveau riche*. I'm nouveau riche! I know what it means, I know how you feel, I know how others feel about us nouveau riche—particularly the not-nouveaus, the old money, to whom we are a threat. But Benito...there's just something too...too...

I don't know what.

She chose a new, sumptuously beautiful dress and prepared for dinner.

A footman escorted her to the small dining room where she was seated to Benito's right, as usual. Benito was already there, standing with two other guests, a man in his thirties and a woman who looked some years younger. Both were dressed in the latest fashion. As they were being seated, a second couple was escorted in and seated.

Dinner was five courses: a savory *soupe* followed by *moules marinières*, then *blanquette de veau*, and camembert. The conversation was light and forgettable until Benito brought up the subject of art, particularly ancient art, that of Greece and Rome, but also of the Phrygians, Phoenicians and Hittites. The two other men at the table were not experts but they clearly had an interest, and discussed the discovery of ancient works, their transport and preservation.

Dessert arrived, a luscious-looking Paris-Brest: delicate pastry filled with praline cream.

"But I can see that we're boring the ladies with this talk of old stones, pots and beads," Benito said. "Gentlemen, we have with us this evening three of the finest works of art of which the human race is capable: the ladies!"

He raised his glass in a toast. The other men did the same.

"Tomorrow, if the weather is fine, I suggest that we ride. Not a hunt, but a ride across the countryside. The beauty of May is upon us! We should ride out, welcome it, and appreciate its magnificence. So. Riding dress, please. Breakfast will be ready at seven o'clock, and we mount at nine."

The next morning, a few minutes before nine o'clock, they left the house and walked to the stables. Clive Harrows greeted them, with a knowing glance and smile at Amaleen.

"How're yuh doin'?" she asked.

"I am pretty well," he said with a smile, "thanks to you."

He showed her to her mount where they checked the bridle and saddle girth.

"Kurnos, the same horse as you had on the hunt," he said. "You and he got along quite well, I believe."

"We shore did! Thanks. We'll have another good ride."

Mounted and ready, they set out across the fields and through the forests of the château estate, then through villages and along the edges of farmers' fields just showing the early growth of summer crops. It was a beautiful morning of bright, warm sun, clean fresh air scented with wildflowers and, along the fields, the pungent acrid animal smell of fertilizer.

Passing through a copse of trees, Amaleen heard the song of the cuckoo and chuckled, imagining a hokey cuckoo clock hanging from a tree branch—but the song was from a real bird.

Out of the copse the terrain beckoned, so Benito spurred his horse and took off at a canter. The others followed and kept up.

After several hours' ride with Benito in the lead, they entered a village and walked their horses slowly along the main street to an inn. Dismounting, Benito handed the reins to a waiter who emerged from the inn. The others did the same, and followed him into the dining room.

"A simple lunch today, a country lunch," Benito said, "but a hearty one. I'm hungry!"

Waiters served *boudin noir aux pommes de terre* (blood sausage with potatoes) followed by grilled lamb chops with root vegetables, then a selection of cheeses, all accompanied by the local red wine. Several times during the meal, Benito looked at Amaleen, caught her eye, smiled, raised his glass, and continued to look at her as he sipped.

The ride back to the château was slower, with the men in front conversing, and the women behind making occasional comments to one another, but the ladies had little in common.

They arrived back at the château by mid-afternoon. As they approached the château, Clive Harrows rode up next to her.

"Miss Amaleen, may I speak with you for a moment when we reach the stables?"

"Shore."

"I'll be in the tack room."

As they dismounted and handed the reins to the grooms, Benito spoke.

"I'm sure we'd all like a little rest," he said. "Please make yourselves at home until dinnertime."

After the two other couples left, Benito looked at Amaleen.

"Before you go for a rest, I'd like to show you a part of the château that few have seen."

"Shore. Whah not? Jes' lemme thank Mr Harrows for a fine ride."

"Certainly! Please meet me in the library in a half hour."

She went to the tack room. Harrows was sitting behind his desk. He rose as she entered.

"Miss Amaleen, I must thank you for saving my life…"

"Aw, 'twernt nuthin'. Jes' a accident."

"Not at all! I saw what you did. I recognize your courage and bravery. And just as much, I appreciate your discretion. Benito congratulated me on making the kill after I was wounded. He said that makes me a hero. We both know it's not true. The kill was yours! Yet you yielded the credit to me and saved my position. I am eternally grateful! I could not have continued as hunt master if Benito had been told the truth. He does not want…failures…around him."

"Y'all ain't a failure!" Amaleen countered, "it was a accident!"

Harrows held up his hand for quiet.

"According to the code of honor, I must surrender my dagger to you. The kill was yours. The dagger with which you performed it is now yours as well."

He held out the heavy knife in its sheath for her to take.

"Aw, Mr Harrows—Clive—ah cain't take yore knife. Ah'm jes' a girl, an' a foreigner even!"

"Miss Amaleen, my honor does not allow me to keep it. I must award it to you following hunt custom. Please do not refuse me the right to honor you according to tradition."

"Well, ah know that the tradition thang is important here in France. Shore, I'll take it, jes' as a souvenir of the hunt, an' yore leadership. But ah'm jes' holdin' it for you. It ain't mine. Ah dunno if ah'l ever go on another hunt like that. But ah'll think o' you ever' time I look at it."

She took the knife from him and drew it out of its sheath. It was heavy. The long blade gleamed. The edge, which she knew must be keen as a razor, had been worn down by many sharpenings. It's a knife that's been used for its intended purpose dozens of times, she thought.

"Thank you, Miss Amaleen."

She slid it back into its leather sheath. He came around the desk and showed her how to lodge it in the top of her right boot so it was secure but ready for use when the time came for the kill.

"Anybody gives me trouble in Paris, ah'll whip this thang out an' scare the pants off 'em!" she joked.

He laughed with her.

"No man in Paris—no stag in the forest!—would be wise to threaten Miss Amaleen!" he smiled.

"S'cuse me now, Benito's waitin' for me in the library."

"Of course. Enjoy the rest of your stay at Château Corsique."

22

Perversity

Benito, still in riding habit, was coming out of the library as she approached.

"Ah! Amaleen! Please come with me."

He led her through hallways and doors, along a corridor and down a narrow spiral staircase to a heavy door in the cellar. He slid the heavy cast-iron bolt, pulled the door open, switched on the lights and they walked in.

The lights were dim. It took Amaleen a moment before her eyes adjusted and she could see several pieces of exercise equipment.

"Yore gym, exercise room," she said. "Benito, you got ever'thang in this place!"

"Yes, my...exercise room. It is a special place for me. I only show it to special guests. You are one of my favorite guests, not to mention the most beautiful! I think we can enjoy ourselves here. I tend to...perspire after exercise, so I thought I might show you the special features of this chamber before we wash and prepare for dinner."

"But...we're still wearin' these fine ridin' outfits! Won't they git damaged?"

"Puh! Riding dress adds to the enjoyment of the exercise. I am always in riding dress here. You will see. Clothes are just clothes. We have plenty."

He took her hand and led her to a machine attached to the rough stone wall.

"We have many ancient traditions in Corsica, where I come from. This apparatus has been used for centuries there for...well, to be honest, for...discipline. Some would even call it punishment, or even torture. But even psychologists know that pain and pleasure are two sides of the same coin. Pain and pleasure, ecstasy and fear, call on the same physiological mechanisms to flood the body with hormones that make our hearts race, our blood pressure rise, our breathing increase, and our emotions grow to the heights of stimulation and excitement. Soldiers in the thick of battle, when danger is all around and death could catch them at any moment, experience this sensation. People making love come to climax and call it 'the little death' because it achieves the height of stimulation before the collapse of emotions and the exhaustion after pleasure."

"I will show you how this device is used, and I ask for your help in the exercise. It would please me greatly."

"Shore. Whatever."

Benito turned his back to the wall and stood against the machine.

"Put the straps around my feet and hands," he instructed her, "then lock them."

She saw heavy leather straps by his feet. She wrapped one around each ankle and snapped the latch closed. His legs were now immobilized.

"Now my wrists." He held his arms up bent at the elbows, his forearms vertical, his wrists next to the upper straps. Amaleen looped the straps around his wrists and snapped the latches.

This is kinky, she thought, but I've seen lotsa kinky before. So far, I think I can handle it. He's the one who's strapped in, after all.

"You may think this is unusual," Benito said, "but when you think of what I explained about pleasure and pain, it will make sense. The leather strap behind my head goes around my neck."

Amaleen hesitated, then lifted her hands and fastened it. It was snug against his skin.

"The handle on the front of the neck strap tightens it. Each time you turn the handle, you hear a click and the strap tightens a little more. During the exercise you will...stroke my manhood as you tighten the strap once, twice, three times—but no more than three times! If you tighten it more, I cannot breathe, but at three clicks the pressure is such that I must work very hard to breathe. This stimulates the hormones and gives me great pleasure—to climax!"

"As you see the tension mount, you will turn the handle on the neck strap. If you perform these duties just right, I will experience the height of ecstasy shortly after the third click. You will have given me the greatest pleasure! After the climax, turn the handle on the neck strap back to the beginning quickly, and wait. I will tell you when I am ready to be released."

Amaleen paused. Holy shit, she thought, I've never done sado-masochism before. Should I do this? He's trussed up and can't get out. I could run outta here and never come back. But... what's it hurting? It looks like it should hurt him, but he says he's gonna get a lotta pleasure.

What the hell. Give it a try. I know what he means by "stroke" him. This sure ain't my first weird lover, just my craziest.

She stroked him sensuously and felt him harden beneath the sheer cloth of the tight riding breeches. His breath came more rapidly.

With her right hand she continued to caress him. With her left she reached up and slowly turned the handle on the neck strap until she heard the click. He gasped. His eyes closed. His breath came rasping now. She saw the sweat appear on his face.

She changed her gentle caress to forceful play, slapping and squeezing him. He grunted with each slap and his breath came faster. She saw the top of his riding shirt darken with sweat running down from his neck.

Her right hand stroked him in a regular rhythm as her left reached for the handle and slowly turned it for another click. His body was racked with spasms. He jerked his arms and legs against the constraints. His eyes bulged and rolled in their sockets.

Jeez, I hope he knows what he's doing, she thought. What if I kill the guy? This damn machine could do it, choke off his windpipe completely. You can't last more than a minute or so without air, and I bet he's already oxygen-deprived.

I better get this crazy shit over with.

Her hand moved frantically as she turned the neck strap screw for the third click. Benito made a choking noise and jerked powerfully against the restraints, making the whole apparatus creak and groan. His elbows and knees flexed with such strength that Amaleen expected his legs to kick free. How could those straps hold?

Suddenly he was still. His bulging eyes stared in shock straight ahead and his body was rigid as Amaleen felt the lump in his pants stiffen to rock-hard.

Though it was less than half a minute, the orgasm seemed to go on forever. When it finally stopped, Amaleen quickly turned the handle on the neckstrap in reverse and released the clasp. Benito gave a choked, gasping sigh, and all the muscles in his body collapsed. He gasped again and shook as he took huge, rapid, rasping breaths, eyes closed, head bent, his body sagging in the restraints.

Amaleen waited.

After several minutes his breathing was regular, though still faster than normal. He slowly raised his head, looked at her, and smiled weakly, exhausted.

"Feet first," he said in a rasping whisper.

She released the clasps on the ankle straps, then reached up to release the wrist straps. As his hands came free, his arms grabbed her for support as his body sagged against her, his legs too weak to support him. With difficulty she struggled to hold his weight and shift it to a bench next to the apparatus.

He sat with a thud.

"Water!" he gasped.

She scanned the room and saw a jug and glasses on a shelf. She brought them to him, filled a glass, lifted it to his lips and helped him drink.

Jeez, she thought, there's some weird shit goes on in this world.

But she said nothing.

After a quarter hour, Benito was able to stand. He adjusted his riding pants, drank another glass of water, wiped away some of the sweat with a handkerchief, and patted her on the shoulder.

"My dear, I think you realize the great pleasure you have given me. I thought that you would be an exceptional woman, but I really had no idea how exceptional. You may have given me the greatest pleasure I have ever known!"

They left the dungeon, Benito shot the bolt on the heavy door, they climbed the stairs to the main floor, then to the upper floor.

In the hallway, Benito held her hands tightly in his, smiled at her, and kissed each of her hands.

"Thank you, sweet Amaleen."

At dinner, Benito, dressed in his perfect tuxedo, was his charming self, ebullient and humorous with his guests. Frequently he glanced Amaleen's way, smiled and winked.

As she readied for bed, Amaleen wondered if this was the night. No one could say they had not already been intimate. But what would it be like? Would he bring his sado-masochism into her bed? Was she in danger?

She lay in bed, conjuring up nightmares of the possibilities.

The next morning, when the housekeeper woke her, she had only been asleep for two hours.

23

Josie & Jean-Paul

Early evening. The street door buzzer sounded in the apartment on Rue Claude Bernard. Josie pressed the button on the intercom.

"*Qui est là?*"

"*Jean-Paul.*"

She pressed the latch release for the street door and opened the apartment door a crack. She heard him on the stairs. He entered and closed the door.

"This is a surprise!"

"Martine gave me your address. I was in the Latin Quarter for negotiations with the Ministry and the university, so I came to give you a message from Martine."

His gaze surveyed the apartment. He walked around and looked in the rooms.

"You live alone?"

"No. Well, yes, alone at the moment. I have two roommates, but they're not here. They're not in Paris. You can speak freely."

"Martine would like to see you again. She can't come out yet, it's still not safe, so you would have to go to our apartment."

They looked at one another.

"I'm glad. Of course I'll go. How is she? I mean medically."

"Much better! I'd say her recovery is…miraculous!"

They both laughed at the thought of a communist believing in miracles.

"Medically, she could go out for short periods now, even though she tires easily, but we believe the police are still looking for her. Of course they have hundreds of photographs of the barricades and the people around them. We feel certain they have identified her. She was on top of the barricades! Leading the fight! We are negotiating an amnesty for all students who participated in the demonstrations, but we have not agreed on the terms yet."

He slumped into a chair with a deep sigh.

"You sound tired. What do you need? Water? Coffee? Tea? Food? Wine?"

"Water, and wine."

"What about food? Not fancy, but why not rest, have a glass of wine and I'll make a simple supper. You look exhausted."

"It has been a difficult day. A difficult week. Month! Year! My god, it has all been so difficult!"

Josie brought a bottle of water, a bottle of red wine and three glasses. He drank off two glasses of water and poured a third as she filled his wine glass and her own.

"To the revolution!" Josie said, raising her glass and smiling.

"Oh well, to the revolution, I suppose." He looked at her with irony.

"You are doing great things," she said. "I admire you."

"Sometimes it is simply too much. Too much! The arguments never end. Arguments with the university, with the government, with the other student groups—they cannot agree on anything! Constant arguments!"

"You have Martine. She's a solid support even when she was nearly murdered by police. She has enough strength for all of us!"

"Yes, yes…but how does she use her strength? What will come of it? She has a dream of a better world and it is all she cares about, but is there any chance it can be achieved?"

"She cares about more than the revolution, Jean-Paul. She cares about you."

He looked at her with sad, tired eyes, lifted his glass and took a long drink of wine.

"I suppose she does care for me, but I am not at all as important to her as the revolution. I am useful to her in her battle, at least at the moment."

They sat and sipped in silence for some minutes.

"I admire you as much as I admire Martine," he said.

"Why? I did nothing!"

"You fought with us, not by throwing stones but by caring for our wounded. You are not a strong man, you are a young woman, and not even French! You are American, and you are *une négresse!* This is not your fight, and yet you risked your life to help us."

"International solidarity," she said.

"It is more than that. It is what your heart told you to do—to help those who badly needed your help. You put yourself in danger to do it. If the police had broken through the barricade, they would have beaten you along with everyone else. Look what they did to Martine! Without you she would have died! If they arrested you, they would have beaten you and then deported you."

"France is not my country, and you're right, the fight for a better university is not really my fight. But I've grown up fighting, like all the colored Americans of my generation. Our people have been trampled for centuries, and we won't take it any more! Maybe you're right. Maybe in your barricades I saw a struggle like mine, and needed to participate. I'm glad I did."

She stood and went to the kitchen to prepare dinner, vegetable noodle soup, toasted bread, salad, olives, pâté and cheese. She left the soup to simmer and returned to the salon.

Jean-Paul, his head flopped back and to the side, his mouth open, was deep asleep in his chair.

Two hours passed. She decided to wake him.

"Jean-Paul... *Le dîner est servi.*"

Startled, his body jerked as he came awake. He looked around frantically until he remembered where he was. Slowly he rose from his chair and joined her at the dining table.

He was calmer now. The hot soup was a tonic, as was the wine. Soon the first glass was finished. Josie poured another.

"You live in luxury!" he said.

"This apartment is comfortable, but I wouldn't call it luxurious."

"You live in luxury!" he repeated.

"Three of us share the rent. The dollar is strong. Paris is cheaper than Boston or Chicago."

"I thought all American Negroes were poor," he said, "except the famous musicians. Louis Armstrong, Nat King Cole, Duke Ellington...Josephine Baker!"

They laughed.

"I must ask. Is she of your family? You resemble her so much."

"We are related in soul, but no, she is not my relation, and I have no money from her. I'm just an American student."

She chose not to tell him about her parents' large five-bedroom Craftsman-style house in Oak Park, with its rich woodwork and spacious carriage house behind, nor of her father's shiny 1968 Buick Electra 225, or her mother's more modest—but almost brand-new—Chevrolet, or of the live-in maid who cared for the house while her father the busy judge and her even busier mother the lawyer were pursuing the struggle for civil rights in Chicago.

She didn't tell him these things, but he was curious about America so she told him about Chicago and the Great Lakes, the rich prairies of Illinois, Indiana and Iowa, the wild, forested beauties of Wisconsin and Michigan. She told him of New York City, and Washington, and New England, and Florida, all of which she had seen.

The food and the bottle of wine were gone.

"Oh! It's so late! I had no idea!" she said.

"I must leave," he said, getting up from the table.

"No! I didn't mean that. I mean, of course, if you must..."

"It is not that. I do not have to leave. I planned to stay with friends in the Latin Quarter tonight."

They stood looking at one another awkwardly.

"Well...there's plenty of room here. We have three bedrooms! You could stay here...."

They looked at one another. Their eyes connected, and did not disconnect. The silence was complete, they stood like statues, all their energy in their gaze. Josie felt her heart pounding and feared it was so loud he could hear it.

He approached her. Their bodies were only inches apart. She was breathing harder, her chest heaving. She looked at him with eyes full of confusion and expectation.

He looked deep into her eyes, their faces ever closer. He saw her eyelids begin slowly to descend as he touched his lips to hers. She did not pull away. He kissed her. He opened his eyes and saw hers still closed. He kissed her again, more committed this time, forcefully.

"Oh!"

She drew in a huge breath, coiled her arms around him and kissed him with passion.

It had been so long....

She had boyfriends in Chicago, black boyfriends, but in France most men were white and fewer of them approached her, and she didn't encourage those who did. She knew the Frenchman's reputation for mistresses and brief affairs, and that's not how she lived. She was serious. She believed in love, not just sex, wonderful as sex is. There had to be a bond between her and her lover, a meeting of minds and hearts. It didn't have to be marriage, not yet, but it had to have meaning, not just playing around.

And here she was in Paris after a year as a celibate student, a secular nun, friendships but no affairs, and his lips felt so exciting on hers, and his body felt so good against hers, and his embrace was strong and fervent, and she knew his heart was good.

This is like a drug, this is what heroin must do to you, she thought. I can't stop it. I can't stop it! I don't want to stop it....

I want it to happen.

24

Martine & Josie

"What did you tell Martine?" Josie asked Jean-Paul when he returned to the apartment on Rue Claude Bernard the next day.

"I told her not to expect me tonight. That the meeting would run late. That I would stay with friends in the Latin Quarter again."

"It is late," Josie said, furrowing her brow and frowning at him in mock accusation. "I've been waiting for you."

He took her in his arms and kissed her, kissed her again deeply. She sighed and clutched him close.

"We have such strength when we're together," she said. "I can feel the weakness when we're apart."

They knew their dizzying infatuation was dangerous, a bomb waiting to go off. This made it all the more thrilling, every kiss a shot in the dark, every embrace a treasonous moment of exaltation headed toward tragedy.

The thrill of risking everything, *everything* when they made love. All or nothing. Ecstasy or agony! And yet, every time, it was ecstasy that awaited them in the darkness, and the daylight did not bring agony—yet.

Josie set the table for their simple dinner. As they dined, Jean-Paul told her about the day, the meeting, the acrimony on both sides of the discussions, the accusations, charges and counter-charges, demands made by the government and university administrators, counter-demands by the students.

"There is no way they can understand us!" Jean-Paul said. "It is as though we are speaking French and they are hearing Chinese."

He felt the relaxation come upon him as he ate, drank and talked with her.

He finished his wine and looked at her. She was so beautiful! She was exotic: American, and *nègre*, and sophisticated, but she knew boldness and courage as well as the sweetest tenderness. She knew what it was like to battle police in the streets.

"You're here now, and safe, and I want you!" Josie said, taking his hand and pulling him toward the bedroom, leaving the littered dinner table to fend for itself until morning.

The next morning, after Jean-Paul had gone back to his meeting with university administrators, Josie made the long journey to Martine's hideaway in the Paris suburbs. When she arrived at the door, her knock was light, tentative, but Martine heard and opened. Josie stepped into the room and Martine surrounded her in an all-encompassing embrace, pressing her lips, her body, her groin forcefully into Josie.

"I've wanted you so much!" she said.

Martine took her by the hand and led her to the bedroom. They stood by the bed, Josie in shock, her arms dangling at her sides, as Martine kissed her passionately and worked at the buttons on Josie's blouse. Josie raised her hands to gently to press Martine away, but her hands didn't do that. She held them suspended, just barely touching Martine, as Martine's tongue explored her mouth and their breaths mingled.

Martine slipped Josie's blouse from her shoulders, and quickly lifted her own blouse over her head. She wore nothing underneath. She reached behind Josie's back, unhooked her bra, dropped it to the floor and eased her breasts against Josie's.

Oh my god, oh my god, Josie thought. Oh my god.

Josie's hands slid along Martine's body around to the back and held Martine tentatively, only fingertips. Martine was kissing Josie's face, her neck, her shoulders, her breasts....

Oh my god. Oh my god.

"This is the way it will be when we achieve the revolution," Martine said as she and Josie lay in bed, exhausted. "Everyone can express their love as they feel it. No bourgeois conventions, no restraints. Complete honesty. When you are in love, you express your love in every way. Poetry. Music. Kindness. Sharing. Physical love—sex! This is how I feel about you Josie. I want you to know, so I showed you."

Josie looked at her, so confused she had no idea what to say.

"In the new world, after the revolution, free love will be the rule. Everyone will love everyone as they wish. Everyone will share what they have. There will be no rich or poor, no police, no government. We will all work for everyone. If a problem arises, it will be debated in council and decisions reached by consensus."

"Sounds like heaven on earth," Josie said.

"It will be. It will be! It is worth struggling to achieve, don't you think?"

25

Thieves

"Those *nouveau-mariés*…I don't believe them," Monsieur M said to the others as they moored the motorboat at the dock in Les Eyzies at the end of the day. "They found something up there. 'Newlyweds?' *Merde!* They were not newlyweds. They had no rings! Have you ever heard of newlyweds without rings? They are the only people *certain* to have rings! They may have been looking for caves. If they found something, they would want to lie to us—*nouveau-mariés*—to keep it secret. But we will find it too."

He told them what to do, then went to the café to place a long-distance telephone call to Paris.

"Everything ready?" Monsieur M asked the next morning as they prepared to enter the boat.

"Yes."

"You have extra fuel and oil for the chainsaw?"

"Yes."

"And the water for the cooling jet?"

"Yes."

"It is all packed in the van inconspicuously?"

"Of course. Do you think we are fools?"

Yes, Monsieur M thought, I think you are fools, but I need you now.

"You drive the van and meet us at the rendezvous," Monsieur M said to one of the men. "We will take the boat."

They motored along the swelling waters of the Vézère to where they had docked the day before. The van was already there, off the road in the bushes, below the dark spot on the cliff face.

They covered the van with bushes as well as they could and started up the slope toward the dark spot. Monsieur M wanted to see for himself.

"What's this?" Monsieur M said as they came to the rockslide. He looked at the ground. It had been disturbed. That couple of "newlyweds" had been here, scuffing the earth.

"Move that bush aside," he told them.

"Now the rocks."

As they removed them, they easily recognized the cave entrance.

Monsieur M handed a flashlight to the smaller of the two men.

"Go in. Penetrate for a few minutes, then come back and report."

The man went in. He was back in only a few minutes.

"There are pictures."

Monsieur M tried to enter, but the opening was not large enough for his bulk. He swore as he stepped back from the opening.

"Enlarge it!"

The other men hefted rocks away until it was big enough for Monsieur M. The small man led the way. Monsieur M struggled on behind him, huffing and blowing as he contorted his large body to navigate the narrow passage.

When he stood up to see the colored paintings, his face broadened into a wide grin.

"Ah! Just what I want," Monsieur M said.

"Shall we cut it out?" the men said.

"No, we shall leave it there and stand in quiet contemplation of it for hours...you idiots! Of course you should cut it out! Why else have we come here? We have found it! Go get the tools! Do you want to get paid or don't you?"

The men left the cave, stumbled down the steep slope to their van, and returned to the cave, puffing and sweating, carrying the chainsaw and the other equipment.

"Get to work!"

The noise of the saw was deafening in the small, hard-surfaced space. As they cut around and behind the auroch painting, the water from the jet cooling the ferocious stone-cutting blade sprayed over them.

The man with the saw stopped and shut it off to take a rest and let the overheated blade cool.

"You remember the plan," Monsieur M reminded them, their ears ringing. "When we have cut the picture from the wall, we brace it with the wood strips, put it in the padded tarp, and carry it out *carefully*. We set the explosive charge and trigger it to seal the cave entrance."

What a waste, Monsieur M thought. All this cave art that could be sold...but to whom? No customers—except one—asked for cave art because it was impossible—well, nearly impossible— to find. It was illegal to obtain or to possess and, being illegal, it had no real market value because you could not sell it on any legitimate market in the world. No museum would touch it without *provenance*, without careful documentation of where it had been found, under what conditions, who had found it, and whether excavation and removal of the art had been legal. Only wealthy—*very* wealthy—clients requested it because they wanted it for status. They would only show it to people like themselves whom they wanted to impress with their status. People they could trust to keep the secret. They would say nothing about how or from whom they purchased the art, but it was important to them to know it was real. It must be authenticated by an expert. Monsieur M's client told him that would not be a problem.

This is a one-time sale, he thought. No more cave art after this. Though it will be very profitable, it is too dangerous. Yes, it is possible today because most of the police in France are in Paris or busy with other disruptions. But the wealthy who buy such things are also a danger: if something goes wrong, they would not help me, they would probably have me eliminated to cover their own part in the theft.

Deep within the cave, Gaston and Charity were working silently in the big chamber, documenting the artwork with notes and photographs. Suddenly Gaston's hand stopped writing. He raised his head, turned it, stood completely still, and held his breath. His eyes moved nervously as he listened.

What is that?" Gaston whispered. "I heard something. People!"

"Yes!"

"Mon dieu!"

Gaston put down his notebook and stepped slowly and silently through the large chamber to the tunnel which led to the cave entrance. He heard them talking. He crept back to Charity.

"Stay here. Do not make any noise. I will see what's happening."

He crawled quietly along the tunnel toward the cave entrance until he saw them: three men with some sort of equipment. They cannot be archeologists, he thought. They can only be art thieves.

Charity had the same thought. Oh god, she thought. She made her way silently toward the tunnel and Gaston.

The three men were standing together, talking, and pointing at the wall of the cave. The bull! They were looking at the painting of the auroch.

Two of the men opened a large bag and took something out. Gaston couldn't see what, the light was weak and the men were moving around, but when one of them jerked his arm backward, Gaston knew what it was.

A chainsaw!

Gaston lifted his camera to take a photo of the men. The chainsaw noise would cover the noise of the shutter. He was careful to move slowly so as to avoid flashing any reflection from the lens toward them. He took one photo, then another. He moved the advance lever for another exposure, but it moved too easily: the roll of film was finished.

Gaston let the camera fall to his chest on its strap and started to move toward the men. Charity grabbed his shoulder and pulled him back.

"Gaston, don't! They will kill you!" she said in a frantic whisper over the noise of the chainsaw.

"I must! They will destroy it!"

"It's not worth your life!"

She pulled him away from the men as hard as she could. He fell backward into her. They both lay still, hoping the men had not heard or seen anything.

"Gaston, they will kill you, and me too, and after they kill us they will leave us here and take the art away and cover the cave entrance and no one will ever find us! We cannot save the art. We will be lucky to escape alive. If we escape, we may be able to find them and punish them. If we die, we can do nothing."

Gaston's soul was on fire. His love of art, his sense of values, his professional ethics, his duty to civilization were all being destroyed by these thugs as surely as they destroyed a priceless historic art treasure. But Charity was right. Damage would be done, but he could not prevent it. He could only die, die a needless and useless death.

Yes, Charity was right. They can't take more than a small portion of the art today. If they only take some of the paintings, we can save the others and maybe bring the thieves to justice. We don't even know how many art treasures this site may contain. Perhaps we can save the rest.

"We must hide our equipment and ourselves in case they come farther in and find the large chamber."

Returning to the large chamber, Gaston used the wide brim of his leather hat to smooth the dirt of the cave floor and obliterate their footprints.

They helped one another put on their knapsacks. Charity led the way from the large chamber deeper into the cave as Gaston effaced their tracks. Any sound made from their movement was smothered by the terrible grinding and clatter of the stone-cutting chainsaw as the thieves carved the wonderful auroch from the rock wall, damaging the art to its left and right as they worked to cut behind it.

Their emotions were tortured for an hour by the horrid racket of the chainsaw as it gouged and broke the cave wall, destroying art that had been undisturbed from before the time of human civilization.

The noise stopped. Gaston could hear the men talking and grunting as they moved the heavy slab, then hammering, then the rasping sound of sliding a heavy object out of the cave.

The voices, the scuffling of feet and the dragging of their burden grew fainter, but then stayed at the same low level. They must be outside the cave.

Gaston could still hear them talk. They shouted. Arguing? One man was shouting at the others in anger. Eventually the voices faded.

Gaston waited silently without moving for five more minutes, then crept quietly back through the large chamber and along the tunnel toward the cave entrance. No sign of the men. When he reached the wall where the bull had been he saw the huge rough rectangular hole. He swore violently under his breath.

Outside, Monsieur M lifted his binoculars and scanned the river and the roads for movement. Nothing.

"Now!" Monsieur M said. The man with the detonator pressed the switch, a hurricane of dust and sound belched from the mouth of the cave, and tons of rock cascaded down on the cave entrance.

They descended the hillside to the van.

"Now we will get rid of the tools as I told you."

26

Trapped

Gaston was thrown back into the cave by the explosion. Within a minute Charity was there, cradling his head in her lap. He was gasping, his eyes wild. He could not hear her cries. She soothed his hair and forehead with her hand and touched his cheeks gently to comfort him.

"Gaston!"

He heard her now, faintly, her voice ringing like a thousand bells and making the blood in his head pound.

"Oui, oui," he whispered. *"Je t'entends..."*

Charity held him for many minutes. Slowly he became calm. He closed his eyes.

"Charity, I am here. I can hear you. Please give me time to recover."

Charity waited, his head in her lap. When Gaston opened his eyes again, he started to move. She helped him to sit up, propped against the cave wall.

"They have destroyed the cave entrance. We cannot get out," he said.

She went to the large chamber, brought her knapsack back to the tunnel, took out a bottle of water and helped him drink.

"We will see," she said.

After an hour, the ringing in Gaston's ears subsided.

"No need to whisper now," he said.

They made their way to the cave entrance, passing the wall where the auroch had been. The floor of the cave was a muddy mess from the water jet used to cool the stone-cutting saw. Gaston clenched his teeth and held his breath to keep from crying when he looked again at the desecration of the ancient art.

"I will find them! I will make them pay for this!"

They reached the entrance, now covered by a cascade of rock. No light penetrated from the outside.

"We are doomed!" he said.

They stood there in shock, their flashlight beams aimed at the tons of rock that sealed them in, looking for some sign of a way out.

Charity transferred her flashlight from her right hand to her left and moved her right hand slowly over the gaps between the rocks. After a minute she put her face close to a gap.

"Air is coming in."

They were silent.

"If air is coming in, air is going out," he said. "That is how we first discovered the cave! There must be another opening somewhere. But we don't know where, we don't know if it is accessible, or if we can escape through it."

"Our time is limited," Charity said. "We have little food and water, and the batteries in our lights will only last a few hours, if that."

"I have my *briquet,*" he said. He reached in his pocket, pulled out his cigarette lighter and thumbed the abrasion wheel. Sparks flew, but it did not ignite the wick. He sniffed the wick.

"No fuel!" he said. "It is dry."

They stood staring at the lighter, a symbol of their situation.

Charity reached up and unclipped her long brown hair, let it fall around her shoulders, plucked several of the fine strands, held them by one end and let them dangle. She pointed her flashlight at them. They moved gently toward the depths of the cave.

"There we go."

They put on their knapsacks and made their way purposefully

through the large chamber to clefts in the rock on the far side. As they walked, Gaston swept the beam of his flashlight across the frieze of paintings on the chamber walls. He sighed.

"I hope we will return."

Charity led the way. The climbing was difficult, but they soon realized that it was not as difficult as it could be: someone, ages ago, had moved some of the rocks aside. Someone had passed this way before.

They penetrated deeper into the rock labyrinth for a half hour. They followed a few dead ends, but the strands of hair soon showed them the right way to go.

Now when they held the strands of hair to see the wind, the current was more forceful. It indicated a narrow cleft in the rock. They looked at one another. Charity led on, squeezing through the cleft.

They came to a small chamber with low mounds on its floor.

"Are these burials?" she asked.

"They could be."

Gaston put a fresh roll of film in his camera, photographed the mounds, then carefully swept the accumulated dust from one end of the nearest mound. He revealed a mummified skull.

"Not human," he said. "It looks to be a small sheep—a mummy of a small sheep. The skull still has the skin on it, and the eyes in it, *dessiccée*."

They stood and thought for a minute.

Gaston moved the beam of his flashlight upward. They held the hairs to gauge the current. The air was moving upward.

"This is not a burial!" he said. "These sheep, or lambs, wandered in here, their eyes were not accustomed to the darkness, they missed their footing, fell and could not climb back up. They starved here. If they entered here, there must be a gap!"

"If it's still there," she said. "If it has not been covered by another rockslide since the sheep came in. And it may only be big enough for a sheep—or a lamb."

They explored the roof of the cave with their lights and saw a narrow cleft high up.

"I cannot climb up there," Gaston said, "but perhaps you can if you stand on my shoulders."

From his shoulders, Charity was able to find handholds so she could hold on while he took her feet in his hands and push her up farther. Struggling to get her arms in a secure hold on the rock, the sharp edges cut her hands and forearms. With all her strength she lifted herself into the cleft.

"I can feel the air flowing!"

She shone her light upward, then switched it off. Only darkness.

"I don't see light, but there are gaps in the rock. I think you're right about the sheep."

She thought for a moment.

"We don't know how far it is to the outside. I must keep talking as I go. I'll tell you what I find."

Squeezing sideways through the cleft, she made her way along the narrow, irregular passages, sometimes horizontally, sometimes moving upward. She didn't notice the time passing as she struggled through the irregular openings.

She plucked more strands of hair from her head to monitor the passage of air, but dropped them when she realized that if she licked her lips and spread saliva on her cheeks, she could feel the air current easily.

She shouted the news to Gaston, but received no answer.

Gaston could no longer hear Charity's shouts. They had no communication.

Either she has found a way out, or she has suffered an accident and cannot move, he thought.

I will stay here, where we parted, for one more hour, then I will return to the large chamber and to the tunnel through which we entered. I will go back and forth between these two points until something happens. Or until I cannot move any more.

He waited in the chilling silence of the rock.

After an hour had passed, he made his way back to the large chamber.

I will shine my light on the art once more, then I will make my way in the dark if I can, to save battery power.

He drank from a water bottle as he slowly moved the light

beam along the wall of the large chamber.

If I am to die now, here, it will be the best place for me to die. I will become part of the history of this cave and of this art.

He thought about his life: his childhood, the years at the university, the work in Arizona and New Mexico. He thought about his fiancée Yveline and the grand house in Versailles that he might never step inside again.

He thought of Charity. How fortunate I was to have her as a student! As her teacher, I did not realize who she was. I knew she was intelligent but I thought of her as just a student. She is mature beyond her years, much tougher, stronger and more courageous than the quiet student I knew in the classroom. If I am rescued from this cave, I will owe her my life.

He sat and wrote a short farewell message, folded the paper, and put it in his jacket pocket.

He smiled to himself. They may discover me in a few days, weeks or months, or they may not discover me for centuries.

I will be part of archeology. It is a sad ending, but not a bitter one. An appropriate one.

PART FOUR

Late May

27

Daylight

Gaston hasn't answered me, Charity thought as she continued her struggle through the narrow, rough stone passages in the cave. He must not hear me.

She pushed on faster, almost frantically.

She switched off her flashlight periodically to see if any light penetrated.

This time, she saw it.

The light was faint. She stayed motionless for thirty seconds, flashlight off, eyes closed, to let her pupils dilate. She opened them. Yes! Light! Dimly, without her flashlight, she could see the jagged rocks ahead of her.

She climbed upward, switching off her light often. She could feel the air current distinctly on her cheek. The penetrating daylight grew stronger.

Squeezing around a turn in the passage, she saw daylight winking through broken rock. The mouth of the tunnel was only three feet high, and narrow, and blocked by rock and debris, but she saw the light surely.

She pushed on the rocks at the entrance one by one. They were heavy, too heavy for her to move. Gaston could have moved them, but Gaston could not come. The passages through which she had scrambled were almost too narrow even for her, really just wide enough for a lamb.

One rock moved slightly when she pushed it with her foot. Wriggling into position so that her feet were toward the rubble and her back was against the rock wall, she kicked the loose rock hard with both feet. It tumbled outward, and the rocks above it fell into the gap.

She kicked at the fallen rocks. They were loose now.

The sharp limestone edges cut her shoes and bruised her ankles and calves, but she continued to kick.

She stopped for a moment to catch her breath, sweat covering her face. Wriggling around, she went back to pushing rocks with her hands to find a loose one. She found one, turned again and kicked.

The rock wall crumbled. Daylight flooded in. The rough opening through the pile of stones was much less than a meter square, but by studying the surrounding rocks she decided which ones she should try to push out.

I'm no engineer, she thought. I hope I do this right!

In ten minutes she had opened a hole just large enough to squeeze through.

Careful, she thought. If I dislodge one rock I could be crushed and buried in another rock slide. Whether I died quickly or slowly, no one would know to save Gaston.

As Charity wriggled through the tiny opening at the upper mouth of the cave, the sharp rocks ripped her clothes and drew blood from her skin, but the wounds were not deep. When finally she tumbled to the ground on the far side of the rocks, she was in shade, surrounded by low bushes. She pushed them aside, stood, and made her way toward the brightest light.

High at the top of the cliff, she saw the river and road below.

How to get down there?

If sheep got up here, there must be a way to reach a village, she thought. Well, maybe. If the sheep fell in the cave hundreds —or thousands—of years ago, things might be different now.

With the cliff and river in front of her, she could go left or right. Les Eyzies was to the left. So was the car, far below at the base of the cliff. She went left.

She pushed through the low bushes and scrub. Her thick blue

jeans protected her legs but her shoes had been badly cut apart from kicking the rocks. The ground was scattered with sharp stones, the bushes with thorns. She saw red stains appearing on her white socks.

Making her way along the top of the ridge, she had the advantage of seeing for a long distance, but she saw no sign of civilization. This is Périgord, she thought, not the Sahara. There are villages every few kilometers. I will find one soon.

She picked up two sticks and used them to take some weight off her feet.

After walking for an hour she had made little progress, and was feeling acutely the exhaustion, physical and emotional, from the day, but she did not slow down. When she felt tired, she pushed herself to even greater exertion. I can save Gaston, she thought. I can save the archeological site. I can bring the thieves to justice.

She reached a downward slope. At its foot she could see lines of trees winding through a valley. Streams are in valleys. The trees, the deep verdure, must be along a stream. Along a stream there may be a road.

As she approached the valley, she saw movement. Cattle! A herd was headed back to the farm.

She pushed ahead faster. When she reached the road she followed the cattle and shouted to the herder.

He stared at her in astonishment: a young woman with a sweaty, dirty face, torn clothing, arms soiled by dried blood, feet in ragged shoes dotted with red stains. She was gasping and saying something about life and death.

Charity took a deep breath, exhaled loudly, and spoke evenly.

"I was trapped in a cave. My...friend is still in there. He can't get out. We must get help to save him."

"We must notify the gendarmes!" the herder said. "Five hundred meters ahead is my farm. We do not have a telephone, but there is one at the village two kilometers farther along. I will drive you there on my tractor."

He looked at her, put his huge meaty hands on her slender waist, lifted her like a newborn lamb and set her astride one of the cattle. Clucking and shouting and beating the lead cow, he hastened the herd toward the farmhouse.

It was nearly midnight before the gendarmes could assemble a rescue team and the necessary equipment. Her feet bandaged, with a gendarme to support her, Charity took the lead as they climbed the cliff to the rock-covered cave entrance.

When they arrived at the blocked cave entrance, Charity cried out in dismay. The thieves' explosion had loosened rock all the way up the cliff face to the top.

Captain Gagnier of the gendarmes approached Charity.

"This will take time, Mademoiselle Cabot. We must remove tons of rock and build support structures to prevent more rockslides. We will start at once, but we will also have to bring up more equipment. It will take some time."

The captain sent a gendarme to recruit volunteers from Les Eyzies. Gendarmes closed the valley road and cleared the slope below so that the debris could be rolled down without harm.

They began the heavy work of removing rock and shoring up the rock above with timbers.

The early May dawn was breaking by the time the support structures were strong enough to protect against further rock slides. The hole through the rocks grew slowly as the men worked on it. They removed enough rock to see through to the cave entrance.

Finally, the hole was just large enough for a slender person to pass through.

"I will go in now," Charity said, and thrust her head and shoulders into the hole.

"It is too dangerous!" Captain Gagnier said, but Charity was already wriggling through.

The captain ordered the men to stop work.

"We cannot take the chance of another slide. Wait until she returns."

Charity made her way to the large chamber. Hers was the only light. Wildly she swung the beam around the chamber, and soon saw Gaston lying on the ground beneath the wall paintings, his head resting on his knapsack, his arms folded on his chest.

Charity felt a shiver go through her body. *Oh god, he looks dead, like a corpse in a casket!*

"Gaston?" she said gently. She walked to him.

Startled, he jerked awake.

"It's me, Charity."

"Grace a dieu!"

"Gaston, we're safe!"

He stood up unsteadily, groped for her, wrapped his arms around her, and they burst into tears.

"Time for that later," Charity said after a poignant moment. "Let's get out of here!"

The sun was high by the time the cave entrance had been enlarged enough for Gaston to emerge safely. At the bottom of the cliff, Gaston and Charity gave a brief report to Captain Gagnier.

"You will come to our headquarters later today after you have rested and we will complete a full report," Gagnier told them. "We must not waste any time! The thieves must be found."

The late morning sun was streaming in the windows when they returned to Gaston's cottage.

He built a small fire of kerosene-soaked wood chips in the water heater and added some larger sticks.

"The water will be hot in about 30 minutes," he said.

He went to the kitchen and returned to the terrace with bread, cheese and fruit. They sat and ate.

He brought a bottle of water and filled two glasses. They ate and drank in silence.

"You may shower now," he told her.

When she emerged from the shower, she put on his bathrobe. It hung on her like a tent. She wrapped it around her slender body almost twice, cinched the belt tight, and padded into the salon where he was standing.

"I will set my alarm clock for three hours," Gaston said. "After we have gone to the gendarmes and made the full report, we can truly recover."

He looked into her eyes, but did not move.

She leaned forward and kissed him on the lips, a long kiss full of relief, sincerity and meaning.

"*Nouveaux mariés,*" she said with a wry smile.

He turned and went into his bedroom. Charity followed and lay down on the bed beside him.

They fell asleep within minutes.

28

Suspect

Gaston and Charity sat in Captain Gagnier's office. The captain was behind his desk. Two lieutenants stood to the side. A clerk with a typewriter clacked out a transcript of the meeting.

"You say that you are *Maître de Conférences* Gaston Lagarde of the University of Paris," Gagnier read, glancing at a sheet of notes he held in his hand. "You are an archeologist. This young lady is Mademoiselle Charity Cabot, a citizen of the USA, a student at the university for this year, and a former student in one of your classes. You own a cottage near Sarlat."

The captain slowly put the sheet of paper down on his desk.

"If you are a *maître de conférences* at the Sorbonne, and mademoiselle is a student, what are you doing in Sarlat now?"

"The university is closed, as you must have heard."

"So? Shouldn't you stay in Paris? Will it not open again soon?"

"I do not think so. No one can know. The demonstrations and disturbances in Paris are extraordinary. I did not think they would stop for a week or more."

"So you came to your cottage with one of your students…"

"I decided to leave Paris. I encountered Mademoiselle Cabot at the Gare d'Austerlitz. She had been wounded in a confrontation between police and workers. She asked my help to leave Paris. She had no destination in mind—she was just looking for a safer place—and she decided to come to Sarlat."

The captain was quiet for a moment, looking at them.

"What were you doing in the cave with the prehistoric art? This is not a cave that has been registered with the government as containing archeological features of value."

Gaston told him of his interest in finding new caves with evidence of prehistoric life.

"Mademoiselle mentioned to us that you discovered the cave not yesterday, when you became trapped in it, but the day before. Why did you not report it to the museum in Les Eyzies on the day of discovery as required by law?"

Gaston was silent for a moment.

"We wanted to do a preliminary documentation of the cave's value before reporting it—so that the authorities would realize its great importance," Charity said.

"Mademoiselle, please allow Monsieur Lagarde to answer questions directed to him."

"*Pardon,*" Charity said.

"*Monsieur le capitaine,* it was a mistake for me not to report the discovery on the day it was made…"

"It was!" Gagnier barked. "If you had reported it, the cave could have been secured! It would not have been despoiled! You would not have been trapped! Mademoiselle Cabot would not have suffered the grievous injuries that she has!"

"But it was late in the day, *mon capitaine.* The museum was closed. If we had gone to report it…imagine: we contact the museum director, or you, late in the day, and we say that we, a young *professeur* who claims to be from the Sorbonne, and one of his students—a foreign student—have discovered a marvelous prehistoric cave, one to rival Lascaux. Without knowing who we are, without any documentation, without some evidence of the cave's value, would the museum director have believed us? Would you have believed us, modified the deployment of your officers and posted guards to a remote cliff, in the middle of the night, to protect it?"

"Of course we would have posted guards!"

"With all of the gendarmes summoned from the provinces to Paris and to other cities to cope with the disturbances all over France, do you have a force of sufficient size to be able freely to reassign at least two men and post them high on a steep cliff, for the entire night, to protect a hole in the rock which a young *professeur* and an American student had discovered and had told you contained prehistoric art of value, having shown you no evidence?"

The captain was silent. He looked at the notes in his hand again.

"What is done is done. Let us get on with the report. You returned to the cave the following day—yesterday. You entered and began to document the site taking notes and measurements, and taking photographs. Do you have these records?"

"Our notes and measurements are at my cottage, as are the rolls of film. Ah! I was able to take two exposures of the thieves! I cannot tell if the exposures are good enough to provide evidence, but they should be examined as soon as possible."

"What sort of film did you use?"

"Ektachrome."

"Then it can be developed here in our laboratory at once. This officer," the captain indicated one of the lieutenants standing to the side, "will drive you to your cottage so you can surrender the film, along with your notes and measurements."

Gagnier got up from his desk. Gaston stood, Charity also.

"We will continue the report after the photographs have been developed and examined, probably tomorrow morning. I would like you to come to my office again before noon."

As Gaston, Charity and the lieutenant prepared to leave Gagnier's office, the captain stood and looked at Gaston.

"*Monsieur*, please do not leave this *département*, Périgord, until I have given you permission to do so. I make this a legal requirement."

The sun was low in the sky as Gaston and Charity brought food and a bottle of wine out to the terrace. They slumped into their chairs heavily and sighed at the same time. They began to eat, in silence, their minds so dizzy with the events of the last two days they didn't know what to say.

"Look," Charity said. "The valley is beautiful, the sun is warm, we're both safe, we have food and wine, and we can sleep as long as we like tomorrow—or at least until we have to go see the captain again."

She looked at him directly.

"Think of the possible alternatives. We should be ecstatic," she said in an even, no-nonsense tone.

Gaston looked at her without expression, then refilled their glasses of wine, handed her glass to her and picked up his own. Looking her straight in the eyes, he smiled and raised his glass. They clinked.

He leaned his head back and drained his glass in one long pull. Charity watched him, then took what was for her two rather large sips and set her glass down.

They got up from the table, went to the bedroom and closed the door.

Cloudy morning. The sun did not wake them.

"We've got to get up or I will be late going to headquarters," Gaston said after he rolled over and looked at his watch.

Charity sighed and wrapped herself around him under the covers, holding him so close, so tight.

They stayed that way.

"I'm not sure it matters to me at all," she said.

"I fear that it does matter," he said. "You see, I am a suspect in the theft."

Charity shot upright.

"WHAT?"

"You can understand the captain's logic," he said. "You and I discovered the cave. We were the only ones who knew of its existence. We also knew its value. We did not report it to the authorities as required by law. Someone steals a priceless work and damages others. You escape, and bring help to save me."

"You mean…"

"It is possible for Gagnier to believe that the whole incident was planned. A stage play. If the authorities did not find us and rescue me from the cave, our colleagues in theft could return and save us."

"Or perhaps…" he went on, "perhaps they believe that I was one of the thieves, and you were an innocent pawn in a complicated chess game—an innocent girl to make the play appear more credible. What if I knew there was another way out of the cave, and that you, being small and slender, could get out? What if I planned the whole sequence of events to fool you, and to make the police believe that I had nothing to do with the theft?"

"But you DIDN'T!" Charity shouted at him, close to tears. "You couldn't! That's absurd!"

She fell on him weeping, her body heaving with sobs. Her heart was already near the breaking point with all of the emotion of the past few days—and weeks! And last night!

Ecstasy or agony, she was not sure she could take any more of either.

He wrapped his arms around her and held her tight to comfort her.

"Charity, of course I had nothing to do with this, except the discovery—with you! You were actually the one who found the cave! I am just trying to understand how the captain thinks, so I can know how best to help this investigation. It is his job to be suspicious, to examine all possibilities. Right now, we are the only people that he is certain were involved in these events. Thus, we are automatically suspects until he discovers evidence that leads to others, to the real thieves."

29

Happiness

"We have examined the photographs," Captain Gagnier told Gaston. They were sitting together in the captain's office.

Gagnier took large color photo prints from a folder and handed them to Gaston.

"Ah! These developed much better than I had anticipated!"

"They clearly show the value of the art," Gagnier said.

"But...I don't find the two exposures of the thieves."

"All of your photographs are now in the possession of the gendarmerie as evidence in this case. Prints may be returned to you at the conclusion of the case at the discretion of the investigating authorities, but the original negatives will not be. They are now the property of the state. The negatives have been sent to Paris for further examination, investigation and safekeeping."

Gagnier held out his hand in a gesture indicating that Gaston was to return the photographs to him. Gaston did.

"I am not required to show you any of the photographs seized as evidence. I have shown you the photographs of the art as a gesture of goodwill. I have decided that if I showed you the photographs of the person or persons you have term 'the thieves' at this time, it might adversely affect the investigation."

"But...I might be able to help you! I might recognize the thieves!"

"How might you recognize the thieves?" the captain asked, looking at Gaston intently.

"I…I don't know. I do know that if I cannot see the photo, I cannot help you."

"I appreciate your concern, *monsieur.* We will decide if you will be allowed to view the two photographs at a later time."

Gagnier went to the door of his office, signalled to a staff member, the clerk came into the office and seated herself at the typewriter.

"Now, let us continue with the report."

Charity heard the MG drive up to the cottage. The engine noise stopped. She ran out to the terrace as Gaston was getting out of the car. He approached her and enfolded her in a fervent embrace. They kissed, deeply, for a long time.

Gaston collapsed into one of the chairs on the terrace.

"I am emotionally exhausted!"

Charity fixed him with a steady gaze. He turned and looked at her.

"Oh, Charity!" he said, rising from his chair to embrace her again. "I can't imagine what you have been through! You are the true hero of this adventure! I must not complain about my adversity. You saved my life! *Mon dieu!* You saved my life!"

He held her in his arms a long time, silently. Tears came to her eyes. She held her breath, trying not to sob.

"You've been gone for hours. You've missed your *déjeuner.* You must be hungry," she said after several deep breaths, and went to the kitchen. She returned with a carefully-prepared plate of whatever was in the kitchen fruit bowl and the propane-fuelled refrigerator. The stale bread was toasted and buttered.

"I think we need this," she said as she started to pour wine into his glass, the bottle in her right hand. "It is from Château Tirecul La Gravière near Bergerac. Semillon and Muscadelle grapes planted on north-facing slopes—mostly Semillon, but with some Muscadelle to give it sweetness and the scent of flowers. It is *not challenging* to the palate. I think you will enjoy it."

He burst out laughing. She couldn't contain herself and laughed along, jerking the wine bottle back and forth and sloshing wine on the table. Calming, steadying her right hand with her left, she filled the glasses right to the brim. Ignoring the mess, they lifted their glasses, clinked and gazed into each other eyes. He made the gesture of putting his glass down hard and racing for the bedroom, and she exploded in laughter again, spilling more wine.

"No! Later!" she said, barely in control of her laughter and her tears.

With a sigh, Gaston collapsed into his chair. They ate and drank.

Soon the food was gone. She poured the last of the wine— very little, as most had been spilled. They looked at one another, drained the little bit in their glasses, set them on the table, and looked intently at one another again.

"Now!" she shouted, and raced for the bedroom.

He was so close behind her that he fell on top of her on the bed.

They slept right through the night, exhausted by the love-making that banished, if only temporarily, their current adversity.

The early sun woke them, coming through the bedroom door and into Charity's eyes. She sat up in bed and turned her face toward where he lay beside her. The golden rays felt warm and gentle on her cheek. She gazed at Gaston, her lover. Her first real lover. I'm in a dream, she thought. My fantasies never come true. Why has this one come true? Should I trust it?

She was immediately angry with herself. Don't you deserve happiness? Lots of people experience ecstasy, why not you? You deserve it as much as anyone else. You've never experienced agony and ecstasy like this in your little protected life. This is *really living!* Take it for the miracle it is!

She thought about Paris, about the apartment, her roommates. Oh, that was *so* far away! A thousand years away. She pictured herself and Josie and Amaleen sitting at the Café Aux Tours de Notre-Dame talking about how their lives had changed during their year abroad. That was nothing!

He stirred.

"Bonjour, monsieur le professeur" she said. *"Bon matin!"*

He opened his eyes sleepily, and when he saw her, he smiled and wrapped his arms around her.

She kissed him, wriggled free of his arms and scrambled out of bed.

"Today we are going to have fun, nothing but fun! We are going to eat, and drink, and hike, and talk, and make love, and eat and drink again, and…well, we are going to act like… *nouveaux mariés!*" she laughed.

She went to the bathroom to wash, then to the kitchen to make coffee.

She turned on the transistor radio in the kitchen.

"Students have seized and occupied the *Théâtre nationale* and declared it to be the *parlement* for mass debate," the reporter intoned. "The sit-down strike at the Sud Aviation plant in Nantes continues, with the officers of management locked in their offices. The Renault factory outside Rouen has declared a strike. Other Renault factories at Flins and Boulogne-Billancourt may follow."

Charity smiled and felt her heart beat faster. No going back to Paris and returning to the life of a simple student for awhile, that's certain.

30

Yveline

Gaston and Charity sat in the warm sun, lingering over brunch with a second cup of coffee. Other than the music of the birds and the occasional breath of wind, it was quiet.

They heard a car climbing the unpaved road to the cottage. A large, late-model black Peugeot sedan appeared at the top of the road and stopped next to Gaston's MG.

A tall, blonde woman in a fashionable dress emerged from the Peugeot smiling.

"Ah, Gaston! I thought I might find you here."

"Yveline!"

Charity's heart sank.

"Yveline! What are…why…?"

Yveline approached Gaston and embraced him, kissing him on both cheeks.

His arms stayed at his sides.

"And you must be…the American student?"

"Charity Cabot," Charity said, stepping toward Yveline and extending her hand boldly. No kiss on both cheeks.

Yveline ignored Charity's hand.

"Yes, I have heard about you. I trust you two are enjoying the cottage? It is so lovely at this time of the year—the spring!"

Gaston's face was red. He frowned.

Glancing at Charity with distaste, Yveline took Gaston's arm and led him toward the cottage door.

"Let's go inside and talk," she said, looking at him and ignoring Charity.

"I was just going for a walk," Charity said. "I'll let you two catch up."

She walked down the road away from the cottage, her heart pounding.

Gaston and Yveline took seats in the salon. Gaston did not offer Yveline anything to eat or drink.

"Why did you come?" he asked.

"To tell you the...*conversations* between our attorneys have concluded. I have decided that I will cede all of the contested points in the *testament* so long as I can live in my father's house in Versailles. I'm sure you recognize that the only reason my step-father left the house to you is that he expected us to be married and to live there. He saw no reason to deed it to both of us because deeding it to you would be the same as deeding it to both of us when we are husband and wife. So all I am asking is that his wish be honored—that we both have the legal right to live in the house. I am not asking for legal ownership, just for a guaranteed life tenancy—that I may reside there so long as I live. When I die, the house reverts to you and/or our heirs."

"*Our* heirs?"

"Of course! We are engaged to be married. Don't you remember?" she smiled. "You proposed! We have a legal agreement to be married, you may recall."

Yveline shifted in her chair, getting comfortable.

"Your little fling with a student does not bother me...well, not much. She is so...*plain.*"

Yveline grimaced.

"You and I have not been close since the legal disagreements began. I understand. It has been difficult for both of us. And a man has his appetites! You have only done what many men...and certainly professors...do. Professors—surrounded by luscious, budding womanhood—although I must admit I think you could have made a better choice than that naive, skinny little American girl."

She curled her lip, but then brightened and smiled at him.

"I am willing to overlook such small matters. We will be happy together when we are properly married."

Gaston stared at her. He said nothing. She stared back, but shifted her gaze before he did.

"Well...I suppose that's all I have to tell you," she said, rising from her chair. "We can talk about the details with the attorneys when we're both in Versailles."

She walked to the door.

"I wouldn't want to interrupt your little...*adventure*. Miss...what was her name?...will be returning to America soon I suppose. Just as well."

Gaston stood and followed her out to her car. She got in and drove down the road.

He made no sign of farewell.

Walking along the road, Charity heard a car approaching behind her. She stepped out of the road to let the black Peugeot pass. Yveline smiled and wiggled her fingers at her in sardonic greeting through the windshield. After she passed, Yveline stepped on the gas. The wheels spun gravel behind them, covering Charity in dust and grit.

Charity walked quickly back to the cottage. When she entered, Gaston was seated in the salon with a grim look on his face. She kneeled next to his chair and took his hand. He squeezed her hand firmly, looked at her and smiled.

"You bring me joy," he said.

They decided to go to a restaurant for dinner, one of Gaston's favorites, to be among other people so the memory of the day would have more difficulty haunting them.

Gaston suggested *terrine de fois gras de canard* for the first course.

"Duck liver pâté..." Charity mused. "Then I'd like something lighter for my main course."

He suggested the scallops with leeks for her, and a glass of white wine. He ordered his favorite grilled *filet de boeuf*, and a glass of red.

Charity held up her glass.

"Together!" she said, smiling at him.

"Together! Yes! We are together, and that is what matters."

As Charity sipped her wine, she wondered…how long would they be together?

"We can talk about Yveline if you like," she said as they waited for their first course to arrive. "You don't have to bear the burden alone. I'm a good listener."

"I don't want to put any burden on you, *cher Charité*—you are well-named, do you realize that? *Charité* indeed! It is my burden, I will carry it to its destination, and then I will put it down and be free of it. But you deserve an explanation, at least."

He took a sip of wine. The waiter approached with their *fois gras*. They were silent until he had served the plates and gone away.

"Yveline is no longer my fiancée in my heart. It is finished! She has changed, changed into a person I do not recognize or understand. I do not know why this change has occurred, but for me it is now definitive. However, we still have certain legal agreements that we signed in anticipation of our marriage. As I have told you, she has sought to modify—manipulate!—the matters between us to her great advantage. She continues in this behavior."

Charity was silent, listening intently, looking at him between bites of *fois gras* and sips of wine.

"There is a substantial amount of wealth involved, the property and bequests of my late uncle, Yveline's step-father. In principle, I do not care about such things. They are not the reward for my own labor and effort, so I have no moral right to them. It is as though they have dropped as a gift from heaven."

Gaston took a bite of *fois gras* and savored it.

"In spirit, I could give everything to Yveline," he continued, "but two things keep me from such an act. The first is my uncle's wishes. I believe we have a moral obligation to carry out his wishes. He created this wealth, he should be able to direct its use. Second is that I am not an idealist who believes money is not important. Camus has said there is 'spiritual snobbism' in believing that money is not necessary. Poverty is servitude. To have money is to have time, to be free to live as one thinks best—

not to be tied to a university salary, to be able to pursue archeology as I wish, to be free to make changes in my life, and…well, to pursue happiness."

They ate in silence for several minutes, finishing the first course.

The waiter came and removed their plates.

"So I want a proper conclusion to these legal matters. I want Yveline to receive her fair share, and me my fair share, however we can agree on the details. I also want an end to our engagement. In fact, I'm not sure I ever want to see her again."

"Then you know what you want," Charity said. "This is important."

"Yes! Exactly! I see it clearly now. I have my goal. I will work to achieve it."

Their main course dishes arrived, along with full glasses of wine.

"Now we will talk of other things," Gaston said. "Of the beautiful Paleolithic art we have discovered. Of the lives of the people who made it and lived it thousands of years ago. Of the beauty of spring in Périgord."

He raised his glass.

"To the noble ducks and geese of Périgord who have sacrificed themselves for our happiness!"

They laughed and their hands wobbled from the laughing as they touched glasses and sipped.

After making love that night, they slept long and soundly until the sun streamed into the bedroom around seven o'clock the next morning. Charity arose, washed, and before making coffee, switched on the transistor radio in the kitchen. The announcer recited a long list of factories that had been occupied or closed, and the news that hundreds of thousands of workers were now on strike all over France.

Charity smiled to herself. Many more days together in Périgord.

31

Emmanuel's Boat

Gaston drove into Sarlat to check with Captain Gagnier about progress on the criminal investigation. When he returned to the cottage, he said "The captain requested that you come with me to headquarters for a short meeting."

They drove to headquarters. They entered Captain Gagnier's office. He did not ask them to sit.

"This will not take long," the captain told them, sliding two photographs out of a folder. "Here are Monsieur Lagarde's photographs of the alleged antiquity thieves. I have received permission to show them to you."

Gaston and Charity looked at the photos. The thieves' flashlights were pointed at the wall they were working on—destroying! There was very little light on the men themselves, but the fast film had at least picked up grainy images of their faces and clothing from the light reflected from the wall.

"Our laboratory has attempted to improve the recognition of the faces," the captain said, handing them several more photos, close-ups of the faces with slightly better resolution.

Gaston and Charity looked at one another.

"I do not recognize any of these people," Gaston said.

"I don't either," Charity said.

The clerk began to type and soon had produced two sheets of paper which she handed to the captain.

"Would you please sign these statements to the effect that you do not recognize any of the persons shown in these photos?"

They signed.

"You may go."

"So. Three men," Charity said in the car returning to the cottage.

"Yes, and most probably not local men. I assume that the captain has shown the photos to others in the town and the area and received a negative response. They could be from anywhere in France—anywhere in the world!"

"Because we did not recognize them, this should help convince the gendarmes that you had nothing to do with it."

"Not at all, dear Charity. I could have been lying. After he handed me the photographs, Gagnier was watching my face intently to see if I displayed emotion. As for the statements we signed, these can be used against us under a charge of perjury if the gendarmes prove that we did know these men."

They sat pondering the seriousness of the situation.

At the same moment they exclaimed "the *boat!*"

"It *must* have been those three men in that boat!" she said.

"We thought we had fooled them, but we failed. They must have climbed up the cliff and found the cave. The next day they brought their tools and cut out the auroch painting."

"Do you think they knew we were in the cave?"

"I do not know…but it does not matter! It would be better for them if we had died in the cave! We were the only others who knew of the cave's existence!"

"We must find out more!"

Charity's mind raced. Gaston was under great pressure from all sides except one: her. She must do something to dispel the clouds that darkened his mood and his future. She could do nothing about Yveline, but she might be able to do something about the police investigation.

"Would you drive me into Les Eyzies this afternoon?" she asked.

"Certainly. I'll go to Sarlat for supplies also. But…you want to go to Les Eyzies alone?"

"It's a surprise."

A little smile moved his lips.

"Certainly. I would like a surprise! A good one for a change."

Charity dressed as Americanly as possible: blue jeans, sandals, T-shirt, hippy-style bead necklace. Her hair in a pony tail, she packed clothing in a backpack to fill it out, stowed the pack in the MG and they drove into Les Eyzies.

"Pick me up in two hours," she told him.

Walking in the village she found a shop that had a small rack of tattered travel guidebooks. She bought one that was in English, took it to a café, sat and ordered a Coca-Cola, and took little sips every now and then, making it last. Every few minutes she turned a page of the guidebook, but she limited her movements to a minimum.

She was not reading, she was waiting and listening. After a half-hour, everyone in the café had long since forgotten her presence. She was just some little American tourist trying to figure out what to do, where to go.

She took out a pocket notebook and, appearing to consult the guidebook frequently, began to take notes.

The hours passed. Her Coke was only half gone, and warm now. She looked at her watch, closed her guidebook and notebook, put them in the backpack, paid for the drink and walked out to meet Gaston at the Musée National de Préhistoire.

Driving back to the cottage, Charity said "I have news."

She took out her notebook and read her notes.

"The Périgord accent is a little funny, but here's what I overheard in the café: three men arrived in town last week and asked about renting a *gabarre,* which I guess is a boat?"

"Yes, yes, it is the traditional workman's boat on the river here."

"Well, according to what I heard, these men were willing to pay 'a good price.' They said they would need it for 'several days of geological surveying' on the river. They didn't know exactly how long. They paid by the day. The boat they rented is owned by a man named Emmanuel. They didn't return it to him. They just let it float down the river."

"Did they find the boat?"

"I did not hear."

"Charity, you amaze me!"

"No one pays any attention to a little wide-eyed American tourist girl," she smiled.

Gaston stopped the car, turned around, and started back toward Les Eyzies.

"We will find Emmanuel."

"Espèce de gros cons!" Emmanuel swore when Gaston asked him about the men. "Those bastards! They did a lot of damage to my gabarre, they didn't pay for the last day, and then they just let it float down the river! My friend Hyppolite, a boatman in Le Bugue, saw it floating along and grabbed it for me."

"Puh!" he spat.

"I'm glad I made them pay at the end of each day, but on the last day they just let it drift, out of gas, all the way to Le Bugue! And they just disappeared. *Connerie!"*

"Do you know their names, or where they came from?"

"They said they were government men, doing some sort of geological survey. I don't need their names, only their money. Those bastards have plenty of it. I charged them a fat price because of their Paris accents. I s'pose I did all right, except for the last day, the trouble of getting the boat back, and the gas."

"Well," Charity said as they drove to the gendarmerie headquarters, "that makes it easy! We only have to find three guys in a city of eight million."

"Not eight million," Gaston said. "Very few people in Paris are interested in prehistoric art, and even fewer are going to come here searching for caves, and even fewer are thieves. We must look for those few people—and I know who they are, or at least some of them."

Gaston made a quick report to Captain Gagnier, who said he would communicate this news to headquarters in Paris.

"We will also interview Monsieur Emmanuel ourselves," the captain added.

32

Arrest

Gaston and Charity were sitting on the cottage terrace in the May sun. They had finished their breakfast.

This is our honeymoon, Charity thought. I couldn't be happier except if we were really married.

Noise of a vehicle climbing the hill to the cottage. A dark blue gendarmerie van pulled up in front of the cottage and stopped. Three gendarmes got out.

"Ah, news of the investigation," Gaston said. "But why three of them?"

The three gendarmes approached them. They were not smiling.

"Gaston Lagarde?" the officer said.

"Yes?"

"You are under arrest for destruction of antiquities and theft of antiquities. You will come with us. You need bring nothing with you except means of identification."

"*What?* What are you saying? This is a mistake! I am the one who discovered the theft!" Gaston said, rising from his chair.

Charity leapt to her feet and stood between Gaston and the officers. One of the officers stepped up to her, took her by the arms and pulled her aside.

"Lagarde, come with me. You will talk to the captain who will pronounce the charges officially. After you have been charged, you will be allowed to make one telephone call. You will be held in Sarlat until word comes from headquarters in Paris as to the next steps."

As the officers strode toward him, Gaston stepped back, but caught himself. I am innocent, he thought. They can have no evidence for this charge. I will show them how wrong they are.

The officer led Gaston to the gendarmerie van, opened the door, looked at Gaston and tilted his head to signal "Get in."

The other officers sat next to Gaston on each side. The van drove away.

Charity ran into the cottage shrieking, rushing around the room, unable to comprehend what had just happened. She threw herself on the bed and sobbed, huge hungry gasps followed by wails of shock and pain.

Charity dragged herself out of bed, physically and emotionally drained, shuffled into the salon and collapsed on the couch. This is where it all started, on this couch, on that terrible night of rain and cold, when I was wounded and terrified and exhausted. He saved me and took care of me.

She stood and wandered in the salon.

This was our honeymoon! she thought again bitterly. Perfect, perfect happiness! How could this happen?

She leaned against the rough stone wall. Its sharp uneven surface dug into her shoulder. Her slender fingers went up and moved along the jagged rock, its stark coldness, hardness and sharp edges a symbol of what she felt in her heart.

She stood straight, lowered her hand and went to the window looking out across the terrace to the valley and the river.

I can't let it happen.

Strength. I need to be strong now. For Gaston. For us.

I will not let them take away my happiness, my future, my dream-come-true.

She went to the bathroom, washed her face, brushed her hair and made herself presentable. Taking the car keys from the table, she went out to the MG.

She got in the little sports car.

Uh-oh, standard shift. Do Cabots do standard shift? My father showed me once in a truck at the factory.

I see R, 1, 2, 3, 4 on the shift thing.

She looked down at the floor. The pedal on the left is the clutch. You gotta push that in, then do the shift thing, then take your foot off the clutch.

But first I have to start the motor.

She pushed the key into the slot and turned it. The car lurched.

Oops. Push in the clutch first, then start the motor.

She pressed her foot down on the clutch and turned the key. The engine started. After pushing the gearshift lever to '1' she slowly let out the clutch. The car bucked and lurched. The engine stopped.

Oops. Parking brake on.

She released it.

Try again.

This time she accelerated as she was letting out the clutch. The engine roared and the car surged forward, bucked back and forth several times, but kept going.

I can do this!

By the time she was half-way to Sarlat she had confidence and the car was going along smoothly, with only occasional jerks when she shifted.

She drove to the gendarmerie headquarters, parked the car and went in.

"I must see Captain Gagnier *now!*" she shouted at the duty officer.

"It is not possible," he told her. "He is in a conference."

Ignoring him, she pushed past his desk, charged down the hall to Gagnier's office and flung open the door. The duty officer came running after her.

Gagnier was sitting at his desk. Another man was seated across the desk from him. They looked at her in surprise.

"Captain, I must speak with you!" she said.

The duty officer caught her arms, but she struggled.

"It is all right, sergeant," Gagnier said.

The duty officer released her.

"Please excuse us for a moment," the captain said to the man seated before him.

The man rose and left. The duty officer stood by the door.

"You have made a big mistake! I…"

"Mademoiselle," he interrupted her, "we have important evidence indicating that Monsieur Lagarde took part in the destruction of, and theft of, the cave art."

"You can't have any such evidence! I was there in the cave with him! We saw the thieves enter with stone-cutting equipment! We saw and heard them cutting the stone!"

"The equipment you mention was found behind Monsieur Lagarde's cottage."

Charity's eyes widened, her mouth opened.

"What?"

"We received intelligence indicating the location of the stone-cutting equipment. Investigators found it behind the cottage."

"That's impossible! We were trapped inside the cave! We thought we were going to die there! We have no idea who the thieves were, where they went or what they did with that equipment!"

She was silent for only a moment.

"This is a frame-up!" she said in English.

"Pardon?"

"I don't know the word in French. What I mean is that someone put that equipment behind the cottage so that Monsieur Lagarde would be accused."

Her mind was racing.

"Look, *capitaine*, the thieves must have known that we had discovered the cave. After the robbery, they disposed of the equipment behind Gaston's—Monsieur Lagarde's—cottage so that *he* would be suspected of the theft. They must have believed that he would not be found, at least not alive. The investigation would not be pursued. The real thieves would never be found."

"This is a possibility, *mademoiselle*. There is also the possibility that Monsieur Lagarde arranged the entire scenario you have described, knowing there was another way out of the cave, or anticipating rescue. Perhaps the other thieves you speak of could have sent an anonymous message to us, or to someone else, with information about the cave and the person or persons trapped within. We would have responded with a rescue effort. He would emerge as innocent—how could he be guilty if he were trapped in the cave, likely to die, and the tools used in the theft were not in the cave? Thus he escapes suspicion, and we spend weeks and months, and millions of francs, searching for the 'real' thieves, when the actual leader of the theft is not a suspect."

Charity listened intently. She was quiet after the captain finished. Then she spoke in a serious, patient tone.

"Monsieur le capitaine," she said, placing her hands flat on his desk, leaning over and staring into his eyes, "I understand what you are saying. I understand the logic of your theory. I understand that you are responsible for finding the criminals. I understand that you must allow for all possibilities. I understand that you must report to your superiors in Paris. But I *know* that Monsieur Lagarde is not a criminal."

She leaned over the desk, her face close to his.

"Monsieur le capitaine, there are only two people in the world who know everything that went on in that cave. Monsieur Lagarde is one of them. I am the other. We have told you what happened. If you do not accept it, your investigation will fail to find those who are guilty. It will be a miscarriage of justice."

She stood up straight, turned, walked out of the office and out of the headquarters.

The duty officer looked at the captain.

"Paris wanted an arrest," Gagnier sighed. "With all the conflicts in France, and the criticism of law enforcement now, they wanted to give the press some good news, a law-enforcement success."

"Well, we have made an arrest," Gagnier said, standing up from his desk. "The young *Américaine* is passionate, but perhaps she is in love. What she says may be true, or not. We must discover the truth."

Driving back to the cottage, confused, fighting back her tears, Charity missed the turn for the cottage road and drove into Les Eyzies. By the time she realized her error, she was driving along the bank of the Vézère. On an impulse she swerved to the side of the road, stopped the car, switched off the motor, and sat staring straight ahead.

Her mind was in chaos.

She noticed a path running along the riverbank. She got out of the car and started to walk, looking at the river. She walked faster. She started to run. Her bone bruises telegraphed their pain, her wounded feet stung, but her legs were strong and her lungs sturdy. She ignored the pain and ran faster. Pain was her enemy. She would not allow it to win. She pushed herself until she knew she must stop.

Gasping for breath, dripping with sweat, she sat on a boulder overlooking the river.

The river was in flood and the current still swift from the April rains, its powerful flow ever changing. The rushing water hit rocks and flowed smoothly over them, or coursed easily around them, increasing in speed. At the edges, collections of boulders shunted the flow into eddies, reversing its course, but the water always curved back downstream again, rejoining the flow.

Where there were no obstacles, the surface of the water was smooth as a mirror, but she knew that underneath the placid surface was limitless power that could not be stopped.

That's me now, she thought. That's how I must be. Strong. Inevitable. Irresistible.

The next morning she drove to the gendarmerie headquarters and asked if and when she would be allowed to visit Monsieur Lagarde. An officer led her through the jail to a small room with a table and three chairs. He went away and returned with Gaston a few minutes later. Gaston and Charity sat across the table from one another. The officer sat in a chair by the door, not far away.

Gaston smiled weakly at her. For a moment, they just gazed at one another and their hearts spoke softly together.

Charity broke the spell.

"How did the thieves know where to leave the tools so that they could be used as evidence against you?" she asked him.

"I simply do not know," he said, his face marked with emotion and fatigue. "Did they know we were in the cave? I do not know that either. Did they intend to trap us there?" He shrugged his shoulders. "So much is a mystery!"

"The captain told me they 'received intelligence' about the location of the tools. Some tip I guess. An anonymous tip?"

Gaston sat back, smiled wanly and sighed.

"Perhaps an anonymous tip, but because I am a suspect, the gendarmes would have investigated my cottage in any case. I have no reason to go behind the cottage except to check on the water supply, so I would not have discovered anything placed there."

"If they only wanted to hide the tools, they could simply have left them in the cave. After they dynamited the entrance, no one would discover the theft or the tools if we did not escape. We—and the thieves—were the only ones who knew about the cave," she said.

They sat in silence.

"But...how did they know who *you* were?" she asked. "How did they know where to leave the tools to incriminate you?"

"I do not know. We must find out!" He caught himself and smiled. "I mean, you must find out. I can do nothing here."

"You *can* do something here! Think of who in Paris—or in the Vézère—knew that you often explored for caves?"

"*Oh la la,* everyone in Les Eyzies knows, anyone I know in Sarlat knows that is why I come here. Before the demonstrations in Paris, and before...before I met—came to know—*you,* looking for caves was the only reason I came to the cottage."

"In Paris..." he went on, "I usually mentioned my trips to other archeologists, and to the staff of the *faculté* if I had to take leave. Of course, Professor Noireau knows I come here. He was the one who encouraged me to do it. He helped me to acquire the cottage. There are so many people who know!"

"Noireau. Do you think he could help you now? Tell the captain about you, vouch for you?"

Gaston smiled weakly.

"Perhaps. But how does Noireau know that the captain's suspicions are not valid? This is the problem. If you look at what happened, and the evidence, my arrest is a logical result. Besides,

I am not sure that the great professor would want his name to be mentioned in any connection with a criminal matter, especially not one which involved desecration and theft of precious cave art! We must ask—*you* must ask for his help, of course. What else can we do? But I would not be surprised if he said some nice words to us, then took no action at all."

Charity thought for a moment, and leaned over close to Gaston.

"My roommate Amaleen used to, uh, *date*, the professor—you may remember I mentioned this?"

"No whispering!" the guard barked. "Speak up!"

"Ask her. We need all the help we can get."

Gaston reached across the table and took Charity's hand. She saw his eyes glistening.

"Charity…"

"No touching!" the guard barked.

Gaston withdrew his hand. They looked into one another's eyes.

I love you, she said with her eyes. *I love you!*

Charity left the jail, drove to the train station and checked for trains to Paris.

"Yes," the ticket agent told her, "there are now several trains daily. They are locals. They take much longer than usual, but they have been operating more or less regularly, and reaching Paris."

Charity bought a ticket.

33

Amaleen & Clive

When Georges brought the box with two dozen blood-red roses to her, Amaleen asked him to have Marie bring a vase with water. When he had left, she sat down, looked at them, and pondered what to do.

Another weekend with Benito meant doing the S&M weirdness with him again, she was sure of that. She could see now how he had prepped her for that role. I guess there were others before me, she thought. He said I had given him the greatest pleasure. Does that mean there were others who didn't do it as well?

Who were they? Just girlfriends? How long did they last at Château Corsique?

In one way, Benito's sado-masochist perversion was a pretty small price to pay for experiences that were otherwise extraordinary: the hunt, the riding, the clothes, the meals, living in a castle. High life, indeed. And Benito was a charmer, the least demanding lover—if that was the word—that she had ever had.

What to do?

I want to give Clive his dagger back, she thought. It was gallant of him to 'award' it to me, and I guess that's customary, and I'm glad I went along with it last time,…but what the hell am I going to do with a razor-sharp hunting knife? Cut bread? It should be with him. He's done his honor duty. Now it should go back to him.

That decides it. Hell, I'll go. I can handle it.

I wonder what new 'pleasures' Benito has in store for me this time....

This time it was a tour of the towns and villages of the region with Benito in the Rolls. No other guests. Benito pampered Amaleen, joked with her, was cozy and sweet.

The next morning at breakfast, the butler told Amaleen that Mr Vénière had to attend to urgent business and would be unable to accompany her for the morning. He expressed his apologies, and hoped she would be available for pleasant activities in the afternoon. In the morning, the château was hers to do whatever she liked.

She would like to take Kurnos for a ride in the country, if that would be all right.

"But of course, mademoiselle. I will inform the stables."

When she got to the stables, Clive Harrows was sitting at his desk in the tack room. He saw her, smiled, and stood to welcome her.

"Miss Amaleen!"

"Clive! It's a pleasure to see y'all again."

They looked at one another, smiling. Amaleen's smile was the first to fade. She looked at him seriously.

"Clive, ah've decided that it's time for yore dagger to return to its rightful owner. It was gallant of y'all to award it to me. You done it, but it ain't right. This here dagger has a proud an' noble history. You prob'ly used it on lotsa terrific hunts. You gotta have it."

He looked at her, looked down at his desk, and shook his head slowly from side to side.

"Ah insist!"

Amaleen reached down for the dagger and its sheath in her boot.

He was silent for a moment, then looked at her earnestly.

"Miss Amaleen, I understand what you're saying. It shows again the nobility of your mind and heart. I can see that you're determined."

His expression relaxed, and he smiled at her again.

"I'll accede to your wishes and accept the dagger, but not today. If I accept it, I must give you something of equal value in return. No, no, I insist! You're right to say that a mighty dagger is of little use to a beautiful lady, but I have seen the beautiful lady armed with the dagger, and my opinion of 'the weaker sex' will never be the same!"

They both laughed.

"My honor requires me to offer you, in exchange, a gift of equal merit that befits a lady of your beauty, talents and courage. Amaleen, please remember: you saved my life, and indeed also my honor. I can never forget that, and never repay you adequately. Please give me a little time to consider an appropriate gift."

Amaleen smiled.

"Y'all are *trop gallant, monsieur!*"

Clive smiled at her, but then his smile faded. He stood up and looked at her without blinking.

"Amaleen, I think you should keep the dagger with you when you are at Château Corsique."

She gave him a quizzical look.

"Our château is paradise, yes, with pleasures galore, but it also has its...perils. There are certain situations that can be....not what one might expect."

He was silent as he thought for a moment.

Amaleen could see that he was trying to give her a warning.

"I realize that it is impossible for a beautiful lady to carry a weapon with her at all times, but she can at least be aware that not everything is always...as peaceable as it seems."

They looked into one another's eyes and saw communion, an understanding.

"Ah hear what yore sayin'."

With Benito away there was little activity in the château. Amaleen wandered from room to room and finally settled into a large wingback chair in the library. The chair was off in a corner of the vast room, facing a window that looked out over the château park to the forest beyond.

The view was beautiful. The chair was comfortable. It was warm and quiet.

Amaleen sat and thought about her life.

She dozed.

The sound of the library door opening and men's voices woke Amaleen slowly from her nap. She didn't understand much of their rapid French. One of the voices was Benito's. The other sounded vaguely familiar as well.

She sat still, not wanting to interrupt.

She heard the rattle of papers on Benito's desk and brief comments separated by silence. She noticed that the movements at the desk were reflected dimly in the window in front of her. She could see the light on Benito's desk clearly, but the figures and their actions were distorted and dim.

The unknown man left.

She heard Benito dial the telephone on his desk.

Another man entered and spoke to Benito in a mixture of English and French. Some business matters: customers, products, shipments, revenue.

She heard the word *narcotique.*

"What are you giving the police?" Benito asked.

"The usual," the man said, quoting a large sum of money.

What? Suddenly it all clicked for Amaleen: they were talking drug deals!

She sat completely still, breathing silently.

After the man left she heard Benito shuffling more papers on his desk, opening a drawer and closing it.

The light on the desk was extinguished with a click and disappeared from the reflection in the window. She heard the library door open, Benito walk out, and the door close.

Amaleen peeked around the side of the chair. Nobody. She tiptoed to Benito's desk and surveyed the papers on it. One was a photo of some artwork, a bull's head. Another of some men in a dark place. Nothing about drugs.

She tiptoed to the library door and peered through the keyhole. No one. She opened it slowly, watching for movement.

None. She stepped out into the hall, pulling the library door closed gently behind her.

When she reached the main staircase she walked boldly up to her room.

"Have you seen Mademoiselle Amaleen?" Benito asked the butler, smiling.

"No, monsieur. She may be in the library. A gardener working on that side of the château mentioned to me that he saw her in the library some time ago, asleep in a large chair by the window."

Benito stared at the butler for a moment. His smile faded, replaced with a grim expression.

34

Amaleen's Turn

When Benito led Amaleen down the spiral staircase to the dungeon, she was still in her riding clothes. She knew it would be over in less than an hour, and she could go to her room…alone, thank goodness.

After they entered the subterranean stone chamber, he smiled at her.

"This time, it is your turn to experience the ecstasy," he said.

"But…ah'd rather give you the pleasure!"

"No, no, I insist!" he said, taking her arm and moving her toward the torture apparatus.

She looked at him, and saw the difference in his face. This was not the suave, generous, beneficent Benito, ready to do anything for his beautiful lady. This was Benito the Corsican mafioso, knowing what he wanted, what he had to do, ready to do it, to get what he wanted.

Amaleen was terrified. Something had gone horribly wrong. Is this what happened to the other women who humored him in his perversion? Is this what Clive was warning her about? Other women were brought down here, clueless, and ended up suffocated on Benito's Corsican torture machine? Her roommates didn't know where she was. There were no other guests at the château this weekend. A search would produce no results. Benito could easily deny any knowledge or involvement.

She would…disappear.

She thought quickly.

"Shore! Wha' not?"

She stepped toward the apparatus, turned, and positioned herself so he could attach the ankle and arm straps.

"Your neck is more slender than mine. I think it may take four or more clicks to…give you the pleasure," he said, smiling at her.

"Whatever. But ah have one improvement to make. You leave mah right arm free so ah can…uh,…stimulate you while y'all are stimulatin' me."

Benito smiled wickedly. Why not? Maybe he would achieve ecstasy at the moment of death! What a triumph!

He strapped her ankles and her left wrist into the contraption and put the strap around her neck.

"Gimme some time to enjoy the first part," she said.

She began to fondle him. She was breathing hard.

He closed his eyes as he felt her hand on him. Ah, this would be superb! Simultaneous orgasm and death!

He opened his eyes, looked hard at her, and with his right hand reached up and turned the handle on the neck strap to one click. Amaleen felt the grasp of the strap around her throat.

As she fondled, he reached up and turned the handle again. Click.

Now it was hard for her to breathe.

He's gonna kill me if I don't do this right.

She fumbled in her fondling.

"Ah cain't reach you like ah want to!" she said in a whisper, her throat constricted by the torture mechanism. "Ah gotta have more reach! Let mah right foot out!"

He frowned at her. He had imagined her death as coming when she was bound hand and foot in the apparatus. When he thought about it, he felt his manhood stiffen. But he had not foreseen that she might actually give him an orgasm at the moment of her death. That would be unprecedented!

He would do what she asked. She was still bound by the left foot and ankle straps and the neck strap.

He reached down and released the clasp on her right ankle, then reached up and turned the neck strap handle to its third click.

Amaleen gasped as the strap strangled her. She could hardly breathe. She had little time left. If he turned the handle one more time, and left it like that, she would die. Her next few actions had to be perfect or they would be her last.

Gasping for breath, she fondled him vigorously to arouse him as much as possible. Her eyes bulged from the lack of oxygen, but her hand was sure and expert. Benito must think she was aroused, not about to die.

He reached up and turned the neck strap handle to the fourth click. Now she could not breathe at all. She had seconds of life left, only seconds.

She saw him close his eyes: the ecstasy was coming.

Now!

She raised her right leg, dropped her right hand and with her remaining strength fumbled in her boot for the dagger. Her fingers found it, but could not grasp it.

She was fading.

Her thumb and forefinger wrapped around the end of the knife and slowly drew it from its sheath. The sight was fading from her bulging eyes, but she saw Benito before her, eyes closed, breathing heavily as he felt the ecstasy flood over him.

Don't drop the knife! Hold onto it, don't drop it!

She felt her fingers weaken as they slowly crept along the handle of the knife. They wrapped around it. She could no longer feel her fingers, but she could pull her shoulder upward. As she did, the knife came free of its sheath. Just get your hand up, get your hand up! She summoned the last bit of breath left in her lungs and with the last of her strength thrust the knife toward Benito's groin.

He shrieked and grabbed at the wound.

Quick now! He would fight back!

With her right foot she kicked out at Benito. He fell backward onto the stone floor and lay still.

She flung the knife aside and willed her hand to reach the handle on the neck strap. One click, two clicks, three clicks, four! She could breathe!

She sucked in air with a loud shriek, then another, and

another.

Her hand gripped the clasp on the neck strap and sprang it open. She snapped the clasp on her left hand, thrust herself downward and fumbled with the clasp on her left ankle.

She staggered forward, falling onto Benito's body.

Benito moaned beneath her, his hands still gripping the bleeding wound. She rolled off of him, grabbed the dagger and staggered toward the door. She wrenched it open, pulled it closed behind her, and shot the cast-iron bolt closed.

Her right hand gripping the door handle, her left holding the dagger, she bent over and vomited. She wiped her mouth and started up the spiral staircase.

I have minutes to get out of here. Only minutes.

At the top of the staircase she stood and composed herself. *I must look normal. No one must get any idea of what just happened, or I'll be dead.* She slipped the dagger back into its sheath in her boot and swept the hair from the front of her face.

She walked at a normal pace down the corridor and to the back door which led to the stables, then out the door and across the gravel drive. The lights were on in the stable, but she saw no one. She went to the tack room. Clive was not at his desk. She wiped most of the blood off the dagger and slipped it into the drawer of his desk.

Pulling a heavy saddle from its stand, she grabbed a bridle and hurried to Kurnos's stall. He looked at her knowingly and neighed softly. She patted his nose and whispered to him, then quickly hefted the saddle onto his back, attached the girth, put on the bridle, and led him toward the door. In a corner she saw the bin of oats. Grabbing a feed bag, she scooped a mass of feed into it and tied it to the saddle.

Out the door, she mounted and rode at a quiet walk, avoiding the noisy gravel drive, away from the château and into the countryside. It was late in the evening but still light—the longest day of the year was only weeks away. Twilight lasted until nearly midnight, and the sky began to lighten again before 4 am.

She rode north, toward the darkness, away from the southwestern light.

They won't be able to find me. They won't hear Benito in that dungeon for awhile—if he's still alive—and then it will take more time to find Kurnos gone.

But they have the dogs, she thought. They can follow any scent.

She spurred Kurnos to a trot, then to a canter, always heading north, away from the fading light.

35

Flee!

Amaleen rode. When she came to a creek or body of water, she did what a stag would do: travel up or downstream along it so the dogs would not be able to follow the scent.

She came to a country road. Which way? Don't know. Go one way or the other. She turned right.

After a few kilometers she came to a crossroads with signs.

Paris. Yes!

She went that way.

She had ridden for hours. It was now dark except for a slender crescent moon. She no longer feared that Benito would find her in the countryside. She was too far. She stopped in a copse of trees by a pond, dismounted, and sat on the ground with her back to a tree. Kurnos went to the pond, took a long drink, then browsed in the grass on its shore.

She went to the horse, took down the feed bag and strapped it to his head. After he had fed she tied the reins to a bush, sat down, and leaned against the tree.

She woke with a start at a sound and looked wildly around her.

Only Kurnos snorting, she decided. She looked all around her and saw no danger, but she did see a faint dawn light in the sky to the southeast.

Back in the saddle, reckoning roughly the direction north, she started out again.

The morning was beautiful and still. She rode, looking at her watch about every hour. Five o'clock. Six o'clock. She rode for another hour and felt hunger. Better get something to eat.

She rode into a village, found a café, and tied Kurnos to a lamp post. Striding purposefully in her riding clothes, she approached the bar. Three workmen in blue smocks were leaning against it, chatting to the café owner. They all looked at the blonde amazon in her riding costume and fell silent.

She put her elbows on the bar, and in her atrocious American accent demanded a café au lait, a croissant and a pain au chocolat.

The café owner paused, staring at her, nodded and went to prepare the coffee. One of the men slid a basket of croissants toward her. The café owner set down the coffee in front of her, took a pain au chocolat from under the counter, put it on a plate, and set it down before her.

All the men watched her as though she had just landed from Venus.

She took a long drink of the coffee, wolfed the croissant, took another long drink of coffee, and shoved half the pain au chocolat into her mouth. Then more coffee, then the other half of the pastry.

Wiping her mouth with the back of her hand, she set the coffee cup down and said "Mah money is on mah horse."

She strode out of the café, mounted, and trotted out of town.

In the café, the men looked at one another.

"Un rouge, et que ça saute!" one of the men barked at the café owner. A glass of red wine, quick!

It was afternoon when Amaleen rode slowly through the farmland outside Chartres.

I can't take a horse into Paris, she thought. That's too bad! I'd love to do that sometime!

She imagined herself mounted on proud Kurnos in her slick Hermès riding outfit, trotting briskly along the Avenue des Champs-Élysées, smiling to left and right, watching little French cars collide around her.

I better not make a stir there. I gotta hide out from Benito.

When she could see the steeple of the Chartres cathedral, she dismounted at the gate of a farm, opened the gate, walked Kurnos through, gave him a slap on the rump and watched him trot away toward the farmhouse. He stopped and looked back at her, but by then she was jogging toward the town.

When she reached the Gare de Chartres, a train was boarding for Paris. She got aboard.

The conductor came through the car checking tickets. He stopped and looked at her. He had seen many things on trains in his career, but not a beautiful young woman in riding habit.

"Shucks!" Amaleen said in her best hillbilly English, "mah horse ran off an' all mah money an' mah ticket was on it."

The conductor sighed and moved on. *"Touristes,"* he grumbled under his breath.

At the apartment building on Rue Claude Bernard, she rang the doorbell to call Madame Chambond, the concierge.

"J'ai perdé mon clé," she told her.

Madame Cambond winced, whether from the loss of the key or from Amaleen's French, she didn't know. Madame let her into the apartment and offered her the spare key. Her roommates weren't there.

I can't stay here for too long, she thought. *Benito probably thinks I went to Olivier's château. He doesn't know my Paris address...but he could probably track me down here. That will take his thugs some time, though.*

She took a hot shower, changed into normal clothes, wrote a note to her roommates, took some money and the spare key, and went out. She walked to a nearby bistrot, Le Languedoc, and sat down to an early dinner.

What now?

She knew she had seriously wounded Benito with the hunt master's dagger. Even if he recovered, he would never forgive her for assaulting his manhood.

Benito was incalculably wealthy and powerful, and also a mafioso who ignored laws and morality. He had tried to kill her once, she felt sure of that. Now he would put out a hit on her, have his thugs find and murder her, perhaps after torture.

But why? Had he discovered that she had been in the library? She didn't really understand much of what they were talking about, but he didn't know that. Maybe he believed she could provide testimony on his drug deals to the police. But what could she tell the police about her escape? That they were engaging in sado-masochism and she thought it would go too far?

So what now? Time would pass before the château staff would find Benito. The torture chamber was the last place they'd look. He told her few knew about it. That must be true. He would want to keep it secret. If others knew about his perversion it would hurt his *amour-propre,* and others could even use it to blackmail him.

It might take hours, or even a day, before the staff decided something was unusual and began to search for him.

His staff would see to his wounds. He would spend time in a hospital. "It was a hunting accident," he would say, even though the doctors would hardly believe such an explanation.

Benito would carry on as normal as he planned his revenge carefully so there would be no slip-ups. He would not be in a hurry. That's the sort of man he is, she thought. What would matter to him was success, not haste.

If she fled back home to America, would the thugs follow her? Some morning, walking out of her apartment, would three men waiting in a car kidnap her?

At least I have a little time, Amaleen thought. Not a lot, but I have time, a few days, a few weeks, maybe more.

I need a plan.

The next morning, her train left Paris at 7:00 am and arrived in Marseilles at lunchtime. Amaleen left her first-class seat, walked out of the Gare Part-Dieu and strolled around the streets of the city looking into shop windows, sitting in cafés, going into clothing shops and trying on clothes but not buying. She asked several policemen for directions in her thickest hillbilly talk. She bumped into people walking along the streets and made a fuss in a loud voice that got everyone within earshot to look at her.

In short, she got herself noticed in Marseilles.

As the time for her departure neared, she went to the central post office and handed a letter to the clerk. He put the required postage stamps on it and cancelled them. She paid him, left the post office, walked back to the Gare Part-Dieu and sat in a café, her face behind a newspaper, until it was time to board her return train to Paris.

Dear Olivier,

By now you may have heard of Benito's 'accident.' I'm afraid that he doesn't want me around anymore, so I'm taking a ship to Italy, then to Greece. I'm sorry I won't see you again soon, but I want to thank you for all your generosity and for being my friend.

Love,

Amaleen

The black car drew up to the door of Olivier's château. Three men got out and knocked on the door. When Georges opened it, they pushed past him into the house.

Marie ran to tell Olivier he had visitors.

Olivier came to the foyer.

"How may I help you?" Olivier asked them, but he already knew what they wanted.

"Tell us where she is!"

"I do not know."

"You will tell us. You can do it now, or afterwards. You would be wise to tell us now. You will not feel so well afterwards."

"We don't want you, we want her," another of the men said.

Olivier looked at them, then looked away. One of the men grabbed him by the shirt and shook him.

"All right!" Olivier said. "Let me get something. It is all I have."

He began to walk away. They followed him closely.

In the library, Olivier went to his desk, picked up the letter from Amaleen and handed it to them.

The first man looked at the envelope and the postmark.

"She does not deserve…"

One of the men punched Olivier in the face. He fell to the floor, bleeding from the nose.

They walked out of the château and drove away.

"Oh mon dieu!" Marie said as she glanced into the foyer and saw Olivier lying on the floor, blood running from his nose.

"Monsieur le baron! Qu'est-ce qui se passe? Oh mon dieu! Apocalypse!"

She and Georges helped him to his feet and walked with him to the kitchen. Georges went to fetch ice as Marie prepared cold compresses.

"Your face will swell greatly, *monsieur le baron! Oh mon dieu, quelle douleur!"*

Georges returned with the ice for the compresses.

"It is nothing, Marie," Olivier said to the woman. "A small price to pay…"

"I will make sure that they have left," Georges said, and walked toward the front door.

"I'm sure they have left, Georges. They got what they wanted."

"But…what did they want, monsieur?"

"They were looking for…someone. They think that they will find her…but they won't."

As Marie applied the icy compress to his face, she saw him smile.

"She is too *intelligent* for them."

36

M. Plouff

Josie and Jean-Paul woke late, and slowly, touching one another gently, lazy.

"Oh!"

They had made love over and over, burning away all of their worries in a fiery ecstasy. As they woke in the morning the passion of last night rose again. Jean-Paul's hands wandered over Josie's body and she responded, opening herself to him. Afterwards they both collapsed, satiated.

Someone had to start the day. Josie got up and went to the shower. Afterwards, swaddled in her thick terrycloth bathrobe, she wandered to the kitchen to make coffee.

When she returned to the bedroom with two large cups of café au lait, he was sitting up in bed. He nodded when he took the cup she handed him.

They didn't have to talk. They knew. They had betrayed Martine, over and over. But they felt true to each other. A dizzying mixture of elation, affection and anxiety inhabited and unsettled their minds.

They were silent for a long time.

"Eh bien, continuons," Jean-Paul said, quoting Sartre, the last line of *Huit Clos,* the author's story of hell as a bourgeois living room.

They looked at one another over the rims of their coffee cups. They set the cups down and made love again.

"Josie said she would come today," Jean-Paul said to Martine, back in their apartment.

"Ah! Fantastique!"

"I must go to the meetings in the Latin Quarter. Please give her my best wishes."

"Of course."

Jean-Paul went out. He climbed into the bus, found a seat, and thought of how he couldn't be in their apartment when Josie came. Their betrayal of Martine would be too painful. And it was dangerous. For all her talk of free love, Martine was highly sensitive—and jealous. She was sure to sense the emotional connection between them. When she did, the explosion would be terrible.

Jean-Paul sat in the meeting room with student leaders, university administrators, and officials from the Ministry of National Education. The older men droned on about 'order' and 'adherence to principle.'

He looked at the older men. All, he knew, had lived through the Depression. Many had fought in World War II. Some had fought in the *Résistance*, knowing that if they were discovered by the enemy they would be murdered after an eternity of excruciating torture.

He imagined the horrors they had seen, and lived through, the terrible suffering some of them experienced.

For that they must be respected, he thought.

No wonder they and De Gaulle, the war hero who governed France with a firm hand, wanted order, and calm, and quiet, and a system that ran smoothly and everyone performed their assigned functions.

But their world was not Jean-Paul's world.

The peaceful world for which they had fought was not the world the old men had known as *jeunes Français* in the 1920s. The world had changed. They could not recreate the world of the 1920s, and they did not know how to create the world of the 1960s. The students were creating it in the streets!

All of the old men's attempts to push the world back to the

Good Old Days of their youth would fail. It was time for them to step aside and to allow today's youth to shape and live in the world they knew they could—and must—create.

Returning from the meeting with the university administrators, Jean-Paul walked along Rue Monsieur Le Prince. At the other end of the street he saw three riot police. They saw him. They shouted for him to stop. He was afraid—other students had been severely beaten just for being on any street near the university, no questions asked.

They started running toward him.

He ran around the corner, down Rue Dupuytren and ducked into in a shop doorway. The screen in the window of the shop's front door was pulled down, but a faint light illuminated its edges from behind. He pounded on the door. The police rounded the corner of Rue Dupuytren. As they stood looking for him, the shop door opened, a hand grabbed his shoulder, pulled him in, and quietly closed the door.

"In the back room, *now!*"

Jean-Paul hurried past a cluttered desk, through a ragged curtain and into a dark hallway. Feeling his way along, he came to a door, opened it, slipped through, and quietly closed it. It was pitch dark. He felt for a light switch, found it and switched on the weak bulb hanging from the ceiling. A metal bedstead topped by a rumple of grey sheets and blankets. A cheap dresser. A cracked wardrobe. A washbasin. A door which probably opened on a toilet. He took a mental picture of the room, switched off the light, draped the old blankets carelessly over the front of the bed and hid beneath it.

Ten minutes later the door opened, the light was switched on, and he heard a voice say "They've gone."

He emerged from beneath the bed. His savior was an old, bald man with a salt-and-pepper moustache, dressed in a threadbare, rumpled suit and wire-rimmed glasses. The old man smiled.

"I am Plouff. Perhaps you should stay for a little while in case they are still looking for you. I will make tea."

He signalled for Jean-Paul to come back to the front room of the shop.

Monsieur Plouff came tottering in carrying an ancient tea tray bearing a cracked teapot and two cups of different patterns. He glanced at the decrepit, cluttered wooden desk in the center of the shop, looking for a place to set the tray. Jean-Paul cleared a place on the desk, pushing aside a dirty Duralex water glass, piles of newspapers, documents, books, photographs, unopened envelopes, and an ashtray with a small briar pipe which emitted a powerful odor of stale tobacco.

Plouff poured the tea.

"This is green tea from Mariage Frères, the oldest tea company in Paris. One does not drink green tea with milk, but I have some sugar if you should want some."

"Thank you."

Jean-Paul lifted the cup, eyed it suspiciously, avoided putting his lips on the chip in the rim, and took a polite sip.

"Thank you, *monsieur.* I am not a criminal. I am only a student. But they would have beaten me anyway."

"Yes, yes. I've seen so much of it! All the other shops on the street are closed, but I have nowhere else to go, really, so I stay here and watch. Such confusion! I can't believe this is indeed our Paris! But it has happened before, of course. The revolution, the Commune, the protests before and after the wars. I did not expect it in 1968."

"You understand why the students are protesting."

"Oh, of course! Conditions are bad! I was never a Gaullist... nor a Socialist. Truth is, I'm not political at all...."

The old man lifted his cup and took a gulp of tea.

"I suppose you could say I live in another age. Sometimes I think I was born in the wrong century."

He smiled at Jean-Paul.

"You are an *antiquaire?*"

"Yes, as you can see," Plouff said, sweeping his arm across the clutter of the shop.

"Are you an archeologist?"

The old man fixed Jean-Paul with his eyes.

"No. I never had the opportunity to study at the university. Everything I have learned, I have learned on my own."

"So...you travel the world collecting these ancient objects? To sell?"

"Ah no! I cannot afford to travel. It is my most fervent dream to be able to see the pyramids and temples of Egypt, the Acropolis at Athens, Eternal Rome....Ephesus...Palmyra... Ancient Assyria, the Hittite cities, Phrygia! But I cannot afford it. You see how I live. I have no money."

"But...you are surrounded by ancient objects here! I assume they are valuable, and for sale."

"They are, but there are few buyers. I established the shop after World War I when I was a young man..."

Plouff chuckled to himself at the thought of being young.

"There were buyers then, and sellers too. I would buy from the estates of the wealthy, people who had traveled in the last century and built collections, or perhaps just picked up a few ancient figurines. One could buy—or even find!—ancient objects at the archeological sites then: kick the dirt, find an object and take it! Of course the best objects, found by organized expeditions, went to museums, but there were so many objects, so many! Farmers plowing their fields would pick them up and give them to a boy who would find a tourist and offer them for sale. The art and crafts of entire bygone civilizations! Thousands of years of making figurines of gods and goddesses, kings and queens, religious and occult symbols!"

Plouff took another mighty gulp of his tea, now lukewarm.

"I bought from the estates, and wealthy young customers came to my shop to buy from me. They wanted ancient objects to lend prestige to their décors. My business was thriving! Then came World War II and everything stopped. After the war—you are too young to remember how poor we all were. No one had money except the American soldiers, and they had no interest in antiquities, only in wine, women and war souvenirs. Now, the wealthy do not come to me, they travel to the destinations themselves. And they do not buy little things. They must have *real* status symbols! Marble statues from Greece and Rome! Russian icons!"

Plouff picked up his tea cup, saw it was empty, and put it down with a clack.

"They must have large, *museum-quality* artifacts in order to attain the status they desire, not little brown clay figurines, or Roman coins to make into cufflinks."

"Yes. It's terrible, the *nouveau-riche!*" Jean-Paul said. He thought for a minute. "We have many ancient sites here in France. Roman cities, medieval cities...."

"Yes! And they are beautiful! I have visited a few of them. But we protect our antiquities. Any discovery of an ancient site is immediately protected and nothing can be taken from it. The artifacts are displayed in fine museums...but that does not help an antiquities dealer!" Plouff said with an ironic grin.

"I will never get to travel," Plouff said with a sigh. "I will never have the money. I could sell everything in this shop and still not have enough to achieve my dream of seeing all the places these objects came from."

Plouff rose from the creaky swivel chair, lifted the tea tray from the desk and carried it to the back room. When he returned, Jean-Paul was replacing on the desk the paraphernalia he had cleared to make room for the tea tray.

"This is not Egyptian," Jean-Paul said, holding up a color photograph.

"That? Of course not! That is far, far older than the antiquities of Egypt! More than three times older!"

The old man took the photograph from Jean-Paul's hand.

"Look at the artistry in this head of an auroch. It is superb! It was created by someone with no artistic training. Ha! Someone who did not even have a civilization! An ape! But what an ape! What sensitivity! And it was created without paints, or brushes, or tools of any kind. It is a miracle. So beautiful!"

"Do you have this for sale?"

Plouff looked at him with derision.

"Such an absurd question! An object such as this belongs in a museum! It is priceless! Of course I do not have such an object. It is..., ah,...it is from...Lascaux! The Paleolithic cave of Lascaux."

"I thought that Lascaux was closed to the public. This is not a professional photograph. Did you go to Lascaux when it was still open and photograph it? It must have been thrilling for you to see it!"

"No, I did not take this photograph. I have not seen Lascaux. I was planning a trip, but then they declared it closed. Someone else took the photograph. I don't know who."

Plouff went to the front door, opened it slowly, and peered up and down the street.

"I think you can go now. But be careful."

"Thank you so much for helping me. I will not forget your kindness."

"It was nothing, young man. Go in peace."

"I hope your dream of travel comes true."

"Ah, yes, so do I. So do I."

Plouff closed the door quietly behind him.

37

Society Tell-All

The three members of the Secret Society sat at the dining table, the first time they had all been together in the apartment since the Society's last meeting weeks before. So long ago....

Josie brought out snacks, a bottle of wine and two glasses.

"Where's my glass?" Charity said.

Josie raised her eyebrows, stared at Charity, glanced at Amaleen who raised her eyebrows and smiled. Josie returned to the kitchen for another glass.

They sipped and glanced at one another.

"Where do we even start?" Charity asked.

Her roommates were silent. Lots to tell, but how to tell it, and how much to tell? Not everything. Certainly not.

"Okay, I'll start," Charity said.

She told them of her stealth walk to the Gare d'Austerlitz, of being trampled, of glimpsing Monsieur Lagarde in the crowd, the train ride to Versailles, the long uncomfortable car ride to Sarlat, recovery in the cottage.

When Charity described her cave-hunting expeditions in the Vézère valley, her roommates smiled.

"Sounds pretty lovey-dovey," Josie said, grinning at her.

Charity looked deep into her wine glass, blushed, looked up and continued her story.

"I can't give you all the details. In fact, I can't tell you much at all. Just trust me! I'll tell you everything when I can, but for the moment, I just need to know that you're with me. Girls, this is the *most important thing in my life!*

"Then it ain't about ol' pots 'n' caves 'n' stuff," Amaleen smirked, "it's gotta be about that professor, Lagarde."

Charity looked at her seriously.

"It's both Amaleen. Very definitely—*hugely*—both! And you're important to the story because you know Noireau and maybe you can help us. I need to talk to Noireau as soon as possible! Can you set it up?"

"Don't see wha' not. We're still on pretty good terms. In fact... funny thing is, I think I just heard him the other day at Benito's."

"Who's Benito?" Josie asked.

Amaleen told them about leaving Paris with Olivier, going to his château, then to Benito's party, and the weekends at Château Corsique. She told them about the hunt, but not the kill. She left out the torture dungeon. She mentioned napping in the library, being awakened by Benito and another man, and thought she recognized Professor Noireau's voice.

"What was Noireau doing at this Benito guy's château? He sounds like a mafioso."

"He prob'ly *is* a mafioso. Ah don't know what Noireau was doing there—if it was Noireau. Ah think it was. Come to think of it, ah saw a picture on Benito's desk that mighta been up Noireau's alley. It was some kinda painting like they find in caves, the kinda thing Charity likes? It looked like a cow. A cow's head."

"A bull's head?" Charity asked—almost shouted.

"Yeah, maybe a bull."

"Describe it!"

"Well, what do ah know? It was like one o' them bull's heads yuh showed us in that book about that place. What's its name? Race car? Something like race car?"

"Lascaux!"

"Yeah, that place. Where's that book?"

Charity rushed to her room and returned with the book. They paged through it. Amaleen pointed to a photograph of an auroch's head painting from Lascaux.

"Was it just like this?" Charity asked.

"Naw, not the same. It was diff'rent, but it was, like, the same kinda bull. But a diff'rent picture."

"And you said you saw it on Benito's desk?"

"Yep."

"Did Benito and Noireau talk about this picture, or caves, or cave art, or anything like that?"

"Ah dunno, honey. Ah was asleep an' when ah woke up they were talkin' so fast in French. You know mah French ain't like yours. I dit'n catch much of what they said. I guess it coulda been about the picture. Come to think of it, ah don't remember seein' the picture on Benito's desk when ah went into the library —not that ah was lookin' for it, y'know. But ah do believe Noireau prob'ly gave Benito that picture."

"Amaleen, I've got to talk to Noireau *now*! Could you call him tonight?"

"Ah'll try, honey, but what if he's away? Oh mah lord, ah may have to speak to his wife…"

"Please, Amaleen! Please!"

"Of course, honey. Ah'll try right now."

She went to the phone and began to dial.

"If a woman answers, ah'm throwin' the phone in yore lap."

"Ten o'clock tomorow mornin', in his office," Amaleen said, putting the handset back in its cradle.

"Thanks, Amaleen! Some day you'll realize what you've just done for me. For us."

Josie and Amaleen looked at Charity. She blushed.

"Do you think you could go back to Benito's château and find out more?" Charity asked.

"Well, no honey. Ah cain't go back, ever. Uh…we dit'n part on good terms, shall we say. In fact, he may be comin' after me. I may be in danger. He's mafia, like ah told yuh."

"What about y'all, Josie honey?" Amaleen asked. "You were fightin' on them barricades I guess, an' here y'all are in one sweet li'l piece. Ah don't see a nick on ya."

"I was a medic, kind of. Took care of wounded students. The

medical students were the 'doctors,' and the rest of us just helped as we could. The police were vicious! You should have seen what they did!"

Josie described the fights on the barricade, the scene in the café-infirmary, and Martine being hit in the head by a tear gas cannister purposely aimed to shoot her down.

"How could you stand it?" Charity asked.

"I grew up in Chicago. Under the great Mayor Daley? Police brutality? I know what that looks like. I'm no stranger to it. Mostly the boys got it there, but here the cops were beating boys, girls, kids, old people. It didn't matter. It was unbelievable. They tried to kill Martine! It was criminal is what it was. That doesn't make it any easier to bear, but it didn't surprise me. I know how to deal with the violence."

They sipped their wine in silence, their thoughts ranging over the weeks since that bell-clear morning at the Café Aux Tours de Notre-Dame when they felt themselves so sophisticated and worldly from their year abroad. Was that only a month ago?

38

Confrontation

Charity walked from the train station in Sarlat directly to gendarme headquarters. She was escorted to the gendarmerie jail meeting room by a guard. She took a seat at the small table. After a few minutes another guard brought Gaston in, seated him across from her, and took his seat in the chair near the door.

"I met with Noireau," Charity said, choosing her words carefully. "I think he knows."

"He knows?"

"He didn't say so, not directly. In fact he denied any knowledge, but when I brought up the subject he was nervous. I could see it in his eyes and his movements. He knows."

"There's another person involved, a…crime figure," she went on. "Powerful. He would have the resources to do the job, to make it happen."

"But why would he want to do such a thing?"

"I don't know. Maybe I can find out."

They looked into one another's eyes.

Charity could see his suffering. She knew he was suffering because of *her* suffering, of her struggling to deal with a huge problem beyond her experience. Her heart was melting, but she showed only resolve.

Gaston looked at Charity and fought back his tears. She was so young, so fragile, her slender body, her thin face. She seemed so…naive. But in her eyes he saw an iron resolution, a power he had not noticed before, the power that got her out of the cave, the power that saved his life. The power that, he hoped, might save him from years in prison and restore his reputation, restore him to the world.

The power that could bring them back together.

Charity went to the Café de la Mairie and asked the owner to put through a phone call to Paris. She ordered a café au lait and sat. After a half hour, the owner pointed toward the phone booth in the corner. She went in and picked up the handset.

"Amaleen?"

"Charity honey? Is that you? It's hard to hear."

"It's me. I'm in Sarlat. I need more information. This Benito, the guy with the château. Did he ever talk to you about antiquities, archeological stuff?"

"Oh yeah, honey. He showed us his big collection of old stuff. It was like a museum! Big marble statues, old li'l statues, old pots, jewelry, them stone tool things. He had ever'thang."

"Did he have anything like that cave painting of the auroch, the bull?"

The line was quiet for a moment except for the long-distance crackle and hum.

"No, ah don't remember anything like them cave paintings. No bulls or nuthin'."

"Do you think he would want to add something like the bull's head painting to his collection?"

"Benito? Are you kiddin' me? Benito wants ever'thang, an' only the best of ever'thang. If you had a cave paintin' to sell him, he'd whip out the cash from his back pocket. Don't matter how much."

The next morning, back in the meeting room at the jail, Charity looked at Gaston.

"The powerful man I mentioned? He has the resources *and* the motivation."

"Can you tell this to Captain Gagnier, give him evidence?"

Charity stared at him in silence, then spoke.

"Not yet. There are...complications. It could put a friend in danger. But I'm confident we're on the right track."

"*You* are on the right track. I curse the fact that I can be of no help. It is such a burden on you!"

"It's worth it," she smiled. "You are helping. By inspiration."

"Labor of *love,*" she said, emphasizing the word as she stood up to leave.

Charity returned to Paris, to her apartment, wondering what to do next. The members of the Secret Society decided to prepare a real French dinner rather than buying ready-made foods from a *traîteur* or getting by on hors d'oeuvres or sandwiches. They chatted as they worked in the kitchen.

"Charity, I remembered something while you were gone," Josie said. "I heard about another picture of a bull's head."

She told them her friend Jean-Paul had mentioned seeing a photo of a bull's head in an antiquities shop.

"Where?"

"Rue Dupuytren."

Plouff, Charity thought. It must be Plouff. There are no other *antiquaires* anywhere near him.

"So...who's this Jean-Paul?" Amaleen asked, turning from the pot she was stirring on the stove. "This here tale is thickenin' faster than this ol' sauce I'm makin'."

Amaleen and Charity looked at Josie, who lowered her eyes.

"Ah hate the fact that colored folk cain't blush, because if y'all could blush, you'd be red as Charity's freckles now, honey, an' we'd see it an' know what's goin' on."

"All right. We're friends."

Amaleen and Charity looked at Josie and rolled their eyes.

"All right, all right! We're more than friends."

They stared at her hard.

"All right, all right, all right! We're lovers! There! It's out! Now you know!"

"Whoopee! Josie's got herself a boyfriend!" Amaleen shouted, waving the sauce spoon in the air and spreading droplets of gooey sauce all over the kitchen and her friends.

Josie turned back to her cutting board and chopped. Yes, a

boyfriend, a *copin*, she thought, and a *copine* too. And my *copin's copine* is the same as mine. What am I going to do?

At dinner, Charity was silent.

"Okay, what's goin' on in that brainy li'l head of yore'n, Charity?" Amaleen asked. "Ah can almost smell yore hair burnin' from the heat."

"I've got to go to that shop on Rue Dupuytren tomorrow first thing," she said. "Josie, can I talk to your…friend Jean-Paul?"

"I…I'll see," Josie said, looking at her plate. "He's really busy with these negotiations at the university. I'm never sure where he is. Maybe he'll stop in and you can meet him."

It was so much easier when I had the apartment to myself, Josie thought. If he comes now and wants to spend the night—and I want him to spend the night—what do I do?

The next morning Charity was outside the front door of Plouff's shop when he raised the shade on it. He saw her standing outside, opened the door and welcomed her, his small eyes peering over the tops of his wire-rimmed spectacles.

He settled into his swivel chair amid a symphony of squeaks and creaks.

"Yes, *mademoiselle,* how may I help you? Another Roman medal?"

"*Monsieur Plouff,* I need your help in a very important matter."

"At your service, mademoiselle!" the old man said.

"A few days ago, you protected a young man, a student, from the police."

Plouff's smile faded. He lowered his eyes to his desk and said nothing.

"While he was here, he saw a photograph of a paleolithic painting of an auroch…"

Plouff looked up at her in surprise.

"I need to know where that photo came from. It is of the greatest importance."

"I have no idea what you are talking about, *mademoiselle,*" he said, lowering his gaze to his papers once more.

Charity stooped over the desk and put her face close to his.

"Monsieur Plouff, tell me about the photo or I will go to the police. I need to know *now!*"

He stared at her, his teeth clenched, his expression one of determination. He said nothing.

She started rummaging through the piles of stuff on his desk, soon uncovered the photo and held it up to him.

"Tell me!"

His face was grim.

"It is an auroch, yes. I do not know the provenance. In fact, I know almost nothing about it."

"Tell me! Did you get this photo from Professor Noireau? Or did you give him one just like it? Do you have the antiquity here in your shop? Are you trying to sell it?"

He looked at her in shock, but said nothing.

She pushed her face to within inches of his.

"Tell me!"

He jerked backwards and almost upset his chair, then regained his balance and rose from it defiantly.

"Mademoiselle, this is a very sensitive matter. I cannot talk about it. You have no right to ask. Goodbye!"

He was an old man, but if this crazy young woman wanted to fight, he was twice her size, and ready to defend himself.

Charity glared at him.

"I will find out! You will be sorry!"

She stormed out of the shop, slamming the door, nearly breaking the glass.

39

Report

After her confrontation with Plouff, Charity took the next train back to Sarlat.

The next morning she went to the gendarmerie headquarters and gave Gaston her report.

"Old Plouff! You're sure the photo on his desk was of 'our' auroch?" Gaston asked.

"Of course. What do you know about him?" she asked.

"Plouff? He's been there in that shop forever. As young students—like you—we would go there and look at what he had for sale. We were conflicted. On the one hand, here were objects that we normally saw only in museums, but from Plouff we could buy them, take them home and look at them whenever we wanted. What he sold were not very important artifacts. I believe some of them were *truqués, faux*, not true artifacts, simple modern copies sold to tourists. And the real articles he sold had no confirmed provenance, which means they were probably stolen… but stolen a long time ago, before stealing antiquities was recognized as a crime. He told us he acquired most of his objects from the collections of 19th-century travelers who had died."

He gave a little laugh.

"Some of the *truqués* were *so good!* It was difficult to tell the difference from real artifacts. The artisans who made the *faux* artifacts were probably the descendants of the original artisans! They used the same materials and methods!"

He was serious again.

"I wonder…. Could the thieves have stolen the auroch painting just to make copies to sell? No, having copies on the market would reduce the uniqueness, the value of the original. No, they wanted the original to sell to a wealthy collector who could boast he had the only one in the world. The only one in human history!'"

"Could Plouff have it and be trying to sell it?"

"Oh, I doubt it. Yet…his shop is certainly in difficulty. *Il est pauvre!* He has no money! He has always wanted to travel the world visiting archeological sites. He is an old man now. If he *did* sell the auroch painting, he would have plenty of money to realize his dream before he died."

"When I mentioned the great professor's name, Plouff looked surprised. The great professor said nothing about Plouff when I spoke with him, but I wonder if they have been talking."

Gaston thought for a moment.

"The professor would be able to provide an estimate of value for the stolen painting. He does that for museums all over the world, for insurance purposes. Such a work of art is priceless, of course, but insurance companies demand a number for their purposes."

"Underwriting," Charity said.

"What?"

"Insurance. Estimating market value. So if Plouff had it, he might go to the professor to learn its market value?"

"Yes. You see, for a work of art without clear provenance, the estimate of value is almost as important as the work of art itself. If it is a fake, some paint slopped on a rock by an amateur, it is worthless. But if, in the absence of reliable provenance, the greatest archeologist in the world confirms that it is a genuine prehistoric work—*that* is what gives the work of art its value!"

She looked at him, her lips compressed, her jaw set.

"What are you thinking? That the greatest archeologist in France would do such a thing? Would assist in the sale of a stolen artifact? Charity, I really think that is impossible!"

"The professor likes to live the luxury life. How do you do that on a professor's salary? Some professors are demonstrating in the streets now for higher pay! They don't even earn enough to pay their bills! How can the great professor support his luxury lifestyle? Where does the money come from?"

Charity looked at Gaston. He was shocked and upset by her accusation.

"Gaston, I know the professor has been good to you, a mentor. More than a mentor! A friend! I don't want to believe these things, but nothing makes sense in this matter. I've got to ask anything that comes into my head."

"Of course, my love. I understand. I just don't want to believe such a thing."

My love, Charity thought. Did I just hear him say that?

Charity returned to the cottage. It was sad, so empty. Tears came to her eyes. We were *so* happy here!

She went into the bedroom and allowed herself catharsis. She moaned as she wept. Her moans turned to shrieks until, exhausted, she fell asleep on her wet pillow.

"Bonjour! Monsieur Gaston?"

She heard someone in the salon. Quickly wiping her face and straightening her hair, she left the bedroom and went into the salon.

"Ah bonjour, mademoiselle! Is Monsieur Gaston at home?"

"No, Monsieur Séraphin. He is not here."

"Is everything all right? The cottage is all to your satisfaction?"

Charity held back her tears.

"We have no problems with the cottage, *monsieur.*"

"I came to ask because I noticed people driving up the hill to the cottage in recent days."

"People?"

"You had visitors, I think. Do you need anything to entertain them? Are they staying here? Another bed?"

Charity thought of Yveline's visit and frowned.

"I think we have had only one visitor, *monsieur,* a woman in a black car, and she returned to Paris."

"Ah yes, Mademoiselle Yveline. She had called the café in Les

Eyzies a few days ago to see if Monsieur Lagarde was at his cottage."

"And they told her he was here?"

"*Ehe oui, mademoiselle!*" the old man said with a look of mock surprise. "Because he is here!"

"But I saw more than her car," he continued. "I saw a small truck, much newer than mine. Several men. They drove up to the cottage, but did not stay. Perhaps you were not at home when they came."

"A gendarme van came…"

"No, it was not a blue van, the kind the gendarmes use."

"Several men? Tell me more!"

Séraphin looked perplexed.

"I did see these men sometimes in Les Eyzies. They spoke like Parisians. They had some tools and instruments. Government scientists or engineers, perhaps. Taking a survey? But I am speculating. I do not know. This is just what men in the café are saying."

"You saw them come here to the cottage?"

"I saw their little truck. They did not stay. You must not have been at home."

"Can you remember when they came? What day, what time?"

"Let me see… I came to see you on Sarlat market day because I saw Monsieur Lagarde coming home from the market. Then the next day, and another day…"

The old man counted on his fingers and told her.

"*Monsieur Séraphin!* You must help me in a matter of extreme importance!"

"Of course, mademoiselle. What can I do?"

"Drive with me to the gendarmerie headquarters. We must speak with Captain Gagnier. You have heard about the discovery of the ancient cave and the theft of artwork from it?"

"*Mais oui, mademoiselle!* It is all they talk about in the café now."

"What you have just told me is extremely important information!"

"I don't see how it is important, but of course I will do as you say."

Charity drove the MG. Séraphin rattled along behind her in

his ancient Citroën van.

The had to wait only a quarter hour before an officer escorted them to Captain Gagnier's office.

40

Inferno

"Tomorrow we go back to battle," Martine said.

Jean-Paul looked worried, but said nothing.

"You're not well enough!" Josie said. "Give it a few more days."

They were sitting in Martine and Jean-Paul's apartment drinking wine after supper.

"We are going back to battle!"

Jean-Paul knew there would be no convincing Martine to do otherwise. He knew to choose his arguments with her. Josie was learning, too.

"In that case, I think we should go to bed," Josie said, hoping at least to give Martine sufficient rest to get through whatever tomorrow might bring.

"Yes," Martine said.

"Where shall I sleep?" Josie asked.

"You will sleep with us," Martine said.

Josie and Jean-Paul looked at one another.

"Come," Martine said.

She took their hands and pulled them toward the bedroom.

Martine embraced and kissed Josie first, then she wrapped her arms around Jean-Paul, giving him fervent kisses.

She began undressing Josie.

"Take your clothes off," she said to Jean-Paul.

When Josie was half-naked, Martine stripped her own clothes off quickly, then finished undressing Josie. Holding her hands, Martine fell on the bed pulling Josie on top of her.

Jean-Paul lay on the bed next to the women.

Martine was a dynamo of sex, kissing, fondling, stroking, slapping, grunting, heaving, first Josie, then Jean-Paul. He responded to her attack, and when she went back to attacking Josie, he joined her.

Josie was swept away in pure physical sensation and the excitement and terror of the forbidden.

It couldn't last. Orgasms and exhaustion claimed them.

Jean-Paul could see that Martine was not her strong self yet. The orgy had exhausted her in only a short time. She plummeted into sleep.

Josie looked at Jean-Paul, then at the ceiling. Tears welled in her eyes.

Soon they were all asleep.

Martine was the first to wake. She brewed coffee. The scent of it, the early light streaming through the windows, and the squawk of the radio woke the others.

"24 May 1968. Approximately ten million workers, two-thirds of all the workers in France, are on strike or in control of factories. Reports from government offices suggest that the government is readying tens of thousands of military personnel to retake control of Paris and bring order to the city."

Martine set the coffee pot and three cups on the table along with bread, butter and jam.

"Get up! We must go!" she shouted at the others.

They made their way toward the center of Paris by bus and Metro when they could, hitch-hiking and walking when they couldn't.

I'm in a torrent, Josie thought, like being captive to a flooded river sweeping everything before it, in chaos. I no longer have control of my life, or even of myself.

The thought scared her, but she couldn't break away.

When they reached Place Saint-Michel, Martine talked to

other students.

"*A la Bourse!*" they shouted. "Down with the Temple of Gold!"

The crowd rushed across the Pont Saint-Michel, along the Boulevard du Palais and the Pont au Change, through Châtelet and Les Halles to the Palais Brogniart, the Paris Bourse, the stock exchange. Police and stock market guards stood, armed and defiant, in the classical colonnade surrounding the building, but the mob outnumbered them by thousands. Using military tactics, one group of protesters fought with the police defending the building's entrance while others sought weak points in the defenses. They probed the building's periphery, finally finding a spot where the police were not in force. They broke through and swept around behind the police fighting at the entrance and forced their way into the building.

Martine pushed her way in, Jean-Paul and Josie following. In the great hall, a hurricane of noise. Someone started singing the "Internationale," and the cacophony seemed to shake the antique columns. Josie saw a flash of light, a small flame that soared over the heads of the crowd and burst into a blaze when it hit the wall. The flames ignited the curtains and the documents on desks, then the desks themselves. The shouts of the mob were deafening as they stormed the exits to escape the flames, jamming the doors, pushing, shoving, lashing out at those in their way. Josie felt herself pushed along with the crowd. Elbows thrust into her chest knocked the breath out of her, but Jean-Paul supported her and pushed ahead of her to get them out.

Outside in the plaza, they looked back to see smoke and flames filling the inside of the building.

"Victory!" Martine shouted. "Students and workers are in control!"

Josie looked at Martine in shock: her face was a manic mask, her eyes glistening like those of a vicious animal on the attack, her body out of control, jerking erratically.

"*Victoire! Victoire! A bas les réactionnaires!*" Martine shouted in shrieks of force and animal brutality, her voice now a primal scream.

I have to get away, Josie thought. She's crazy! She's going to get us killed!

Martine and Jean-Paul's eyes were fixed on the burning building. Josie eased herself behind them, then into the crowd, then away, against the tide of more students running toward the Bourse. Avoiding protesters and police as best she could, she made her way back to Rue Claude Bernard.

PART FIVE

End of May

41

Release

Charity was sitting on the cottage terrace nibbling at a salad and planning her next moves when she heard, then saw, Séraphin's wheezy old truck climb the hill and approach the cottage. Séraphin circled and parked pointing downhill as always. He got out of the driver's side and Gaston stepped out of the other side.

He ran to her. She leapt up, overturning the table, and rushed into his arms.

"Charity!"

"Oh Gaston!"

Séraphin looked away, gazing over the valley. Oh, these young couples, he thought.

"What…? How? You're here! Are you free?"

"Yes, I am free, at least for now. I will tell you about it. Let me thank Séraphin for bringing me here."

He went to the old man, patted him on the shoulder and handed him a 50-franc note. The old man's eyes grew wide as he stared at the money.

'Anytime you need a taxi, monsieur, call on me!" he joked before climbing into his jalopy and coasting down the hill.

"Are you hungry?" Charity asked.

"For you!" he said.

He grabbed her, lifted her up, carried her to the bedroom and gently laid her on the bed.

"I am hungry for other things now," he said as they lay in bed, satiated with love-making. "I would like something to eat and drink. The food at the jail was atrocious, and no wine!"

She went to the kitchen, prepared a plate of bread, cheese, and *crudités*—sliced raw vegetables—and took it out to the terrace. He followed with a bottle of white wine.

"I'm sorry. It's not much. I've been busy with important matters," she said.

Before sitting he kissed her, lingering on her lips, kissing again, and again.

They sipped the wine.

"So tell me! I'm going crazy!"

"I cannot tell you much. A guard came and took me to Gagnier's office. He handed me my identification paper and said I was free to go, but I must keep in touch with them to help with the investigation. I was in shock! I asked him why I was being released. He would say nothing. Just 'Go!'"

"From the café in Sarlat I telephoned the café in Les Eyzies. Of course Séraphin was there drinking red wine with his friends. He came to get me. Here I am."

She leaned over and kissed him, a long, deep, probing kiss.

"Then they must have another suspect," she said, pulling away and looking at him.

"Or your work convinced them that I was not guilty."

"Séraphin told Gagnier about the men coming the day we were trapped in the cave. That must be when they dropped the tools here. The boatman—Emmanuel—must have told him about the three men from Paris, the 'geology survey' men. I wonder what the police in Paris have found."

They gazed out over the valley. The sun was still well up in the sky even though it was seven o'clock in the evening.

"Tonight we go to the best restaurant in Sarlat," he said. "We sit outside in the garden. We order the most delicious dishes on the menu. We drink an entire bottle of champagne."

"And afterwards?" she grinned at him.

"Afterwards? We sleep...." He grinned at her. "Sometime... when it's convenient."

42

Assignation

"Meet me at the house tomorrow, darling, same time. I can't wait for you to hold me in your arms! And I have some important news. Good news!"

Professor Noireau placed the telephone handset in its cradle. He stood up from his office desk, went to the window and looked down at the street, at the students walking along, the girls in their spring dresses after the cold winter, the boys chatting them up or conspiring in groups.

Back to normal, he thought, but not really. The rage, the chaos seems to have burned itself out. All of France is exhausted from a month of tumult and conflict. The streets, the university, Paris, looking more or less normal again, but *les évènements de mai* are burned into the consciousness of every person in France.

Good news? I don't think so. He dreaded the thought of what she would tell him, of doing what he had to do, but he knew he must do it. His name would be dragged through the scandal sheets, his professional standing questioned, but he could not avoid what was going to happen. There was no other way.

Gaston drove fast along the highway to Paris: Brive-la-Gaillarde, Limoges, Orléans.... The car was noisy from the speed and the wind. Absorbed in thoughts of their hopes and fears for the future, he and Charity spoke little.

Could they ever reclaim the bliss they had felt during those first days at the cottage?

No, Charity thought. It was too good to last. It won't be the same. Bliss doesn't last. It can't last. It never lasts.

She sighed quietly. We can't go back to that bliss.

But it doesn't *have* to be the same. If we can get past this nightmare we can create another dream-come-true for ourselves, a new one, the next stage in our lives together. Bliss again, but a different bliss, perhaps as good—perhaps even better.

Gaston drove steadily. In Paris, would he wake up from this nightmare? He knew the ordeal wasn't over. The captain had released him, but said nothing about the case being solved, the true criminals identified and arrested. He must assume that the case was still active and unsolved. He might be arrested again.

The university was re-opening, but what did that mean? That nothing had changed? With such chaos, disruption and damage to so many lives, nothing had changed? Many things *must* have changed, or be soon to change. What did that mean?

Then there was Yveline. They had been so in love. Now it seemed not just that their love was dead, but that she despised him. What had come over her? How could he have been so mistaken about who she was?

So many burdens, so heavy. Thank goodness for Charity! What a miracle! A slender student, a mere girl, with such wisdom, courage and determination! In class she had been the best student, yes, and her enthusiasm for archeology was obvious. But he never could have imagined the power and capability within that girl's fresh face and fragile-looking body.

But …his student! He was now involved romantically with one of his former students, a girl ten years younger than he, something he vowed never to let happen. He would not take advantage of the innocence and impulsive romantic nature of young women. It was not right. It was not fair to them. He saw them trying to get his notice, to tempt him, but he had been steadfast. In love with Yveline and committed to her, he found it easy to resist. And yet here he was, deeply involved with Charity. She had been a virgin! How could he not even have considered that possibility? He had not, and by the time he realized, it was too late.

Too late? No, it was the *beginning* of what he felt now, this fierce loyalty to her. Yes, she was young, but so wise! If I compare Charity to Yveline, it's astonishing. Charity is so kind and considerate, so even-tempered—except when she is angry at injustice.

I am still not comfortable with this relationship because she was my student, because she is so young, but I cannot stop it. I am in love with her. I cannot change it. Like the rest of my life right now, I will have to follow it to its conclusion, whatever that may be.

Professor Noireau walked from the train station to the house through the cool evening air, in through the gate and to the front door. He let himself in with his key, and locked the latch open. He climbed the stairs to the bedroom.

She was already there, sitting by the fire in a sheer *négligée*. A bottle of champagne waited in an ice bucket on the table next to two glasses, as always.

She smiled at him.

"Darling, I have arranged everything. All of the...obstacles will soon be out of our way. Soon we won't have to meet secretly. We can live together openly, in complete happiness."

He went to her, kissed her, opened the champagne and poured two glasses.

"Let me tell you the news!"

She came to him, leaned over and kissed him, her négligée falling open to reveal her breasts.

On the street behind the house, a car moved quietly, stopping a block away. Three men emerged and walked slowly around the block, through the gate, and in the front door.

"When you hear my voice, come upstairs," one man whispered to the others.

He climbed the stairs slowly and quietly.

"Yes, my beautiful one, tell me your news," Noireau said calmly.

"I have solved the problem of my father's estate. All of it will soon be mine. And my other project will make you even more famous at the same time. You will be famous throughout the world!"

"Not only that," she said, smiling at him over the rim of her champagne glass, "I have removed all legal obstacles to our marriage. We will be married as soon as you have your divorce."

"How did you arrange all of this?"

"Are your friends in your apartment?" Gaston asked Charity as they approached Paris. "Shall I take you there?"

"Don't you usually leave your car in Versailles?"

"Yes, normally, but I can drive you to your apartment if you wish."

"No, we might as well do what you always do. We can take the train into the city."

"That is probably best," he said. "I don't want to have to think about the car in Paris. I don't know what's going to happen in the next few days."

They arrived in Versailles and he parked the car in the carriage house of the mansion. As they walked toward the back door, he smelled woodsmoke. Looking up, he saw the smoke coiling from a chimney of the mansion. A light shone through the window of a second-floor bedroom.

"Who is in the house?"

Gaston opened the back door with his key. Through the empty servants' quarters and the kitchen, they went quietly up a back stairway. Gaston signalled to Charity to stop and stay where she was as he tiptoed along the hallway. Turning the corner, he saw a man standing outside the bedroom door with his ear pressed to it.

"All you have to do is to authenticate the artifact," she told Professor Noireau at the end of her news report. "I know it is authentic because I know, and now *you* know, exactly where it came from. But we cannot tell anyone—and we don't have to! The man I employed to get the artifact is in contact with a buyer who wants this truly unique art object. He does not need to know

—or even *want* to know—where it came from, so long as it is certified as authentic by the world's most highly-regarded archeologist!"

She smiled at him, leaned down, kissed him, and brushed her breasts across his face.

She is getting tipsy, he thought. But so what? It's almost over.

"If anyone else finds out where it came from, everything is ruined! So we must be careful," she said with a frown, pouring herself a third glass of champagne.

Noireau drained his second glass of champagne and threw the glass violently into the fireplace. At the sound of the shattering glass, the man outside the bedroom door flung it open, shouted to the other men, and walked in.

43

Tragedy

Gaston heard the other two men running up the stairs. He retreated around the corner. After the men entered the bedroom, he crept along the hallway and stood to the side of the open door to listen.

"I am Detective Béranger of the Gendarmerie," the first man said. "Mademoiselle Yveline Guéron, you are under arrest for conspiracy to steal national historic artifacts, to cause damage to national historic sites, and to engage in illegal commerce of antiquities."

Yveline drew the filmy négligée tightly around her and stared at the detective in shock. She turned and looked at Noireau, who eased himself calmly into his chair.

Gaston stepped into the room. Charity followed. They saw Yveline and Noireau.

"What is this? What is going on?"

"Who are you?" the detective shouted at Gaston.

"I am Gaston Lagarde! This is my house!"

"Ah, you are Lagarde. You were the first suspect in this case, yes?"

"Case? Yes, I was a suspect in a criminal case, but I have been released."

"Yes, I know," the detective said. "You were released because we now have conclusive evidence regarding who was leading this conspiracy to commit the antiquities crimes. We have arrested the perpetrators of the theft and they have testified as to the leader of the conspiracy."

Turning to the others, the detective said "Mademoiselle Guéron, you must come with us. Do you have proper clothing?"

"Yveline? What are you saying?" Gaston cried.

"It is true, Lagarde," Noireau said. "She organized the theft."

"Impossible!" Gaston said. "Why would she do such a thing?"

"You will not want to hear the answer to that question," Noireau said. "For me, what is important is that she employed men to follow you, to enter the paleolithic cave that you had found, and to destroy a priceless prehistoric work of art. It is unforgivable!"

"You told the police!" Yveline shouted at Noireau.

"Yes, my dear, I told the police—or, rather, they told me first. They came to me with a photograph of a paleolithic painting of an auroch and asked me to identify it. I could not. I had never seen that particular painting before, and I have seen every known prehistoric cave painting in France. They told me it had been discovered in the Vézère valley by a young archeologist. I guessed it was Lagarde. He is always looking for caves there. I encouraged him to do so."

"That's why they arrested me!" Gaston said. "Did you really think I would destroy priceless paleolithic art, or rip it from its place and attempt to sell it?"

"No, of course I did not," Noireau answered calmly. "But I had to cooperate with the investigation. I was as eager for answers as the police. Such a crime must not be permitted to succeed! The police told me you were the prime suspect because you had discovered the cave and had not reported it right away."

"But, then, why did they release me?"

"Because I was able to collect more evidence. This evidence did not implicate you, it implicated others."

"What evidence?"

"I have a friend who is an eager and ambitious collector of antiquities," Noireau said. "He has employed me to authenticate some of his collection. Though he is a collector, his love of antiquities is genuine and disciplined. He collects only what has already been…abused, shall we say, objects for which the provenance is unknown and an original owner cannot be identified. He was as appalled as I at the thought of destruction in an unknown paleolithic site."

Noireau glanced at Detective Béranger before continuing.

"My friend is extraordinarily well-connected in…shall we say, 'certain circles.' I informed him of the theft and asked for his help in finding the perpetrators. Through his contacts he was able to identify positively the men who actually entered the cave after you and cut the auroch painting from the wall."

"Benito!" Charity exclaimed.

Everyone looked at her.

"Ahem," Noireau cleared his throat and all eyes turned to him again.

"These criminals were taken into custody and interviewed by the police. They revealed that the person who had employed them to steal the painting was none other than Mademoiselle Yveline Guéron, your fiancée."

"And *your* lover!" Gaston said, staring at Noireau.

"Yes, Yveline and I were having an affair. She wanted us to marry. I let her know this was…improbable, that we should just enjoy our time together, but she would not listen to me. She has just told me that getting rid of you was part of her plan. She wanted to have you put in prison so she could get all of her step-father's inheritance and be free to…well, to marry me."

"So it was *you* who ordered your crooks to put their tools behind my cottage!" Gaston said, pointing at Yveline.

She hung her head and did not look at him.

"With me convicted of a crime, our engagement would have been automatically dissolved, and all of my uncle's estate would have gone to you!"

Yveline looked up at him, her face soaked with tears.

"Oh Gaston, I'm sorry! I didn't want to hurt you. I was so in love with him! I wanted him to divorce his wife and to marry me. We would live together in this house so happily! We would be wealthy! You were…in the way, the only obstacle to my happiness. You wouldn't let me have my dream! If you had only given me what I wanted from father's estate…."

"But Professor Noireau is already wealthy!" Charity said.

Noireau gave a low laugh.

"Wealthy? No, young lady, unfortunately, not at all. Archeologists, even famous ones, rarely get wealthy, as you know, Lagarde. Because of my expertise, I can require generous fees for my professional assessments of antiquities, but they hardly generate what you would call great wealth. Because of my renown, I have wealthy friends and connections. They are generous to me. I live well. But Yveline knew that if I divorced my wife and married her, we would live a common life, not much better than a bourgeois, middle-class professor's life. She did not want that. She couldn't bear the thought of it. She wanted a life of wealth with a world-famous husband. She told me that someone she knew, a 'Monsieur M,' was in contact with a wealthy private collector somewhere in the world who would buy the prehistoric painting of an auroch for a very high price—*if* she could obtain my authentication of it. Then we would be rich. She could then live the glittering lifestyle she imagined."

He glared at Yveline.

"It was a despicable plan. I am ashamed to have been involved with it in any way, even without my knowledge."

"Mademoiselle Guéron! Please dress in appropriate clothing. You will come with us," the detective said. "Young lady?" he said, looking at Charity. "Please stay with her until she is dressed. We will wait just outside the door."

"Be quick!" he said, looking at Yveline.

The men went out of the room, leaving the door open.

"Please find some clothes in the wardrobe there," Yveline said to Charity, pointing to a large armoire. "I will return soon."

She went into the bathroom.

There were few clothes in the armoire, but they were all from the best shops. Charity chose the most sober and unpretentious outfit she could find and laid it out for Yveline on the bed.

She sat in a chair.

All in a second, she thought. The world changes completely in just a second, like when the thieves entered the cave behind us. Our exhilaration at having discovered historic art treasures in the cave turns instantly to terror of death from the art thieves. Our blissful morning in the sun on the terrace at the cottage turns to despair in a single moment when the gendarmes come to arrest Gaston. From bliss to bitter fate in a single second. Your vision of a wonderful present and future simply vanishes, all at once, irretrievably.

Charity felt sadness for Yveline. She had no reason to like her. She did not even know her except for what Gaston had told her and from their one brief, unpleasant encounter at the cottage. But still, having had her world destroyed, Charity knew how it feels.

"Hurry up in there!" the detective shouted.

Charity got up from the chair and went to the bathroom door.

"Yveline? They want you to hurry."

Charity heard the water running.

She didn't hear me over the water, Charity thought.

"Yveline! You must hurry!" she shouted.

No response.

Detective Béranger came into the room, fidgeted for a moment, then went to the bathroom door and knocked. No response. He pushed down on the door handle, but the door would not open.

He pounded on the door and shouted for her to open it.

He beckoned to the other policemen and the larger of the two threw himself against the door with all his weight. It didn't open. Two more violent thrusts, the latch was ripped from the door jamb, and the door flew open.

Yveline was lying in the bathtub, the taps fully open, the tub nearly filled with pink water, a broken champagne glass in her hand, her wrists rhythmically pulsing clouds of bright blood swirling into the rising flood.

PART SIX
Early June

44

Declaration

"Come here," Charity said to Gaston when he telephoned her at her apartment. "I don't want to talk in a café."

She knew it would be an important conversation, perhaps the most important of her life. She told her roommates to go out. She wanted no distractions.

An hour later the intercom buzzed and she let him in.

"Your apartment is beautiful!" he said, surveying the scene.

"Let's sit at the table," she said. "Coffee? Tea?"

When he sat without answering, she sat too.

"I have talked with Professor Noireau and Detective Béranger. They told me more about Yveline, Noireau and the crime," he said. "Yveline got to know the professor at a faculty reception that we, she and I, attended two years ago. She seemed impressed by his good looks, his fame and his sophistication, but yes, he is all of those things. I thought nothing of it. She started seeing him secretly. I believe she decided she must have him! She dreamed of a life flying around the world to prestigious meetings and being with rich friends. She must have known he was not rich, so she was determined to claim all of my uncle's estate for herself, and him."

"She knew that I searched for caves in the Vézère," Gaston went on. "We had done a bit of searching together, but she hated it, found it boring. She knew, however, there was a chance of finding a 'treasure cave.'"

"So she sent the men to follow you, hoping you'd find a cave?"

"No, I think she just sent the men to look for a cave on their own. If they found one, her plan was to have Noireau authenticate the art. She knew that would be essential for a work without provenance. His authentication would be worth millions!'

"But then her men saw us, the *nouveaux mariés*. They saw where we had been, and found the cave?"

"Yes, I believe so." He sighed. "Without realizing it, or wanting to, we helped Yveline in her plan."

"So when she had the auroch painting, she had to tell Noireau so he could perform the authentication. He would know that it was not in any officially known cave."

"Yes. When her men succeeded in stealing the auroch painting, she told Noireau. Secretly, without letting her know, he was appalled. And he was also in great danger! If word got out that he had anything to do with desecrating a cave...well, you can imagine! Total ruin of his standing and reputation, arrest, conviction, and many years in prison! So he knew he must act like he was going along with her plan, but he must secretly contact the police at once. The police wanted evidence, so he told them what he knew. He also asked for help from his friend and patron Benito Vénière. This Vénière is...well, he is mafia! He has connections in the criminal world. Noireau showed him my photo of the men in the cave, Vénière made copies and circulated them in criminal circles, and he was able to discover the identity of the men in the boat, the men who came into the cave after us."

"...And tried to kill us!" Charity said. Her body shivered.

"I don't think that was their plan, but they did find the cave because of us. Whether they knew we were in the cave when they dynamited the entrance, I do not know."

He hung his head.

"I cannot allow myself to believe that Yveline, whom I loved, would try to kill me."

"But you see how it would benefit her if they had!" Charity said. "You, the prime suspect, would have disappeared! If anyone ever found the cave, you would have been long dead, and the case would have been closed with you determined as the criminal!"

"I cannot think that way, my dear…but it does not matter now."

He looked up at her and smiled.

"Noireau also told old Plouff about the theft of the painting, telling him it was a recent crime, under active investigation, and if he heard or saw anything about it, he must inform the police, but he was not to tell anyone else about the investigation."

"So that's why Plouff refused to tell me anything about the photo," Charity mused.

They sat in silence, remembering all that had happened.

Gaston straightened in his chair and put his arms on the table in front of him, clasping his hands.

"Charity, it is important that we discuss our situation…"

Charity feared this was coming. She had seen it over and over in her dreams. The dreams started at a huge, lofty castle, a stand-in for Gaston's mansion in Versailles. Yveline was a powerful wicked witch, Professor Noireau was a fearsome judge seated at a high bench like God on His throne. Gaston was an indecisive petitioner, harried by the witch, cowering before the arrogant judge. She, Charity, was a tremulous child shouting at him, her sibling-boyfriend-father figure, to be brave, to defeat evil, to stand up for what is right.

With all the will she could command, Charity clamped her jaw, held her tongue and let Gaston say what he had to say.

"I am ten years older than you are, almost half of your life older! I am French, you are American. I am guilty of having committed an offense which I swore I would never do: I became romantically involved with one of my students. Far worse—let me speak frankly—I have stolen your virginity! I have involved you in a tragedy that was completely my creation, a tragedy which has ended in death, a terrible tragedy which should not have touched your young sensibility at all."

He swallowed hard. Charity felt he was about to sob.

"If you had never met me, you would have had an

unblemished year in France. You would return to America with good memories and a good appreciation of our country, our culture. You could continue your normal development as a fine young woman: education, acculturation, falling in love with a good young man of your own age. Your future would be bright! Instead..."

Charity stared at him with eyes fixed. Not a muscle in her face moved. Here it comes, she thought, and I can't take it. I won't stand for it.

"Instead," she said, cutting him off and speaking in that same firm, direct, don't-interrupt-me tone she had used on Captain Gagnier in Sarlat, "instead, I have learned more in one month than I learned in half my life. Instead, I feel as mature and understanding of life as someone ten years older than I— someone *your* age. Instead, I have found the love of my life, my first and, I am certain, my only love, and I will not give up any of it. I am yours, and you are mine, and I will say this until you understand and accept it."

Gaston was speechless.

"Don't say anything," she said. "There is no need."

Gaston stared at her, his mind racing.

Let him catch up, Charity thought, continuing to stare at him. This is going to happen. It's going to happen.

His eyes fell to the table top. His tense shoulders and arms relaxed. His face too, his whole body threw off its tension.

When his eyes rose and returned to her face, he was a different person. They were brimming with tears.

He's still confused, she thought. I'll take care of that.

She stood, walked around the table and wrapped her arms around him. He raised his arms and held her.

Their bodies moved slowly in rhythm as they wept.

45

The Parting

"You can come over," Josie said, and hung up the telephone.

"My friend Jean-Paul will be coming over in a few minutes," Josie told her roommates.

They looked at her. She was not happy.

When Josie let Jean-Paul into the apartment, the others greeted him, then retreated to their rooms.

Josie and Jean-Paul looked at one another in silence. She took his hand, led him to her room and closed the door.

They sat on the bed.

"Martine is back in the hospital," he said. "The doctors say a blood vessel broke in her brain, perhaps because of the wound from the tear gas cannister. She should not have gone to the protests at the Bourse. By the time she got to the hospital, the pressure from the leaking blood had caused brain damage, a stroke."

Tears came to his eyes.

"She may not recover. She may die. Or spend the rest of her life in bed. That would be worse."

Josie held him in her arms as he wept.

They were silent.

He looked at her.

"I'll be going back to America soon."

"You won't stay in Paris? After all that has happened?"

"My struggle is in America, not France. I have to go and do there what you and Martine tried to do here."

"I must take care of Martine or I would go with you."

"Your struggle is here, not in America."

"The struggle is everywhere!"

"You sound like Martine."

She looked at him.

"Jean-Paul, I can't stay, but I can tell you that you and Martine have given me something I will never forget. Never."

They sat quietly, embracing.

"I must go see Martine," he said, rising from the bed.

She walked with him to the door. They looked at one another.

She gave him a tender kiss on the lips, lowered her eyes, and closed the door.

"This meeting of the Secret Society will come to order," Josie said after pouring the wine.

"We only have a few more days together. We need to hear each other's plans and, more importantly, how we can continue Society meetings after we go home."

"I'm not going home," Charity said. "At least not soon. After you girls leave, I'll be sharing the apartment rent here with a certain friend of mine—and former professor."

"You mean he's movin' in here with you?" Amaleen asked.

"Yes."

"Whoopee! Charity honey, are you gonna marry this Gaston guy or jes' live in sin?"

"We're going to live in love. I don't know what after that. I don't care."

"What about college?"

"I'm going to be an archeologist. I will need to get my degree and go to graduate school. I will. I'll figure that out later. It will happen. I'm in no rush."

"I'd bet my life it'll happen," Josie said. "Congratulations, little girl! That's just great!"

"Amaleen?" Charity asked.

"Well, ah plumb used up all the men in France, ah think, so ah'm goin' home, but ah don't think ah'll last long in Charleston

—that's West Virginia, not the one in South Carolina. How yuh gonna keep 'em down on the farm after they seen Paree, right? So ah'm gonna move somewhere. Don't know where yet. California? Lots goin' on in California."

"Lot of men, too," Josie wisecracked.

"'Bout twenty million, give or take. That'll last me a year or two, ah guess."

They clinked glasses.

"California surfers! Watch out! Here comes Amaleen! You won't know what hit you!" Josie shouted.

They drank.

"I have an announcement to make," Josie said. "I have been invited to visit Madame Josephine Baker at Château des Milandes, her castle near Sarlat."

"Wow! Josie, how'd you do that?"

"I wrote her a fan letter, told her about *les évènements* here in Paris, and how I hoped to carry on the work, the civil rights revolution she helped to start, when I return to America. Next thing I know I get a fancy letter, hand-written by Ms Baker herself, inviting me to come and meet her...in her castle!" Josie squealed in delight.

"You gonna take that boyfriend o' yours, that...what's his name? He got two names."

"Jean-Paul?"

"Yeah, that's the one."

"I...I don't think he'll be able to come. I'll probably go by myself."

"That's *so* exciting!" Charity said. "Josie, you're really a wonder."

"Charity, you're saying that to *me?* Look in a mirror, sweetie."

"Well, ah cain't tell yuh what it's meant to be here with y'all. I mean, what does life have to offer after this? How we gonna have meetin's of the Secret Society? How'm ah gonna live without 'em?"

"We got through some pretty heavy stuff in the last month, ladies. I think we can handle getting together now and then... somewhere in the world," Charity said.

They clinked glasses and drank, but their faces were not

smiling.

Charity put down her glass and hugged Josie, tears filling her eyes. Amaleen stood up, came around the table, and wrapped her long arms around both of them, sobbing with them in joy, and in sadness.

Epilogue

Gift of Honor

The envelope was the strangest that Amaleen had ever received, a mess of stamps, postmarks and scribbled forwarding instructions. She could tell that it had originally been posted in England and sent first to Olivier's château, then to their old apartment on Rue Claude Bernard in Paris, and then forwarded to her old home address in Charleston, West Virginia, and then forwarded again to her current address. It had traveled for months.

It's a miracle it ever reached me, she thought.

She opened it.

Inside was a newspaper clipping. At the top of the clipping was scrawled "Gift of honour. CH."

International Times News
June 30, 1968

Reputed Mob Boss Dies in Hunting Accident

PARIS: Reputed Corsican mafia figure Benito Vénière died accidentally while shooting with friends yesterday on his estate in the Loire Valley.

Vénière, 55, often cited as an important figure in underworld businesses, had been indicted numerous times on criminal charges involving shipment and sale of illegal drugs, prostitution, bribery and conspiracy to commit murder, but was never found guilty.

He was reportedly shooting quail with a party of nine friends on his vast Loire Valley estate, Château Corsique, when an errant shot hit him in the head. He died instantly.

"It was a tragic accident," the estate's hunt master, Clive Harrows, is reported to have said. "We were out for quail in a shooting party of ten. The pointers flushed a covey. The birds rose to our right. Mr Vénière, at the right side of the party, was on the edge of the line of fire, in a good position to bring down a bird, but was hit by an errant shot, apparently from someone aiming too low as the birds gained height."

"Several of our party had never been shooting before," Mr Harrows told reporters. "It was their first time. I instructed them in hunting safety and the use of their guns, but I'm afraid their inexperience got the better of instruction and precaution."

When ask whose gun discharge was responsible for the injury, members of the hunting party could not agree.

"No one knows who fired the errant shot," Mr Harrows said. "When hunters hear the first shot, they all fire, so all of the guns discharged in only a second. Because one hunter shot too early, everyone did. You certainly don't think you're aiming at anything other than the prey, but accidents happen. Perhaps one of the inexperienced shooters, excited by the rise of the birds, pulled the trigger too soon. This is a great tragedy. Mr Vénière was a fine man. He will be greatly missed."

Mr Harrows, as hunt master, is responsible for the organization and safety of the shooting party. He has been detained for questioning, but no charges have been brought.

Château Corsique is the largest and most opulent private château in the Loire Valley. The 150-room castle is the centerpiece of a 10-square-kilometer hunting park and forest. Accusers said it was bought with the illegal profits from criminal activity. Vénière denied such accusations, pointing to his successful legitimate businesses in many parts of the world.

Born in Corsica to working-class parents, Vénière was reputedly recruited by a local mafia group in his teens and rose quickly through the crime group's hierarchy. After a bloody internecine battle among local mafia groups for market share of the illegal drug distribution network, he fled to Marseilles where he founded his own small organization distributing illegal drugs smuggled through the Port of Marseilles. Over the decades his organization is thought to have grown to be among the largest and most successful criminal enterprises in Europe, with affiliated organizations in other parts of the world.

Charity's Letter

Dear Amaleen and Josie,

It's been months since the last meeting of the Secret Society. That's way too long! This letter will have to serve as my part of a "paper meeting."

Gaston and I were married on the autumnal equinox, September 21st, in the Arènes de Lutèce, the 1st-century Gallo-Roman ruins near our apartment on Rue Claude Bernard. I wish you could have been there! I had something old—my Roman medal of the goddess Vesta; something new—a locket with a photo of Gaston; something borrowed—a tiny stone from our cave, which I will return; and something blue, a Middle Eastern anti-evil eye bead Gaston gave me.

I made my parents come to Paris for les fiançailles, *the French custom of engagement, when the two families spend time together to get to know one another. They were here for a week, and were pretty docile. Gaston charmed my mother. I guess she was willing to face up to the inevitable. My father was simply in shock when I told him all that had happened. He has no idea what to do, which is fine. He just smiles, looking a little bewildered. He seems happy enough, and accepting.*

Gaston's parents seemed a bit unsettled by his marrying "a mere girl," non-French, and of unknown status, but I think I impressed them. His mother is already on my side. "She speaks our language…correctly!" she says. His father is less certain, but I'm working on him and I think they recognize that times are changing. He'll come around. So far as I'm concerned, he doesn't have a choice.

We had to move out of the apartment on Rue Claude Bernard, but we found another one, pretty similar, close by on the same street. We bought it— Gaston sold his house in Versailles, so we had the money.

Gaston took a leave of absence from the university so we could work on properly documenting what is now being called "the Lagarde cave" in the Vézère valley. (Remember, my last name is 'Lagarde' now too!) We have the stolen auroch painting, and will be supervising its replacement in the cave. Professor Noireau is helping, but Gaston is taking the lead, with Noireau's approval. We've been spending a lot of time at the cottage near Sarlat, which makes me very happy. It's heaven there!

Because of the cave discovery, Gaston has already been invited to be a visiting professor in archeology at Harvard, so we may move to Cambridge next year. I can finish off my senior year at Radcliffe and then, I hope, begin a doctorate at Harvard. My husband may be one of my professors! Incroyable!

I think of what it's going to be like to go back to North Adams. My mother will show off Gaston, the handsome, famous, rich, exotic trophy that her shy little daughter brought back from France. If any of her friends look askance at our marriage because of the age difference, my mother will glare them down.

Amaleen: how is California? Are you its First Lady yet? You've got to be the talk of the town, or the entire state.

Josie: I guess you're applying to law schools. Have you told His Honor the Judge that you roomed with two white girls in Paris? What did he say?

Enough for now. I hope you're both well. I hope we'll all be in the US next year. If we are, we've got to get together. The Secret Society must meet again!

Until then...

Love to you both,

Charity

Josie's Letter

Dear Charity and Amaleen,

It was so good to get your letter, Charity. Married! Wow! Girl, you don't waste any time! I'm so happy for you!

I think your year abroad was the best, but I did have that wonderful visit with my idol, Josephine Baker, at Château des Milandes. She is such a great lady! She's created a miniature model of what I want the world to look like. She has adopted a dozen kids, all different nationalities and ethnicities and colors and religions. She calls them "my rainbow tribe." This is what I want! This is how the world should be! I'm going to make it that way!

Here in Chicago, I'm in the thick of it. You must have heard about the Democratic Convention here in August. It was Paris all over again! Tens of thousands of students protesting, tens of thousands of police beating them. The brutality was awful, almost as bad as Paris.

There were demonstrations in over a hundred cities. The revolution is really happening here! We got rid of LBJ, but the Democrats are still supporting the Vietnam war. Even Humphrey, who should know better, is supporting it, at least in public. If we have another four years of Nixon, I don't know what I'll do.

I had a hard time last May in Paris, but I'm glad I experienced it because it made me into a better fighter. I understand the dynamics now, and the politics. I'm helping to lead a group here in Chicago that is fighting against the Vietnam war, and for women's rights, and for minority rights. My parents are wonderfully supportive. I know what they lived through growing up, and I can see their vision of the future: a vision of fairness, and understanding, of mutual respect, and building together, not hating and destroying.

It's hard sometimes, but I've got to do it, and it makes me feel good about myself.

I'd like to tell you about my boyfriend, but I don't have one. I do get along well with some of the excellent young men I work with. Maybe something will develop, but right now we're all so busy with work that we have no time for that side of life.

Charity, it's so great to hear that you may be living in the US soon! We've got to get together at the first opportunity. The Secret Society lives!

Take care, you two. I love you so much!

Josie

Jean-Paul's Letter

Chère Josie,

I thank you for all of your help to us in our revolution. It did not happen the way we hoped, but we have made some progress.

When the elections of June gave even more strength to de Gaulle, we were devastated, but we still have hope that we can get rid of de Gaulle as America got rid of Johnson.

There is hope, but it will be a long struggle.

I regret to tell you that Martine died a week ago. She never recovered from the brain injury, she just grew weaker. She was desolated. I also was desolated, as you may believe, but I know that she would not want to live without fighting.

Now she has become a symbol, a martyr of our revolution. Her photograph is everywhere, and artists are designing posters showing her standing on the barricade triumphant. She is our new Marianne, the symbol of the Revolution! I know she would be happy. She is fighting still!

I wish you all the best in your revolutionary work in America. I am honored to call you my friend.

Mes sentiments les meilleurs,

Jean-Paul

Amaleen's Letter

Dear Charity and Josie,

Your letters made me miss you-all something powerful. I, Amaleen Carlile, started to cry! If you can imagine that.

I made a mess of my first letter to you. This is my second try.

I'm in L.A. That's Los Angeles. I went to San Francisco first, but all that hippy stuff is getting real old, and it was too crazy, so I went south to the sun. L.A. is even crazier, but in a different way. I guess it's my way, because I like it here.

It was pretty easy to get a modeling job. People told me that modeling was the best way to get into movies. You model for a spell, and meet people, and they get to know your face, and you sign up to be an extra in a film, or wangle a bit part, and you get noticed. I really don't know yet if that's what I want, but if you're a blonde girl here—or a guy, for that matter—that's what you do. The big question is can I stop talking hillbilly. There's only so many parts call for a hillbilly amazon! We'll see what happens.

I suspect you're wondering about little old Amaleen and her men. Well, I haven't been doing much of that stuff here. I know, you-all have just collapsed on the floor laughing, or in shock, after reading that line. But it's true. Maybe I got an oversupply in France, but I'm a lot more serious about relationships now. I think first and hop in bed later—if I hop in bed at all. I haven't, much, and what surprises me the most is I don't really miss it. I don't even feel that horny, if you can imagine.

Am I growing up? I can't imagine that either, but it may be happening.

Anyway, I'm happy. I'm happy because the weather here is always sunny and warm (compare that to grim old Paris in February!), because I can go to the beach whenever I want, because the modeling thing isn't too hard and it pays good, because all the men here look at me and want to roll me and I guess I like that, and…and because I'm just happy.

What makes me unhappy is missing you-all. Charity, you were such a good example for a wild thing like me. You had it all together, girl. Look at you now! Talk about having it together! And Josie honey, I could never dream of doing the good stuff you're doing, and if I tried, I'd just get in the way of the people—like you—who are really doing it. What you're doing is making the world into a big Secret Society, a place where really different people, people different in just about every way, can not just live together, but be happy together, and support each other, and learn from each other. And, OK, LOVE EACH OTHER!

You're going to make it so people don't need a Secret Society to live together happy.

If you-all ever get to L.A., just holler "Amaleen!" and somebody will point the way to me. And Charity if you get to that snooty old Massachusetts next year, and Josie can make it, I'll seduce a pilot or hijack a airplane if I have to so we can have our Secret Society meeting.

Anyway, I'm going on too long, but at least I didn't cry all over this paper and have to start again. I better stop before I do.

Love you-all! XOXOXOXO!!!!!!!

Amaleen

Afterword

Acknowledgements

Here it is, short, sweet, and what a treat: **Jane**.

Thanks also to the Concord Free Public Library and its genial staff for providing a fine atmosphere for research and writing.

North Adams Public Library

The John Henry Haynes archeological collection at the **North Adams Public Library** is real, down to Charity's favorite, the little elf. The library itself is a gem of New England architecture, culture and education, a tribute to its staff, the town and the region, and well worth a visit. While you're there, visit the other fine museums in the district, all described on NewEnglandTravelPlanner.com.

Isabella Stuart Gardner Museum

Boston's world-class treasure of an art museum does indeed hold an oil-on-wood profile painting of Battista Sforza, Duchess of Urbino. It's a late 18th—early 19th-century copy of Piero della Francesca's 15th-century original painting now in Florence's Uffizi Gallery. Look for it on the Gardner's third floor, Long Gallery. The painting is mis-labeled as being of the "Countess" of Urbino.

Prehistoric Sites in France

The prehistoric caves "discovered by Gaston and Charity" are fictional, but France's Vézère Valley is indeed a real treasure house of prehistoric art.

The village of **Les Eyzies-de-Tayac-Sireuil** boasts the *Musée National de Préhistoire*, the *Pôle International de la Préhistoire*, the caves of *Font-de-Gaume* and *Les Combarelles*, and other prehistoric sites open to the public.

The **Grotte de Lascaux**, discovered in 1940 in the Dordogne's Département de Corrèze near the village of Montignac, was permanently closed to the public in 1963 to protect it from degradation, but a superb replica, **Lascaux II**, was opened in 1983. Constructed to reproduce the shape, ambience and art of the original, Lascaux II is excellent. Also, check online for **Lascaux III**, the international traveling exhibition of cave art, and **Lascaux IV**, the International Centre for Cave Art.

The **Grotte Chauvet** (Chauvet Cave), discovered in 1994 in the Gorges de l'Ardèche region near the city of Orange in Provence, was never opened to the public, only to archeologists and other experts. In 2016 a painstakingly-crafted replica, **La Caverne du Pont d'Arc,** was opened for all to visit. Superbly done, it allows the world to appreciate the artistic skill of our common ancestors in a proper setting. Don't miss it.

For more information on these and many other wonderful things to see and do in France, visit FranceTravelPlanner.com.

About the Author

Born in Pennsylvania, Tom Brosnahan joined the US Peace Corps in 1967, went to Turkey to teach English, and discovered a fascinating land virtually unknown to most travelers. Tom wrote his first travel guidebook, *Turkey on $5 a Day*, (Frommer's, 1970) as a Peace Corps project.

After graduate school and historical research in the archives of the Ottoman Empire, Tom devoted himself to writing and photography. His 40 travel guidebooks for Lonely Planet, Frommer's and Berlitz, translated into a dozen languages, covered Belize, Canada, Egypt, England, France, Guatemala, Israel, Mexico, Morocco, New England, Tunisia and Turkey. He now writes and photographs his own travel websites including FranceTravelPlanner.com, TurkeyTravelPlanner.com and NewEnglandTravelPlanner.com, which receive up to seven million annual visitors from 230+ countries.

Tom has served as a Contributing Editor to *Budget Travel* magazine, and has appeared on ABC's *Good Morning America*, NPR's *Talk of the Nation*, the Travel Channel and Public Radio International's *The Connection*. He has given lectures at the American Turkish Council's annual conference, the Smithsonian Institution, the Cooper-Hewitt National Musem of Design, and other organizations.

Paris Girls Secret Society is his first novel.

If You Enjoyed This Book...

Look for more on TomBrosnahan.com. Likes, dislikes, suggestions and corrections are welcome on Facebook (www.facebook.com/tom.brosnahan.77) or to tom@tombrosnahan.com.

Flora, Julien, Bruce & Sarah

The new novel by Tom Brosnahan...

In 1968, the world is on fire: war in Vietnam, revolution in France and riots in the USA, but not in Istanbul. Few foreigners travel to Turkey, but those who do are in for adventure: Bruce, the American grad student of religion looking for meaning. Astrid, the Norwegian village girl discovering the wider world. A VW microbus full of rollicking hippies in search of fun, sex, and total freedom. US Peace Corps Volunteers seeking adventure and purpose. Yergat, intent on bloody revenge. Even novelist James Baldwin, escaping the oppressive racism of his homeland.

Their lives interact in a beautiful, ancient land filled with cultural treasures that has become a hotbed of spies, drug smugglers and Cold War intrigue. There's Ahmet Kamanbay, the powerful drug capo. His right hand man Korhan Kanlı, suave, sophisticated and deadly. Colonel Zimanskieva, Soviet terror operative. Danny Dracut, the Peace Corps Volunteer turned drug smuggler. Their lives and loves meet just as an atomic cataclysm threatens to destroy one of the world's greatest artistic treasures.

"Aman!" Ahmet Kamanbay gasped.

He pushed a button on the armrest of the car door, it swung open automatically, and he scrambled from his limousine to stare at the cataclysm.

People close to the explosion ran from it in terror, those farther away gaped in shock.

Kamanbay's face was stung by the heat of the inferno sweeping down from Edirne's Selimiye Mosque, the greatest masterpiece of Ottoman architecture.

Two hundred meters away, as the driver of a Mercedes sedan

stared in shock at the fireball, a tall blonde woman sitting in the back lunged forward and grabbed with both hands for the pistol on the front seat. The driver whipped his head around toward her just as she jerked her left elbow violently into his face. When he opened his throbbing eyes he was staring into the muzzle of the gun.

"Let me out!" she screamed.

The driver pushed a button. Click. The woman swung open the left rear door and leapt out. Pistol in both hands still pointing at his head, she shrieked "GO!"

Tires screeched. The car sped away.

She stood on the street corner and stared up the hill at the inferno, staggering backward as an even bigger explosion shot a gigantic mass of smoke and flame into the sky.

In the Soviet Russian Consulate-General in Istanbul, 240 kilometers east of Edirne, GRU Lieutenant Colonel Boryana Zimanskieva glanced at the clock on her office wall, took a long pull on her cigarette and smiled. November 14, 1968, she thought. A good day. A day to remember.

A day of victory!

(Publication in summer 2017)
www.tombrosnahan.com

*   *   *

Made in the USA
Columbia, SC
08 May 2017